Millie
Copyright ©2019 resides with a
ISBN: 978-1-9998650-7-8

First Publication: 2019 AnneMarie Brear.

Cover design by Image: JB Graphics

Published novels:

Historical

Kitty McKenzie
Kitty McKenzie's Land
Southern Sons
To Gain What's Lost
Isabelle's Choice
Nicola's Virtue
Aurora's Pride
Grace's Courage
Eden's Conflict
Catrina's Return
Where Rainbow's End
Broken Hero
The Promise of Tomorrow
The Slum Angel

Contemporary

Long Distance Love
Hooked on You
Where Dragonflies Hover (Dual Timeline)

Short Stories

A New Dawn
Art of Desire
What He Taught Her

Millie

Chapter One

Yorkshire, England
Late August 1919

Millie lightly touched the white rosebuds in her short black curly hair. She smiled at her maid's reflection in the oval mirror. 'You've done a wonderful job of it, Daisy. Thank you.'

'I'm so pleased you like it, miss. It has to be perfect for today of all days.' Daisy, small and thin, fussed with Millie's hair a bit more, tweaking a rosebud or two.

'Are you all packed?' She watched Daisy thread another pearl stud hairpin into place.

'Yes, miss. It's all downstairs ready to go to the station.'

'And you said farewell to your family?'

'I have, miss.' Daisy's smile didn't waver. 'My mother will be at the church, anyway, miss, to see you on this important day.'

'That's so kind of her.'

'The whole village is coming out I should think. It's not often one of the important families of the area gets married in the local church. They want to send you off with their best wishes. You're the first Marsh girl to be married.'

'I'll be happy to see them, and I couldn't have married anywhere else. Prue suggested York Minster, but that's too formal. I wanted to marry in the village, as it's home.' Excitement bubbled up in her chest. She was getting married! She hardly believed it.

'I'm pleased you're having the wedding breakfast here at Elm House, and not in a reception room in York.' Daisy sighed happily. 'It's all so beautiful.'

'And the sun is shining!' Millie laughed, opening a small brown velvet box. Inside, diamond earrings glittered, a gift from her intended groom. It was so thoughtful of him and unexpected. She paused a moment and thought of Jeremy, the man she was to marry in under an hour.

How had it happened so fast? A man she'd known for years, but never really thought of as husband material, had never really thought of him as someone other than her father's friend. A man she had seen at every social event, and at most times seated along the family dining table here at home.

Lifting the earrings from their satin bed, she admired them in the morning light.

'They are lovely, miss.' Daisy sighed dreamily, staring at them.

'I am most fortunate.' Donning them, Millie's gaze went to the door as it opened and in came her two sisters, Prudence and Cecelia, and their cousin, Agatha. Excited voices filled the room as they circled around Millie where she sat at her dressing table.

'You look like an angel, Millie,' Agatha said softly, hesitant as always to make herself known.

Their mousy cousin happily followed in the Marsh girls' wake.

'I doubt that but thank you.' She gazed at their dresses of palest blue satin. 'You all look lovely, too.'

'This is the saddest day of my life!' Prue, always dramatic, flopped onto the bed and hugged a corner post forlornly. 'I cannot believe that tonight this room will be empty forever. You'll never be just down the hallway, or at your place at the breakfast table. Why must you marry? Is it because of the shortage of men after the war? You'll not be left on the shelf you know, not you. You're too pretty, too *good,* to be overlooked by the men who did come back.' She tossed her pretty head angrily. 'That bloody war. And I will say *bloody* because that's what it was. Destroying families, our whole generation of fine young men, or maiming them beyond any use to anyone!'

'Prue!' Cece gaped, her face paling, if that was possible with her porcelain skin which held a hint of freckles that she hated almost as much as her red hair, a legacy from their father. 'Do be quiet. That is cruel. It's not their fault. When I think of those poor men, our *friends*, who will never be the same. It fair breaks my heart.'

Prue sat up indignantly. 'You know I saw Robbie Simmons the other day in the village? Blind. I couldn't, *wouldn't* believe it. He was jolly enough, of course, but I was beside myself with the pain of it. And he could ride so well, and shoot, and now what has he got?'

'Some lovely girl will fall in love with him,' Agatha said softly. 'Some people can see past things like that.'

'Yes, some can, I suppose, but what if the rest of us can't?' Prue snapped. 'Then suddenly it is *we* who are awful with no compassion. It's a disgrace.' She turned back to Millie. 'So, is that why you said yes to Sir Jeremy? Because he came back whole? Well, nearly whole. They say he's even quieter than ever, *tormented*, perhaps, by what he's seen and done.'

'Prue, please,' Cece murmured, giving Millie a horrified look.

'That's enough, Prue. We've been through this.' Millie glared at her sister. 'Do you wish to ruin my day?'

'No... But really, Millie. Why not marry someone young and dashing? There are some left, I assure you. Pick one of our friends instead of Sir Jeremy Remington. Tom Rollings and Henry Pinkerton both came back without a scratch and so did Arthur Healy and—'

'Prue!' Cece's warning went unheeded as Prue launched into another rant on why marrying Sir Jeremy was the wrong thing to do.

'But he's *so* old.' Prue protested, tossing her head, obviously not caring if her hairpins fell out.

'He's thirty-six.' Millie spread her hands out in protest. Anyone over the age of twenty-one was old to Prue.

'He lives in a crumbling old manor in the middle of nowhere.'

'No, he doesn't. Remington Court is perfectly fine. It's the chateau in Northern France that isn't so good. Since his Uncle Louis's death and the German occupation of it, it is in a bad state.'

'And we'll never see you!'

'I'll be only twenty miles away. We will see each other all the time.'

'He's father's friend, not ours.'

'We've all known him for years. And you,' she pointed a finger at Prue, 'have always got on well with him!'

'Yes, I do, but it doesn't mean I'd marry him!' Her blue eyes so like Millie's flashed defiantly.

'He didn't ask you.'

'Well, you cannot deny that he's sour. I swear I've never seen him laugh. All we get are twitches of his lips when something is amusing. He's handsome enough I suppose, if you like them to be cold and distant with it.'

Agatha twitched her skirt. 'Millie has her very own Mr Darcy.'

'Don't talk nonsense, Agatha. Mr Darcy indeed. Everything is not like you read in those infernal books of yours.' Prue glared. 'Millie can do so much better!'

'Prudence Violet Mary Marsh.' Their mother's voice from the doorway had them all turning to her. Prue flushed guiltily.

Violet Marsh stepped regally into the room. 'Out now, all of you. Give Millie some peace. Cecelia go to Grandmama and see if she's ready.'

She stepped aside as the three bridesmaids filed towards the door, but before Prue could leave, their mother touched her arm. 'Not one more word from you today unless it is to say something pleasant. Don't you dare spoil your sister's special day any more than you already have. Do you understand me?'

'Yes, Mama.' Prue turned back to Millie. 'I'm sorry, Millie, really I am. It's just that I'm terribly sad you're leaving us. Nothing will ever be the same again...' Tears filled her eyes.

'I understand, dearest, I do.' Millie walked over to her younger sister and hugged her briefly. 'Everything will soon settle down again though, I promise.'

'Go now,' their mother butted in. 'Your father is waiting outside with the carriages.' Walking over to the dressing table, Violet smiled at Daisy. 'You've done a magnificent job, Daisy. Miss Millie looks just as a bride should. Thank you. And I wish you well in Sir Jeremy's establishment.'

'Thank you, madam.' Daisy bobbed a curtsey and left the room.

When they were alone, Millie took her mother's outstretched hand. 'So, Papa is ready to leave then?'

'Ready and waiting impatiently, as always. He's checked his fob watch a dozen times in the last ten minutes.' She smiled the indulgent smile wives gain after twenty-odd years of marriage.

'Do the carriages look lovely?' Millie patted her hair one more time.

'Oh, indeed. There's enough white satin bestowing the carriages and horses that if the wind was strong enough we could all be flying to the church. I blame your grandmama, of course.'

Millie grinned. 'Grandmama loves a bit of bunting.'

'A bit?' Mama raised a dark eyebrow. 'We'll look like a carnival caravan coming into town. I do not comprehend her at times, truly I don't. Never be one to show off as it is bad manners to do so, that is what my mother has always told us. Yet the minute I mentioned you wanted to travel to the church in the carriages and not the automobiles, she is ordering enough bolts of satin to cover the entire house. I dread to think what the church looks like.'

'It'll look beautiful. Grandmama has excellent taste.'

Mama took a deep breath, the smile coming back into her blue eyes she had passed on to all three of her daughters. 'Are you all set to go?'

'Yes.' Millie smoothed down her narrow ivory silk and lace gown, while her mother adjusted the fine lace veil at the back of her head.

'You do look beautiful, my darling girl.' Her mother's voice caught with emotion. 'Exactly as I imagined you would on this day.'

A flutter of nerves gripped Millie's stomach. 'I hope Jeremy thinks the same.'

'Of course, he will. No male could think otherwise.' Mama's smile slipped a little. 'You are completely certain this is precisely what you want?'

Her nerves went up a notch. 'Yes, Mama. Why?'

'Well, you know Papa and I will support you if you want to change your mind.'

'Why would I?'

'Because Jeremy, as nice as he is, he's not of your set, is he? I mean, he's extremely handsome, but not so full of life as Frank Bloomingdale or Arnold Botham. Jeremy was always your father's friend. He's older. Not a—'

'Mama, please, don't worry. I have thought long and hard about this decision. I confess I was surprised by Sir Jeremy's proposal, but with due consideration and the chance to spend some time with him, I do believe this is a good match for me. I had no interest in any of the young men of my own circle.'

'Some would say it is a very good match. You will become Lady Remington. But have you spent *enough* time with him? He went to the Continent straight after your engagement party. You've barely had more than a dozen days together.'

'It was unavoidable that he returned to France so soon, but he had to find out about his property over there. After years of war, he had a right to be worried that there'd be nothing left of his family's chateau and the winery.'

'He could have waited, what was another few months after not seeing it for nearly five years?'

'He wanted peace of mind. I agreed that he should go and find out what was left of it.'

Her mother sighed. 'All I'm saying is that he could have taken you with him after the wedding.'

Millie shook her head. 'No. Jeremy explained that travelling through a devastated country was not the type of honeymoon he envisaged for us, especially with the Spanish flu epidemic.'

'So, instead you're going to a hotel in Scarborough. Why not London or down to Cornwall, or Dorset? It seems a poor choice to me.'

They left the bedroom and walked along the gallery.

'After visiting the chateau, he knew he couldn't take us there. Jeremy has been through a war, Mama. He wanted to stay close to home, after years away, but he felt I need something to remember the occasion by. The hotel is the best in Scarborough. We won't have to travel far to get there and we'll have lovely walks by the sea. It'll be wonderful and safe. And I think that is what Jeremy needs. Somewhere safe, peaceful.'

'Promise me you'll get in touch if you find he has... if he is... What I mean is that he's... they say he's not...' Her mother blinked rapidly. 'Some say his injuries are not physical, but more mental and I worry enormously that he may not be who you think he is.' She let out a breath, her eyes expressing her concern.

'I trust my judgement, Mama, that and my instincts. Jeremy is a decent and kind person. He would not inflict such a... disability on me. I'm sure of it. Papa thinks very highly of him and he would know if Jeremy is not right mentally. They talk a great deal.'

'Yes, they do talk but like all men their conversations are of little value and consist of subjects such a shooting, politics and cigars!'

They stopped at the top of the stairs. A babble of subdued voices floated up to them from below, where no doubt the entire house staff were waiting to see her off.

Mama gave her a shrewd look. 'And your papa isn't the one marrying him. You are. And you know what that entails. This man. Forever. Sharing your life. Sharing his home, his bed... Marriage can be difficult enough when both parties are well, but should one not be...'

Millie smiled gently at the anxiety on her mother's dear face. 'All will be well, Mama. I know it will.'

'And if it doesn't work out as you expect, then you are to come home. If you are unhappy, you must not hide it from us. Promise me!'

'I promise.' She kissed her mother's soft cheek. 'Shall we go?'

Chapter Two

Jeremy Remington twitched his shoulders as though his officer's uniform didn't fit correctly, but of course it did for it was made by the best tailor in London's Savile Row. The coolness of the church calmed him somewhat, not that he was nervous. He didn't get nervous. Well, not normally, but then, it wasn't every day that you got married.

Married.

He still couldn't believe it. He was getting married. And to Millie Marsh, the one lady he thought he would never have. His heart did a little flip as it always did when he thought of her.

How long?

How long had he admired her, Lionel's eldest daughter? He'd watched her mature from a young lady into a beautiful woman and the whole time he never expected to be the one to take her hand in marriage. He assumed she'd be snapped up the minute she turned eighteen, but the years went by and the war took away the world they were used to. When the war ended, he eventually returned home, eager to see the woman she had become in his absence, and he wasn't disappointed. Millie had turned twenty-three during the summer and it only took one look, a few seconds in her company the day he called to visit them, and he knew it was time. His time to make a move.

He'd been patient long enough. He'd wanted her long enough. Discreet enquiries gave him the answers he sought. She wasn't waiting for anyone to return to her. She'd spent the war doing the good deeds women of her class did at such times, for her father had forbidden her to join the nursing corp, which apparently had been her desire. And he was glad she'd been stopped.

He shuddered slightly. The thought of his lovely Millie seeing the atrocities he'd witnessed filled him with cold fear.

He quickly cleared his head of the images that threatened to blind him. No, not today. Today was a joyous occasion. His wedding day. The nightmares could wait, as he knew they would, ready to grab him in the darkness and choke him. God, could he put Millie through it? Should he have told her? Would she despise him for crying out into the night, for his shakes?

'Ready, Rem?' His best man, Isaacs, joined him by the altar, smiling hesitantly, looking as anxious as though he was the one making his vows.

'I'm ready.' He nodded once, determined to not let his emotions show. He was more than ready to take a wife, to take Millie, to start a life that would fill him, fill the emptiness that had opened up inside him since the war finished. No, he wasn't going to think of the war today. It was done, over. Now it was time for new beginnings. A new life with Millie. If anything could help banish his night terrors it would be her. The sweet smell of her, the soft feel of her lying beside him would cure his dreams, he was certain of it.

His chest tightened at the thought of lying in her arms, sated with love, whispering his heart into the shadows. He hadn't survived the spray of bullets, the blast of bombs, the loneliness of the dark quiet nights in muddy trenches, the boredom, the endless paperwork, the death and the bloody sheer waste of it all not to be rewarded now.

Millie was his reward. She would heal him. He'd never be lonely again.

He turned to look over his shoulder and nodded at several guests taking their seats. The pews were filling up rapidly, the time was approaching.

He swallowed and took a deep breath, straightening his back as though ready for an assault. No, he had to relax, to smile, for Millie. He mustn't do anything to spoil this day, or worse still to make her change her mind. He knew he wasn't like the young men of her circle. He didn't find it easy to laugh at nothing or joke and make fun so effortlessly as her friends did, as *she* did.

Why had she said yes to his proposal?

Why had she agreed to tie herself to him of all people? He knew his faults and was trying desperately to change his ways. People thought him cool, detached, but beneath that hard exterior he was warm, loving, he knew he was, and he would prove it. His mother had died when he was young, but he remembered her kind eyes, her soft voice as she sang him songs in the nursery. Her loving embraces were the last he had received.

He ached to be loved again and to love in return. He cherished Millie and would spend every day of the rest of his life proving it to her, if she gave him the chance.

For years something in her manner alerted him to her gentleness, her compassion. He'd discreetly studied her for so long he knew her inside out. He admired her strength of purpose, her humour, the way she cared for others, her determination to win at tennis, even when she knew she was a dreadful player.

She had character. She went through life laughing and enjoying herself and he wanted to be a part of that. He wanted her happiness to seep into him and change his life.

The organ started to play, and the elderly vicar appeared from a side door with his verger walking solemnly behind him. Jeremy looked up at the stone vaulted ceiling. He wasn't a praying man. He didn't really believe in God, not after the horrors on the battlefield, but now he wanted to ask, beg even, that if there was some deity watching over them that it would grant him this wish.

All he wanted was for Millie to love him.

Could he have that?

Did he deserve it?

He'd killed men...

'Here we go then.' Isaacs coughed quietly and adjusted his uniform sleeves. 'Good luck, my friend.'

Jeremy let out a deep breath and smiled at him, the first true smile he'd felt for a long time. Saying, 'Good luck, my friend,' was what they said to each other before going over the top and into battle and each time they had survived it. Nothing else Isaacs could have said would have been as welcomed as that.

The music swelled, filling the small church. He turned slowly and watched his bride, *his beautiful bride*, walk towards him on her father's arm. In all his thirty-six years he had never felt as proud as he did at that moment.

~ ~ ~ ~

Soft music drifted on the breeze across the garden. The weather was still summery for the last day of August, which Millie was most pleased about, but if it had rained then they'd have just taken the tables inside the house. Her mother would have nothing ruin this day and her staff knew it.

Millie smiled at John, a poor harried footman, who passed by with another tray of drinks. He looked ready for a sit down and a cup of tea. She would have to go thank them all later, before she left.

'My dear, you seem a little lost.'

Millie kissed her grandmama's soft cheek. 'Not at all, Grandmama. I was just thinking, that's all.'

A look of horror came over Grandmama's face. 'Good lord, dear, don't start doing that. You're married now.'

'Grandmama!' Millie couldn't help but laugh. Her grandmama, Adeline Fordham, was a faded beauty, but she had the wit and backbone of a woman who had seen and done things that most could only guess at. Millie adored her. She had grown up listening to her grandmama's stories of her adventures abroad and the men she loved.

Grandmama leaned in close. 'Have you done the right thing, dear?'

'Please, not you, too?'

'No, I don't mean to be nasty, you know that. I greatly admire Sir Jeremy. The man is a war hero, for heaven's sake, and your father's good friend. A decent man all round, everyone knows it, but he's...' she paused, frowning, selecting the right words, 'he's so serious, my dear, always has been, even before the war. It's because he's an only child. They are like that, you see. He's never had the chance to fight with a sibling, and we all know how much that benefits one's character.'

Millie grinned at her. 'He was sent to boarding school at a young age, I'm sure that compensated somewhat in that area.'

'It's not the same at all, my dear. Chums at boarding schools couldn't possibly replace the familiarity of a sibling's emotional blackmail.' Grandmama paused, frowning. 'He's so unlike you. It worries me.'

'I don't think I would want to marry someone the same as me anyway. We'd be bored with each other before the year is out. Please don't worry. We do have things in common, naturally, but it's also stimulating to find out our differences and learn about them, too.'

'Spoken like a true innocent.' Grandmama nodded wisely, adjusting the dove grey lace at her throat. 'You'll learn, my dear. Just make sure you don't let him steamroll right over you. Men do that. They can't help themselves, it's as natural as a dog lifting its leg to pee.'

'Grandmama!' Millie spluttered her laughter.

Grandmama screwed her face up and then laughed with her.

'It'll be fine. I know it will.' Wiping her eyes, Millie shook her head at her grandmama's foibles. 'We have managed to talk quite a bit since his proposal and we get along rather well.'

'He is intelligent and so are you, but you can't talk forever.'

'Why ever not?'

Grandmama sniffed and fiddled with her emerald brooch. 'It's not natural, my dear.' She tapped Millie's hand. 'You'll soon find out that there are times when words are not needed, or useful.'

'You mean in bed?' Millie hid another smile.

Shocked, her grandmama's eyebrows rose. 'Indeed, I do not mean that at all! Talking in bed is most interesting, as you'll find out. I was talking about the times when fate makes life difficult, that's when you will know if you've made a mistake or not. It's those times when you don't need conversation you just need each other and it's in those times when you learn if you can depend on that person or not.'

'And you think I won't be able to depend on Jeremy?'

A long sigh escaped Grandmama. 'I think you can depend on him with your life, my dear, but can he depend on you with the same?'

'I would like to think so.'

'Yes, yes of course you would. I don't doubt it, really. You're my granddaughter, after all, and you're strong like me. Just remember though, dearest, men are funny creatures and not like us at all.' She gave Millie a long look. 'I think you'll find Sir Jeremy is the right man for you despite the differences.'

'Our age difference you mean?'

'Life experiences, Millie. He's a man who has been to hell and back, and not only that, his father, Soames, was a cold fish of a man, especially after his wife died. Now, she was a beauty, and Soames never got over her death.'

'Jeremy told me he and his father weren't close.'

'No. Tragic really. They only had each other and had no relationship at all. It's amazing Jeremy turned out as well as he did, really, but then the army helps shape men, and most times they do a better job of it than families.'

Millie kept silent and searched the crowd for her new husband but couldn't see him.

Grandmama tapped Millie's hand again and then lifted her head and gazed about at the guests. 'I had best go and mingle. Why your mother had to invite half the county is beyond me. The Sherwoods, for instance! He collects birds' eggs and she sleeps with a bottle of gin under her pillow. Their son draws nude women by bribing their housemaids, and their daughter eats chalk. Need I say more?' She tilted her head thoughtfully, giving a tiny smile and a wink before she walked away.

Millie watched her go, laughter bubbling in her chest. Her grandmama was a card, and she adored her.

'It's nice to see you smile.' Jeremy came silently to her side. 'You do it so well.' His own lips twitched.

She looked at him, her new husband, and had a moment of feeling none of it was real. The guests, the marquees of food, the music, the sunny day, and Jeremy himself, it all seemed a dream.

'I hope you will always be smiling,' he said softly, an earnest look in his eyes.

'I'm sure I will.'

'Have I told you how beautiful you look?'

'I don't believe you have. Thank you.' Her heart did the little flutter it always did when he looked at her so intensely. Why had it never behaved in such a way with other men before? There had been numerous opportunities for her heart to be affected by a handsome man, she'd known enough of them growing up. Certainly, she had danced with every man in the district and not once had any of them stirred her beyond friendship.

How had Sir Jeremy Remington done it? The moment he visited Elm House for the first time since returning from France, she had felt a strong attraction to him. She must have been blind to him all these years before, or maybe before the long years of the war she'd not been mature enough to think of him as a man, but simply a friend of her father's.

Jeremy cleared his throat. 'It is near to the time we ought to be leaving. I've already sent my man, Royston, and Daisy, to the station with the luggage. They'll get to the hotel before us and have everything ready.' His gaze roamed the gathering. 'I don't think we'll be missed now, do you?'

She looked for her mother and found her smiling and talking to a circle of friends. Her father wasn't too far away doing the same. No, they wouldn't be missed. 'I shall go tell Mama.'

Within a short space of time Millie had changed her gown into a tailored pale blue jacket dress and wore a small matching blue hat. Their guests crowded around them wishing them well, calling goodbye and good luck.

They were bundled up into Jeremy's automobile, a brand-new cream-coloured Napier and more rice and rose petals were thrown over their heads. Prue and Cece were crying, and Grandmama gave them a stern talking to for being so soft, while her parents gave her anxious kisses.

The Napier's top was down so they could wave all the way along the drive until they disappeared from sight around the curve of elm trees.

Jeremy was driving, something Millie found she was extremely comfortable about. Previously they had gone for a drive with Jeremy at the wheel, and she liked the intimacy of it. No chauffeur to listen to their conversation no matter how discreet they were. Besides, Jeremy told her that he much preferred to be in command of the vehicle himself, have the control of the speed. He relied on his skills, his intuition, and so far, she agreed with him. He was an excellent driver.

She sat beside him in the front and for a while they didn't speak, but lapsed into companionable silence.

She thought of what lay ahead, their first night together. She wasn't frightened or awed by the possibility of climbing into bed with this man, her new husband.

What was wrong with her?

Why wasn't she nervous?

Casting a quick glance at his profile, a tingle of excitement trickled down her spine. Shocked, she realised she was eager to find out what the whole experience would be like. Good or bad.

'What are you thinking?'

She blushed and looked away over to the passing countryside. 'Do you think our hotel room will be nice?' It was the first thing that came into her head.

'Of course. Why wouldn't it be? I asked for the best and paid for the best.' He changed gear as they slowed to turn right onto the road that would take them to the coast. 'These hotels have been closed for the duration of the war. They are eager to get their reputations and businesses up and running again. We'll be treated very well.'

'Yes, I'm sure we will.' She flashed him a smile and was pleased when he responded the same way.

Although money was never a topic discussed by anyone at any time, everyone knew which families of their circle who were in dire straits. And never once had Jeremy's family been talked about in that way, or at least that's what her father said. And he would know. Nothing got past her father when it came to money, those who had it and those who didn't. As an astute businessman, Lionel Marsh would have warned her if his friend wasn't able to provide for her.

They drove in silence for many miles, each lost in their own thoughts.

'Are you hungry?' Jeremy flicked her a worried look after they'd been travelling for nearly an hour. 'We can stop at the next village and find somewhere to eat.'

'But we aren't far from Scarborough now, are we?'

'No, not much further to go, but we have a few hours of daylight left so we can stop if you'd like to.'

'That would be nice. I'm not hungry, more thirsty I think.'

'Right. Will do.'

Within minutes they were slowing into a village that Millie didn't catch the name of but seemed a nice settled place. One of those little communities nestled in the Yorkshire moorland countryside where everyone knew each other and was likely related to them, too.

Parking the motor car in front of the only public house in the sleepy high street, Jeremy helped Millie out and they stood and stretched a little. The sunshine coated the front grassed area of the old stone building, inviting passers-by to take a seat on the wooden benches, and Millie did just that. Another bench was occupied by two old men drinking large glasses of frothy ale.

'May I have one of those, but perhaps not so large?' she asked Jeremy.

He frowned. 'Ale?'

'Why, yes.' She laughed at his shocked expression. 'I've had it before. My cousin, Eddie and I often went riding long distances in the summer and we'd stop at some little place somewhere and have a glass of ale to refresh us.'

'You do surprise me.'

'Good. I'd hate to bore you within hours of marrying you,' she joked.

Jeremy leaned down close to whisper in her ear. 'I very much doubt you'll ever bore me, my darling.' Then he was gone, disappearing into the dim interior of the pub.

A little flustered, Millie looked down at her hands and tried to stop the tingling running through her body. Heavens. A mere whisper from him had her quivering. How did that happen?

She'd known him for years, enjoyed dinners, dancing, picnics, shoots and every other entertainment in the heady days before the war started and not once did she feel like this. Granted, even back then she was aware of him. It was hard not to; such an interesting and powerful man drew attention wherever he went, but never in the way he did now.

If she was totally honest she knew he had watched her, or more accurately observed her from afar. He always made sure he talked to her at least once at any event they attended, and always claimed a dance.

She thought for a moment and realised they had never danced more than once at a party. Why was that? Why, if he ever thought of her as a future bride, did he not dance more than once with her at balls?

She gazed at a fat bee drifting among the flowers planted in the wooden tub by the door. There was so much she didn't know about her husband. Oh, she knew the main things, his pedigree, his family; that his mother died when he was a child, his father last year, and his cousin too, on the Somme. She knew of his Eton schooling, his love of automobiles, yet he was still devoted to his beautiful black hunter, Magic. She knew he liked to read the classics, though he'd confessed to her that sometimes he didn't always understand them and that annoyed him, so he'd read them again to overcome the challenge. She'd seen his sporting abilities on hunts, on the cricket field and on the tennis court – though he'd never partnered her, instead usually picking Prue. From her father she knew he was smart in the business world, having made clever investments. He'd joined the army young and distinguished himself on the battlefield.

But what was in his heart?

Jeremy came back outside and placed a small glass of ale beside her on the wooden table, but held his larger glass. He raised it to her. 'Cheers.'

'Cheers.' She raised her glass and then sipped from it, enjoying the cool invigorating taste. 'Why did you never dance more than once with me? In the past, I mean, before the war. All those parties and we only ever danced just once each time.'

'I think you had many willing partners, don't you?'

'So?'

His honey-brown eyes darkened. 'One dance was enough.'

'It was?' She didn't know what to make of that.

'Discipline.'

'Pardon?' Now she was confused.

'I had to discipline myself.' He glanced away towards the village green where a mother was shepherding her young children away from the duck pond.

'I'm not sure I understand.'

'Why would you?' With a huge sigh he turned his attention back to her. 'I've admired you for years, from afar.'

Millie stared at him, shock rippled through her. 'But...'

'No one knew. I made sure of that. I would have asked for your hand a lot sooner had not the war started. I was terrified of leaving you a widow, had you accepted, which I doubted you'd have done. I was also terrified of leaving you without declaring myself and that you'd fall in love with some handsome young officer.' He gazed down at his ale. 'I spent the entire war terrified of one thing or another, but mostly of hearing the news you'd found a man to love.'

'Oh, Jeremy.' She couldn't say anything more and when he looked at her the depth of his feelings was clear in his eyes, on his face. Shakily, overwhelmed by this quiet man, she stood and took the glass from his hand. On tiptoe she reached up and kissed him softly on the lips. His whole body tightened, and he groaned low in his throat.

She smiled into his eyes. 'Let's go to the hotel.' Taking his hand, she led him back to the Napier.

As they hummed along the dusty winding roads towards Scarborough, all Millie could think about was his declaration. To think all those years, she knew nothing of the depth of his feelings towards her. Admittedly, he had hidden it well.

She turned to stare at him, her heart fluttering a little. The wind ruffled his brown hair that only had a touch of grey in it, and she had to grip her hands to stop them from reaching out to brush it down. She liked that his nose wasn't completely straight but had a slight bump as though once he had broken it. His full bottom lip invited kisses and, just like back at the public house, she had the urge to kiss him again, only this time she didn't want to stop.

This handsome man was hers!

And he had wanted *her* for years. Incredible.

'Why are you staring at me?'

Unable to prevent herself, she laid a hand on his arm. 'We are married.'

'Yes, I know. I was there.' His lips quirked in that half-smile he was famous for in their circle.

'What I mean is...' Lord, what did she mean? Her fingers rubbed the soft leather of his driving coat.

Jeremy's arm moved beneath her fingers as he changed gears, slowing the Napier down until he pulled over onto the side of the road. In one swift movement he turned in his seat and took her into his arms.

His kiss was completely different from any they had shared before, which weren't many and simply chaste kisses of the kind people give when they are not sure of the other. However, this time, Jeremy held her tight to him. His lips were soft, yet demanding, urging, seeking and she instantly surrendered to the delicious enjoyment of being thoroughly kissed by a man who knew how to do it so fittingly.

Every sensible thought flew from her mind as her body responded to the attentions Jeremy was paying her. When his hands encircled her waist, drawing her even closer against his chest, she couldn't help but moan softly into his mouth. She nestled further into his arms, unable to bear any space between them. Everything in her life shifted at that moment. She suddenly became aware of what her body was wanting – and it wanted this man.

After what seemed an eternity, Jeremy drew away, breathing heavily. 'My darling...' His fingers brushed away a strand of hair which had escaped from under her hat.

Try as she might, she couldn't form the words she wanted to say. She didn't even know what she could say. All she knew was that if being married to Jeremy meant enjoying kisses like that, then she would be very content indeed.

'We should go.' He seemed as reluctant to let go of her as she was of him.

'Yes...'

He kissed her again, softly, tenderly, almost reverently. 'We have tonight.'

'Yes.' Couldn't she manage to say anything else? What was wrong with her? 'Jeremy?'

Kisses rained over her face. 'I know, my darling, I know.'

'You feel it too?'

'Yes. I always have.' He stroked her cheek with a finger. 'Thinking of kissing you was all that kept me sane in France. I've imagined doing this for so long.'

'I wish I had known.'

'It wasn't the right time. I didn't want to take the chance that you might not find my proposal welcoming.'

'But you hardly spoke to me, or anyone for that matter. You were always the ''serious friend of father's''. If you had spent more time with me, before the war, I would have thought so differently about you.' She looked down at the brass buttons of his uniform, trying to say what she didn't understand herself. 'I always admired you. I... I did find you... attractive in a distant kind of way...'

He tilted her chin, so she was looking into his eyes. 'You weren't ready back then. I knew that, and so would have everyone else, especially your parents. The war allowed us both to change, I suppose.' His lips lifted into a semblance of a smile. 'I'm still trying to change, be a better man. Not be so... distant.' He frowned, withdrew a little from her. 'Millie, there is something you need to know.'

'Oh?'

'I should have mentioned it to you before, before we were married.'

'I see.' She didn't of course and became worried. Then, seeing the despair cloud his eyes her heart melted. 'You can tell me anything, I won't judge.'

He gripped her hands and stared down at them as though the answers he sought were written on her gloves. 'I have nightmares.'

His simple statement made her fall in love with him even more. Three words. Three little words coming from such a strong man everyone admired, yet he was frightened to death of her reaction.

She let go of him and placed her hands on his face so that he looked straight at her. 'I can help you with that.'

'You don't understand. They occur quite often and can be most violent. I would never hurt you,' he added quickly. 'But I can't control them.'

'Maybe not, but perhaps having me beside you will lessen the severity of them.'

'I can only hope.'

'Jeremy.'

'Yes?'

'I think I have fallen in love with you, I hope you don't mind?'

The dead light left his eyes and was replaced by sheer happiness. 'I don't mind at all, my love, for I feel the same.'

'Good. I think we'll rub along together quite well, don't you?'

It was his turn to touch her face and he cupped her cheek to bring her lips closer to his. 'I'm banking on it, my darling.'

Chapter Three

Flat pewter clouds swept across the sky blown by a cold wind that had no right to exist in late August. The seagulls' cries were carried out to sea as they rode the air currents.

Millie wrapped her blue cashmere shawl around her shoulders tighter. She hadn't expected such a dramatic change in weather and hadn't packed her coat. Her hair was whipped into her eyes, making them sting, but the feeling of being free and happy was like an elixir. How could she be this happy?

'Why are you standing up there in this weather?' Jeremy came up the stairs to the castle wall and stood behind her. He wrapped his arms around her, cradling her close to his chest as the wind buffeted them. He'd been talking to one of the caretakers of Scarborough Castle and Millie had wandered off to explore. The castle was no longer standing, only small areas of ruins but the surrounding walls still remained. High on the bluff the walls offered a view of sea and sky that today were both grey.

'I like the smell of the salt on the air.' She snuggled in closer, not able to get enough of this man she married only two days before. Her body responded to his nearness. Despite only making love this morning, she wanted him again. Did a desire as strong as theirs ever fade? She certainly hoped not.

All that she had wondered about the marriage bed had melted away the moment Jeremy started to undress her that first night. They had sent Daisy and Royston away to find their own entertainment soon after dinner. By the soft glow of a bedside lamp, Jeremy had taken his time to undress her and kiss each inch of revealed skin until she was gripping his shoulders to keep upright. When she was naked, he laid her on the bed and quickly undressed himself before joining her. He took his time exploring, kissing, caressing her body, while encouraging her to touch and become familiar with his body.

Her fingertips traced the odd scar he wore, the bullet nicks from battle, the German bayonet stab in his side. She kissed each scar tenderly, showing him how much she cared about what he went through. Jeremy had refused to rush things and delighted in making her more sexually aware under his attentions. She surprised herself in her lack of modesty, and the freedom she felt. Finally, she'd become a woman properly loved by a man and she was eager to experience it all. She'd not known what to expect, it was a topic never discussed in society, but she had never anticipated feeling her body take over, to demand its own release and when that happened she'd gasped at the enormity of it.

When hours later they lay sated and tired, she sleepily curled against him and Jeremy held her tight to him and whispered he loved her.

He had not suffered a nightmare that night or last night. Perhaps he would suffer them no more.

'I think it's going to rain.' Jeremy murmured into her ear, as the first fat drops fell. 'Shall we return to the hotel or wait it out in the café down the street?'

'Let's go down and walk along the beach.' She grinned.

'Are you mad, woman?' He frowned but his lips quirked into a small smile. 'We'll be wet through before we reach the sand.'

She broke free from his arms and ran down the steps, laughing. 'Where's your sense of adventure?' She raced away, her shawl flying out behind her like a kite's tail.

~ ~ ~ ~

Jeremy carefully drove the motor car down the winding dirt road towards his ancestral home, Remington Court. Misty rain enveloped the shallow valley surrounding them. The car rattled over a wooden bridge that crossed the small stream, which wound itself way through the deer park. Tall chestnut and plane trees littered the fields on either side of the drive.

'It is unusual for a long drive not to be lined with trees,' Millie said, gazing out.

'It once was, over a century ago. But my great-great-grandfather sold all the oak trees to pay debts and to refurbish the house when he inherited. Apparently, the house was falling down from the lack of use, as the family stayed in London most of the time. Wings on either side of the house were knocked down and never rebuilt. So, the house is a lot smaller than it used to be. Perhaps we should select a certain type of tree we like and plant an avenue? What do you think?'

It didn't really bother him about the trees, but it pleased him that she had noticed it. His new wife certainly wasn't a normal woman of his class, who thought of nothing but dresses and entertaining. He liked that she was intelligent and inquisitive.

She turned to him with a dazzling smile. 'I think that would be wonderful.'

His shoulders relaxed a little as the house loomed up at the end of the drive. 'I want you to change anything you want in the house and gardens. It's all yours to do with as you wish.'

'No, we will do it together. We are a team.'

'We are.'

He wished the sun was shining, for the house looked pretty in the sunshine, but today its pale grey stone matched the gloominess of the weather. His heart turned in his chest the closer they got to the house. Why did he always feel this way? Ever since he was a child, he'd felt uneasy in this house, as though it was filled with evil spirits. He knew that wasn't true, of course. The only evil had been his father. No, that wasn't true either. His father wasn't evil, just totally uncaring.

He didn't want to come back here. Last night in bed, he had mentioned that they should perhaps go on to London, but she had wanted to see Remington Court, her new home.

He glanced worriedly at Millie, hoping she couldn't read the reluctance in his manner. 'Not the best homecoming weather I had wanted for you. I should have made the time to bring you here before the wedding. But with me being in France and London, I stayed here only a few days myself.' He didn't tell her that this house was not his favourite. He preferred the family's London townhouse and the chateau in France.

'It's only a bit of bad weather.' She shrugged, clearly not caring. 'Besides, I get to spend the rest of my life here. So, I'll have plenty of time to see the house in all weathers.'

He loved that about her, her positive manner, her lightness of spirit. She saw good in everyone and everything. How did she do it? Well, no matter how she did it, he just hoped she always would.

Slowing the motor car down, rain lashed the windows. He pulled over close to the wide steps leading up to the front door. He glimpsed movement behind one of the drawing room windows on the right of the door then it was gone.

Taking a deep breath, he climbed out of the car and hurried around to open her door. Together they ran up the stairs as the big black oak door opened and the housekeeper, Mrs Jacobs, stood there unsmiling.

'Ah, Mrs Jacobs. How are you?'

She bobbed her head slightly, her eyes cold, her back straight. 'I am well, sir.' She closed the door after them and waited with hands clasped in front of her, while a young maid hurried to take their gloves and Millie's shawl.

Jeremy slipped a hand into Millie's. 'Millie, this is Mrs Jacobs, the housekeeper. This is your new mistress, Millie, Lady Remington. I'm sure you'll do your very best to make her feel at home here as quickly as possible.'

'Indeed, sir.' Mrs Jacobs bent her head slightly.

'A light luncheon, please, Mrs Jacobs. Are the fires lit?' Jeremy walked into the drawing room, the fire at the far end of the room didn't look long established and a coldness pervaded the dark room. The weak electric lighting, installed at the turn of the century, didn't penetrate to the corners of the large room.

He looked at Millie, who stood gazing about the room. 'It'll warm up soon.'

Her smile was tentative, her blue eyes large in her delicate face. 'I'm not cold.'

'So, about Mrs Jacobs…' Jeremy jabbed at the fire with an iron poker, trying to grow the dismal fire into a cheerier blaze. 'She has had full control of this place. There's nothing she doesn't know. You must insist she tells you everything about the running of it.' He added another log onto the flames.

'There is no butler, is that right?' Millie perched on the edge of the blue and cream brocade sofa.

'No, he died not long after my father. I didn't replace him as I was hardly ever here.' He sat down beside her. 'Before the war I spent most of my time in London. My townhouse is in Kensington. To me, that is home. And, if I wasn't in London, I was at the chateau in France. This estate never got the attention, or my affection as the other two houses did.'

'If we are to make this into our home, then perhaps we could redecorate?'

'Yes, of course.' He looked around at the room, seeing it as Millie would see it with its dark red wallpaper, the dark wooden floor, the deep green Persian rugs, the large paintings, dull with age in their heavy timber and gilt frames.

'That's if money allows.' She tucked a curl behind her ear, her expression earnest.

He realised he had never mentioned money with her. 'There is money, my love. I am wealthy. My investments have done well during the war, which I'm grateful for as the death duties from my father were substantial.'

'Death duties are crippling so many families we know.'

'Yes, a dreadful business. Paying those after father died means I'll not be able to restore the chateau as quickly as I would like.'

'Is it very bad, the chateau?'

'Bad enough. There was heavy bombing of the vineyards, destroying the vines. The house received some shelling, but mainly it was occupied by the Germans and they didn't look after it, especially towards the end.' He felt such sadness that his mother's beloved home was wrecked so badly, sadness and anger.

Millie touched his hand. 'Perhaps one day we can restore it?'

He nodded, desperately wanting to do that more than anything. 'Until then, we shall live here, so you are close to your family. We shall redecorate every room in the house, make it modern.' He liked the idea — at least he was trying to like the idea. He could wipe out the past, wipe away the fog of neglect, not only of the house but his own father's lack of emotion.

Millie cupped his cheek and he melted inside. Her touch gave him such mixed emotions, desire certainly, but also strength to face anything life threw at him.

Movement at the door made them turn. Mrs Jacobs stood there, and Jeremy was reminded of a painting he once viewed of an old witch all dressed in black. Thinking back over the years, he didn't think he had ever seen her smile.

'Sir, your luncheon is ready in the dining room.'

'Thank you, Mrs Jacobs.'

'Also, the staff are gathered in the staff dining room for you to introduce the new mistress to them after you've dined, sir.'

Jeremy stood, and Millie rose too. 'Thank you. We'll be down in a while.' Jeremy led Millie across the hall and along the corridor next to the staircase. 'The dining room is here on our right, opposite is the study. There is a parlour opposite the drawing room. But I'll give you the full tour once we've eaten and seen the staff.'

In the dining room, a young maid, unsmiling, stood by the sideboard. She bobbed a tiny curtsy. Jeremy didn't know her.

As always when he was in the room, he glanced up at the large painting of his mother, dressed in a white gown and yellow shawl. Next to her, sitting looking up at her, was her favourite dog, Patch.

'That is a beautiful lady,' Millie said, looking at the painting, as he helped her to take her chair.

'My mother.'

'I see the resemblance.'

'You do?' He liked that she said that. He sat the head of the table, and it felt wrong. His father would be turning in his grave. No doubt taunting him for his boldness to sit in his chair. His severe countenance could penetrate from beyond death.

'Jeremy?'

He blinked, focusing on Millie's face. She was looking at him with a puzzled frown. 'I'm sorry, darling. What did you say?'

'I said, are there more paintings of your mother?'

'No. There isn't.' He waited for the maid to pour their coffee and return to the sideboard. He really must learn the new staff's names. 'My father admired that painting and that was enough, he needed no more, he said.'

Jeremy sipped his coffee and wondered why his father was on his mind. Was it because he was back in this house for good?

He felt his chest tighten at the thought.

Could he do it? Spend months here? He looked around the room, his appetite fading. It was so quiet. So dreary and dark and sinister. His father's shadow haunting the corners.

A bang made him jump and sweat broke out on his forehead. The maid was apologising, picking up a silver tray she'd dropped.

'Jeremy.' Millie placed her hand over his shaking hand. He'd spilt coffee on the white tablecloth.

'Sorry.' He didn't know why he was apologising. A feeling of dread built inside him and he had to fight it. The bang wasn't gunfire. He wasn't in the filth of the trenches, he was home, safe and whole.

'Shall we eat?' Millie stood and went to the sideboard.

Trying to be normal, Jeremy joined her and picked up a plate. He stared at the platters of ham, tongue, cheese and salads spread out. Little glass bowls of chutneys and pickles were at the side and, at the end of the sideboard, stood a large crystal bowl of fruit and tiers of cakes and sandwiches. So much food. Far too much. For the last five years he'd lived off army rations. Even when the war ended, food shortage was a concern and rationing was still in place. Why had this feast been provided, and how?

He looked down at Millie's hand on his arm.

'My love, aren't you hungry?'

'There's just so much.'

She took his plate from him and added a few triangles of beef sandwiches. 'Start with this.'

'I'm not a baby.'

She gave him a look of womanly superiority; the look women give men when they are being stupid. 'Your body needs fuel. Then, we will go meet the staff and afterwards we will have a rest in our room and you will tell me why you aren't happy here.'

'How did you know?'

'Grandmama mentioned a few things, but since entering the house you've been lost in your thoughts and jumpy.'

'I'm sorry.' He was amazed that she already was starting to read his body language.

'Don't apologise. We'll lay the ghosts of the past to rest and start again, shall we? I'm sure if we try really hard we can make this house into a warm family home.'

He took a deep breath. 'I do hope so.'

Chapter Four

Millie lay staring up at the shadows drawn across the ceiling. Beside her, Jeremy slept fitfully, and she suspected he was dreaming.

They had gone to bed early and talked for hours before making love. It had gone past one o'clock before they turned the light out. But sleep didn't come for her. Her mind was too full.

While they had been in Scarborough, Jeremy had been light of heart, happy, smiling. The serious man she had known for years gone, and she had fallen more in love each day with her new husband. However, since returning to Remington Court, she'd watch him retreat inside himself. Only in the privacy of their bed did he soften and talk. By the golden glow of the lamp, he'd open up to her about his thoughts about the estate, his family, the plans to rebuild the chateau in France, but he didn't want to speak of the war.

Yesterday, at the meeting of the staff he'd been awkward, and to compensate she had been overly cheerful and talkative. Her mother would have been none too pleased at her enthusiastic manner, and she'd have been correct. The people she had met in the staff dining room were unwelcoming and silent. The more Millie tried to engage them in conversation the more they closed up. She suspected Mrs Jacobs ran the place like a prison. Each member of staff looked to the housekeeper before making stilted replies to Millie's questions. She thought perhaps the housemaids, Sarah and Gilly might warm to her, but it would take time. Mrs Ellis, the cook, seemed competent and eagerly answered Jeremy's questions, but the whole time Mrs Jacobs watched over proceedings like a hawk, her beady eyes not missing a thing.

The tour of the house had been quick and not very enjoyable. Millie had entered each dreary and unloved room and realised there was no love in this house, nor had there been for some time. It was so different from the home she'd grown up in. Her mother had decorated Elm House with light colours, filling airy rooms with flowers and soft furnishings.

'Get down,' Jeremy mumbled, tossing his arm out.

Millie watched him, his eyelids flickering, his legs kicking out under the blankets. This is what he warned her about. She waited for a moment, and he stopped moving so restlessly.

Relaxing, she snuggled down further into the blankets, resting her arm over him, but he shook it off, mumbling.

Suddenly he reared up. 'Fire! Damn you, fire!' He was pushing the blankets away, trying to escape. 'Get down! They're coming!'

'Jeremy!' She went to grab him as he leapt from the bed. His arm swung backwards, his hand slapping her in the face with such force she fell backwards onto the bed. 'Jeremy!'

He fell hard onto the floor, his feet tangled in the bed sheet. 'Jesus Christ.'

Millie peered over the side of the bed. 'Are you all right?'

Jeremy lay on his back, naked, staring up at her, rubbing his elbow. 'Yes, I think so. Knocked my elbow.'

'Well, at least it wasn't your head.' He looked rather comical lying there on the floor.

'Thanks.' He climbed back into bed.

'Is my face red?' she asked offering the side he'd hit.

'Yes, a little, why?'

'It seems I'm going to have to wear armour to bed from now on.' She tidied the sheet and blankets.

'I hit you?' The colour left his face. 'Dear God, Millie. I'm so sorry.'

'You didn't mean it. You were in a battle.' She smiled to lighten the mood and take the horror out of his eyes.

'Darling, I'm so sorry. I didn't realise. I'm sorry.' He looked shattered by what he had done.

She kissed him quickly, smothering his face with butterfly kisses. 'You've nothing to be sorry for. You didn't know what you were doing.'

'But I hurt you! I would never in my life want to do that to you, you believe me, don't you?'

'Yes, of course. It's an accident, that's all. Do you want to talk about your dream?'

He looked away and straightened his pillows. 'I can't really remember it.'

'That's fine.'

'It's all a blur.'

'Sleep now.' She yawned and turned onto her side, pulling his arms around her.

He curved his body to fit against hers. 'I'm sorry.'

'Stop apologising. It's not your fault. You can't help it.' She yawned again. 'I might go up into the attic tomorrow.'

'Why?'

'To see if I can find some old armour in amongst all the stuff up there. I'll wear it over my nightgown.' She chuckled.

Hugging her to him tightly, he kissed the soft skin below her ear. 'I do love you.'

She heard the smile in his voice and knew she'd settled him enough that he'd sleep.

~ ~ ~ ~

Millie read the letter she'd just finished writing.

Dearest Prue,

Forgive me for not writing sooner. I'm sure you are angry at me for only sending a note to Mama and Papa and not to you and Cecelia, but I have been so busy I don't know where the time has gone since we returned from Scarborough weeks ago.

However, I have a few moments now and thought to catch up on my correspondence and write to you, Cecelia and Grandmama.

The weather has been cool but bright. I'm hoping it stays this way as I have the house being thoroughly cleaned, but October weather is so unpredictable.

Jeremy has shown me around the estate each day, and I am glad to escape this oppressive house – its gloomy rooms and gloomier staff do upset me, but Jeremy has given me free rein to change everything I wish to. And I will! The staff are uninteresting and sullen, Mrs Jacobs rules them like a jail warden. She frightens me immensely, Mama would be very cross with me if she saw it. I can't help it though. The woman is like a witch, always watching, silently appearing at doorways with a look of disdain on her face. We have a mutual dislike of each other. Poor Daisy has a time of it. After happy years at Elm House, she is stuck here amongst these unfriendly people. I feel so bad for bringing her here. Daisy tells me so many tales of how subdued the staff dinners are, and Mrs Jacobs rules with an iron will and no one dare cross her.

I need advice from Mama and Grandmama about the staff. Mrs Jacobs, and I certainly don't see eye to eye and I'm at a loss as what to do about it. You know I don't like confrontation, but the atmosphere in the house is severe indeed. Jeremy has left it up to me to sort out and I must do something. I've never had to deal with such things before. Help!

Jeremy and I regularly visit the local village and the few shops there. The people are friendly and happy to see a returning hero. It pleases me enormously to see how much the village folk want to stop and chat with Jeremy, even though the Remington Estate no longer owns the village as it did in the last century. Over tea and cake, I have learned about families who've known Jeremy all his life, and some whose sons have been lost in battle. After these little chats, Jeremy is always a little silent, his thoughts turned inwards, and I struggle to make him smile. He suffers his nightmares still, but not every night, thankfully.

Invitations arrive daily, and we have dined with many families, some I know, of course, like the Harpers, McDonalds and Winchesters, all who came to our wedding. In return we have hosted a few dinners, but I can honestly say to you that until the redecoration of Remington Court is complete, I am not entirely happy to be entertaining at this time.

Mama has confirmed that you'll all be coming here to us for Christmas and I'm so pleased to hear it. The house will be finished by then. I've enclosed samples of the colours in which the house is currently decorated. Notice the scrap of blood red wallpaper, which is hideous in extreme. You can imagine the work that is in front of me.

Tell me all your news.
Your loving sister.
Millie, Lady Remington – still not used to my title!

~ ~ ~ ~

After church on a cool October Sunday, Jeremy mentioned an afternoon ride through the woods. Millie enjoyed riding and her horse, Jester, had been brought from her old home. Reunited with Jester and eager to spend a few hours alone with Jeremy, she donned her blue riding habit and laughed as Jeremy hoisted her up onto Jester's back.

Beside her, Jeremy mounted Magic and they trotted out of the stable yard.

'Where are we heading then?' she asked.

'I thought we could ride across the fields towards Home Farm, and then turn and cross the stream if it's low enough. I'm sure it is. We've had a week of dry weather.'

'How large is Home Farm?' She had yet to visit Home Farm.

'It's of good size actually, even though the estate as a whole has been reduced in size over the years. My father was a keen country farmer, he hated town life and rarely went to London, which is why I preferred being there.'

'What animals do you breed?'

'Sheep mainly. Father won agriculture prizes many times with our ram. But we have a small dairy herd, too, which as you know supplies the house with all our dairy needs. There are pigs and geese, chickens, doves, and a goat or two at one time. I'm not sure if they are still there.' Jeremy rubbed his forehead. 'I really should take more interest in it, but I'm not a farmer.'

'You'd rather be a vintner, wouldn't you?' She gave him a quizzical look.

'I would, yes.'

She knew his heart really belonged in France at the chateau and vineyard, which he owned through his mother's Dumont family. Often his conversation would veer towards the improvements he needed to make at the chateau, how the war and the occupation of Germans had damaged it. 'Then why don't you do that?'

'It wouldn't be fair to you. To take you away from England, and your family, to a place still reeling from German invasion. No, it's not time yet.'

'But if that's where you want to be, then I don't mind.'

'No, Millie, not yet.'

They rode in silence, skirted the Home Farm buildings and headed along a worn path winding through the trees. The horses trod on a carpet of soft dying leaves sending up the scent of dampness only found in a woodland. A wood pigeon cooed above their heads from a thinning canopy.

Suddenly shots rang out shattering the quiet.

'Bloody hell! Enemy fire! Get down!' Jeremy leapt from Magic and ran to crouch behind the nearest tree before Millie had a chance to know what was going on.

The commotion set Jester prancing sideways as Millie tried to control him. 'Jeremy!'

She swung about in the saddle as more shots rang out. Who was shooting and from where? She could see nothing through the trees as Jester skidded and stomped. Once she had him still, she dismounted and hurried to where Jeremy had scrambled.

She found him hunched down by the trunk, his eyes wide, breathing fast.

'I can't find my gun. Stupid. Are there casualties?' He spoke quickly, like the major he still thought he was.

She gently placed her hand on his arm. 'You don't need a gun. We aren't in danger. We're home.'

He frowned at her, gaze wary. 'Home?'

'Yes, darling. At Remington Court.'

'But the gun shots?'

'I don't know, a farmer perhaps, but not the Germans. The war is over.'

Then as though a veil had been lifted from before him, he sagged against the trunk and gave an embarrassed smile. 'So sorry, I don't know what happened there.' His hands shook slightly as he heaved himself up. 'I thought… I thought it was an ambush, the gunfire…'

'That's understandable. You weren't expecting to hear shots ring out from nowhere.' She took his cold hand in her gloved ones and kissed it. 'Do you feel all right now?'

He nodded and looked around nervously. 'Who would be shooting on my estate without my knowledge?'

'I don't know but we will find out.' She walked with him to where Jester stood patiently. Magic was further away, ears twitching.

Jeremy helped her to mount and then caught Magic's reins. He flinched as another shot rang out some distance away. Whoever was shooting was no longer as close as they were.

'Shall we return home?' Millie asked, nudging Jester to walk on. 'I think we could both do with a cup of tea, don't you?'

Jeremy swallowed. 'Yes. Let us go home.'

Once back at the house, Millie sat with Jeremy in the library, a place he found relaxing more than any other room and rang for Mrs Jacobs.

The maid, Sarah, answered the summons.

'We'd like some tea, please, and where is Mrs Jacobs?'

'I don't know, madam.' The girl looked harried.

Unsettled by the girl's response, Millie left the library and found Mrs Jacobs coming out of the dining room carrying a case of silver spoons. 'Mrs Jacobs.'

The housekeeper sighed as though stopping her was an inconvenience. 'Yes, madam?'

Millie bristled. 'I rang the bell and you did not appear.'

'I was engaged elsewhere, madam. Did Sarah serve you?'

'She did.'

'Then there is no problem?'

'You are meant to be there, Mrs Jacobs, not Sarah.'

'I didn't expect you back so soon, madam.'

'While Sir Jeremy and I were out riding there were shots fired. Have you any knowledge of who would be out shooting on the estate without consent?'

'Consent?' Mrs Jacobs chuckled sarcastically. 'I'm sure it was only Phil Greenway, the gamekeeper. He doesn't need consent to do his job, surely?'

'He should at least give word of his intentions. We could have been shot. It shook us up very much, especially my husband.'

Mrs Jacobs tilted her head. 'Actually, I do believe he sent a note up to the house saying he was rabbit shooting today.'

A flicker of anger ignited in Millie. 'Then why wasn't that note given to my husband or myself? *You* knew we were out riding.'

A sly gleam entered the housekeeper's eyes. 'I must have forgot, madam, being as busy as I am.'

'Sir Jeremy is still suffering some effects of years of warfare. Suddenly being shot at has unsettled him greatly. In future we must do everything we can to prevent that. Do I make myself clear?'

'You do, madam. But perhaps it would be better for Sir Jeremy to return to London for a time, until he is more himself?'

'Remington Court is his home also, and where he has chosen to stay for the time being.' Millie turned and left the horrid woman. She had a suspicion that Mrs Jacobs would rather she had the house to herself just as she did during the war when she could do as she pleased all day. Well, she had a shock coming to her, that was for sure.

~ ~ ~ ~

Straight after breakfast the following morning, Millie set to work in changing the house. She wore a fitted blue woollen dress as the day was cool, and house even cooler. While Jeremy went to visit the estate's Home Farm, she decided to make an inventory of the items in each room. Thankfully the incident yesterday had not brought on Jeremy's nightmares. He had slept soundly after they had made love. It seemed the physical act of love made him sleep better, at least that's what she hoped. He liked the feel of her wrapped around him, he said, and she preferred to be nowhere else.

She started in the drawing room. Going from wall to wall, she wrote down each painting. Next, she listed the cabinets and tables, the chairs and sofas. She noted the curtains and realised she needed to measure them to be replaced.

Mrs Jacobs knocked on the door.

'Yes?' Millie glanced at the housekeeper, before inspecting the peeling paintwork on the window frame.

Standing stiffly in the doorway, Mrs Jacobs frowned on seeing Millie with pen and paper in her hand. 'Will you be wishing to speak to Mrs Ellis about the week's menu, madam?'

'Yes, I will, but later. I've much to do this morning.'

'Mrs Ellis has her half day off today, madam. Unless you wish for her to change it?' Mrs Jacobs's small eyes narrowed with hostility.

'No, not at all. I will see her about the menus tomorrow morning.' Millie gave her a big smile, hoping to win the odious woman over. It failed. She'd never met anyone she didn't like so intensely, and it was a surprise to her. So far, she had lived her life surrounded by nice people and hadn't even realised it. There was the odd associate in her family's circle who might be a bit strange or odd, but no one had ever showed her acute dislike to her face like Mrs Jacobs did.

Mrs Jacobs' face became more expressionless. 'The grocery order goes out today. It needs to be finalised.'

'I see. Very well, I'll go down and speak with Mrs Ellis in an hour.'

The housekeeper sniffed with disapproval. 'Are you requiring my help with whatever it is you are doing, madam?'

'Actually, yes, Mrs Jacobs.' Millie looked around the room. Lord, where would she start? 'We are to have a full house redecoration.'

'I beg your pardon?' Visibly startled, the housekeeper straightened her shoulders. 'Are you implying, madam, that this house isn't to your liking?'

'I'm implying exactly that. Of course, there are some fine pieces we shall keep, and the paintings, but much of what we see is going.'

'Going?' High colour appeared in Mrs Jacobs's cheeks.

'To auction.'

'Auction?'

Millie raised her chin. This woman was irritating. She behaved as though the house was hers and Millie just a visitor. Ever since the staff introduction, she had been barely courteous. 'That's right. I am instructing a full redecoration of every room. We shall start in this room.'

'*Full* redecoration?' Mrs Jacobs huffed, as though she had been asked to do it all herself.

Was the woman going to repeat every word she said? Millie grabbed a handful of the thick dark red brocaded curtain that adorned both windows. 'All the curtains can come down, in every room. I'm having them replaced.'

'All of them? The former mistress only had them made new when Sir Jeremy was little!'

'My husband is now thirty-six years old. The curtains are being replaced.' Millie turned away from the housekeeper's furious gaze and studied the walls, which were lined with moss green coloured silk. 'I want the wall linings removed as well.'

'The former Lady Remington picked that colour herself. I doubt Sir Jeremy will want to change his late mother's choice.'

'My husband is on-board with every decision I make, Mrs Jacobs.' Annoyed, Millie took a deep breath and stepped across the room to the fireplace.

'Madam, this should be done at the start of summer, not at the end! It is a momentous upheaval going into winter.'

'I appreciate your concerns, Mrs Jacobs, but my mind is made up. I want the house finished by spring.' Millie wrote down a few items of furniture on her list.

Glancing up, she noticed Mrs Jacobs still standing in the doorway, her lips a thin tight line. 'Send in some men to remove the furniture, please. Have Gilly and Sarah pack the ornaments. Dust covers will be needed for the furniture that cannot be moved. The paintings can be stored in the attics.' Millie wrote a few more items down. 'Oh, and the men can roll up the rugs. The floor will have a new stain and polish, too.'

Mrs Jacobs folded her arms under her breast. 'Madam, I *must* relay to you my misgivings on this endeavour. I see no reason—'

'When did the chimney sweep call?' Millie interrupted her.

'Er… well, he was meant to come in early summer, but he sprained his ankle.'

'Are you saying the chimneys have not been swept this year?' Shocked, Millie stopped mid-writing. 'You know how much of a fire hazard that is!'

'I had hoped to engage him while you were on your honeymoon which I assumed would be of some months, but since Sir Jeremy and yourself returned very soon after the wedding, it didn't get done,' the housekeeper spat the words out.

Seeing the woman's dislike clear on her face, Millie's attempts to be civil disappeared. She remembered her mother's teachings of dealing with household staff – kind but firm. But Mrs Jacobs came under another heading altogether!

Millie wrote another item on her list, a beautiful blue and white china vase. She would keep that. 'A sweep must be brought in as soon as possible. There will be no fires in this house until he is!'

'No fires? It's getting colder every day. Lady Remington, I must insist—'

'I said no fires. I'd rather be cold than burnt in my bed!'

'What about the kitchen?'

'The kitchen fires are an exception, but when the sweep comes, he will do the kitchen chimneys first. Inform Mrs Ellis that she must prepare for a day of cold meats for our meals.'

Leaving the drawing room, Millie crossed to the parlour. 'I am to go to York tomorrow, Mrs Jacobs, to select fabrics and place orders.' Millie paused by the piano and wrote 'Parlour' on her list. 'The drawing room needs to be stripped bare. Can you see to this please?'

'Madam is that necessary?'

'It is, yes.'

'The staff has been greatly reduced since the war. Most of the girls haven't come back after earning good money in the factories. We don't have enough people to do all that you ask.'

'Then hire some extra workers. I'm sure there are people in the village who need employment.'

'The kind not worth having.'

'I'm sure you'll soon sort it out, Mrs Jacobs.' Millie wrote some more on her notes. 'The bedrooms will need airing, too. My family will be coming to stay in a few weeks, and I want each room repainted and to not be smelling of damp.'

'How many of the bedrooms, madam?' Mrs Jacobs ground out through gritted teeth.

Millie felt her temper rising at the woman. 'At least four. A room for my parents and one each for my two sisters. I'm not sure if my cousin will be with them. I will let you know closer to the time.'

'There is still rationing, madam. How do you expect us to feed a house party?'

Millie clenched the pen in her hand and took a calming breath. 'My husband is visiting the Home Farm this morning to ascertain the slaughtering of animals for our guests. I'm sure Mrs Ellis will cope with what she is supplied from the gardens and the farm.'

Mrs Jacobs tutted, clearly not agreeing.

Millie left the room. 'If you'll show me the linen room. We can discuss what else needs purchasing.'

'The linen? The linen is perfectly adequate, madam. We have no need to purchase more.'

'I will be the judge of that.' Millie headed for the staircase. 'Please show me where it is stored.'

Mrs Jacobs huffed. 'I take offence that you are suggesting I don't know good quality linen when I see it. There is nothing wrong with our linen!'

'That is enough, Mrs Jacobs!' Millie lost her temper, something she rarely did. 'Am I not the mistress of this house? Are you to argue with every decision I make? If you do not wish to follow my orders, you may find yourself another position!'

Mrs Jacobs grew so red in the face that Millie thought she might surely burst.

'Indeed, I shall!' Mrs Jacobs unhooked the large ring of keys from her waist and threw them on the floor. 'You will regret this day, *madam*. I have served in this house for forty years! You have been here barely five minutes. Good luck in trying to find someone else to live out here in this miserable place.' She stomped from the room.

Millie sagged against the wall. That was not the result she wanted. Had she handled the situation wrongly? Would her mother have done better? They now had no butler or housekeeper. What a disaster. She'd have to contact an agency immediately and begin the laborious task of hiring a new housekeeper, for Gilly and Sarah were too young and inexperienced to take on the role.

She looked up as Gilly and Sarah hurried into the room, their eyes wide in fright. 'Yes?'

'Mrs Jacobs, she's in an awful temper,' Sarah said, gripping her black skirt.

'She broke a vase, madam,' Gilly added.

'Did she now?' Millie marched out of the room, along the corridor to the back staircase used by the staff and went downstairs. She could hear Mrs Jacobs yelling abuse in her private rooms located off the kitchen.

'Madam?' Mrs Ellis and her assistant stood standing at the large wooden table, but Millie carried on and into the housekeepers' quarters.

Mrs Jacobs was packing random things into a suitcase, her coat half on. 'I have a right to pack my things!' she snapped, throwing more clothes into the case.

'You do, absolutely. However, you will not damage another thing in this house. So, I will watch you to make sure.'

'Watch me?' Furious, Mrs Jacobs grabbed a box from a drawer and Millie heard it rattle as though filled with coins.

Again, the luxury of the room surprised Millie. Before, on the tour with Jeremy, they had simply glimpsed into the room, but even in that glimpse, Millie had noted how well furnished it was.

Now, she looked properly and was amazed at the items filling the small sitting room and the adjoining bedroom. A thick rug covered the floor, which was better than the rug in the parlour. The furniture was heavy well-made carved pieces of ebony. Paintings hung on the walls, and along wooden shelves were an impressive selection of books and ornaments.

From her dressing table in the bedroom, Mrs Jacobs bundled up a selection of perfume bottles, ivory handled brushes and combs. Poking out of the suitcase were silk stockings, embroidered linen, skirts of taffeta and sateen, cotton petticoats, and a fur muff. The woman lived better than any housekeeper Millie knew of.

Millie moved to the roll top desk in the sitting room, noticing the paperwork, the accounts ledgers, embossed letter headed writing paper, various pens and envelopes.

'I'll send for my things in a day or two,' Mrs Jacobs snapped as she closed the suitcase and shrugged on her coat properly.

'You do that.'

'After forty years, I expect a good reference and a considerable annuity should I decide to retire.'

'Really?' Millie laughed sarcastically. 'I don't think so.'

'I'm entitled!'

'Are you entitled to steal from this house, too?' Millie swept her arm wide. 'You've been living the high life for years, and you know it. Obviously, my late father-in-law gave you full rein of everything and you took advantage of that.'

'I conducted my position in this house with absolute professionalism. Sir Soames was a gentleman who knew he could leave the running of this establishment in my hands as is the proper way.'

'I doubt he would have if he knew you were feathering your own nest right under his nose!'

'I've poured my life into this house. Everyone knows there are privileges that come with this position, they are compensation for the long days and constantly being at beck and call!' Mrs Jacobs glared.

'With my husband away, you've not been at anyone's beck and call, Mrs Jacobs. You've had full run of the accounts and this house. Look at how you've lived, like a queen! Well no more, Mrs Jacobs. The money you've stolen over the years will have to keep you now.'

'You've no proof!' The former housekeeper edged to the door, lugging her heavy suitcase.

'I can easily find evidence if I investigated hard enough and you know it.'

'I knew you'd be trouble the minute I clapped eyes on you.'

Millie stiffened at the insult. 'Please leave!'

'Good luck living here, you're going to need it. Sir Jeremy has always hated it here and you will, too. Sir Soames's ghost haunts the place.' Mrs Jacobs gave an evil smile. 'And I doubt he'd think anything of you.'

'Go! Now!'

Once the older woman had stormed away, Millie sat at the desk. She hated confrontation and her body shook. For the first time in her life she had heatedly argued with someone and she didn't like it. Oh she'd had silly scraps with her sisters, especially Prue, but never had she had someone be so abusive to her face.

'Oh, madam!' Mrs Ellis came quietly to her side. 'Are you all right?'

'Have you been in on it, too, Mrs Ellis?' Millie accused, suddenly worried that she'd have to dismiss the entire household.

Mrs Ellis paled. 'In on what, madam?'

'The feathering of your own nest as Mrs Jacobs has obviously done for many years.'

A flush crept up the neck of Mrs Ellis. 'No, I haven't unless you count the odd extra tin of cake here and there that I took to my brother's house on Sundays. He is not right in the head any more, but he still recognises me and he loves a bit of fruit cake.'

'Taking your brother some cake is not what I meant, Mrs Ellis. You are welcome to do that. I'm talking about living like this.' Millie swept her arms around the luxuries of the room. 'Mrs Jacobs has had a very good life here. The clothes she packed just now would rival my own. How is that for a housekeeper?'

'Yes, I agree. She liked her comforts did Janice Jacobs. I used to envy her confidence in the way she oversaw the house, but I often wondered if perhaps she was taking too many liberties.'

Millie opened one of the ledgers and idly glanced at the figures. 'I'm assuming the accounts will not easily reveal the odd shilling slipped away here and there over the years. I'm certain she has built up a nice little sum while she has been in total control. My husband has been absent too much to keep an eye on the expenses.'

'Both the old master and Sir Jeremy gave Mrs Jacobs full responsibility of the running of the house.' The expression on the cook's face gave away her feelings on that matter. 'They trusted her implicitly.'

'And you believed that was a mistake?'

Mrs Ellis frowned. 'It's not my place to say.'

'I'm asking for you to have your say now.'

'Well, all I know is that the former butler and Mrs Jacobs lived very well compared to the rest of us and Sir Soames simply paid the accounts when they were presented to him and didn't ask questions. Make of that as you will.'

Millie sighed. She had no proof that Mrs Jacobs lined her own pockets, just a very strong hunch, and now Mrs Ellis had confirmed she was right to be suspicious. She gathered all the ledgers from the desk. 'There will be changes from now on, Mrs Ellis. For now, until another housekeeper is found, you will be responsible for the female staff. Is that satisfactory to you?'

'Yes, madam.' Mrs Ellis bobbed her head in acknowledgement.

'Whatever has been going on before will stop today. Let the rest of the staff understand this. I will not tolerate any behaviour which sabotages the successful running of this estate.'

'Yes, madam.'

'My husband has fought for his country and shouldn't have to return home to find his staff stealing from him.' Millie took a deep breath. This was not the start she wanted. Yet, she couldn't show weakness. If the staff thought she was a pushover, then she'd never gain their respect.

Head held high, she walked past the kitchen staff without another word and headed back upstairs.

Chapter Five

Jeremy stopped at the edge of the woodland. Last week's embarrassing episode remained fresh in his mind. It mortified him that Millie had witnessed such a drastic reaction to the gun shots. He hadn't expected to feel like this still. It was many months since he had resigned his commission and demobbed.

He knew at night his dreams would send him back to the battles he'd fought in, that he could understand, but never had he expected that hearing shots in broad daylight in his own home would affect him so severely. Were other men like this a year after the ceasefire?

He'd witnessed the shell shock of men in battle. Many a time he'd pulled a soldier to his feet and told him to run when all they wanted to do was curl up into a ball and cry like babies. He'd seen men shaking and staring blindly after a fierce encounter with the enemy. Officers had a duty to keep men's spirits up, to keep the morale high. He would laugh and joke with them, ignoring the horrors they'd witnessed, the deeds they had done.

So why now, when he was safe and free of command and responsibilities, was he reduced to a quivering mess. He had everything he wanted. A beautiful loving wife, comfortable homes, wealth and freedom to do whatever he wished. Millie encouraged him to talk to her about the war and his experiences, but he couldn't. Nothing he said would adequately describe the horror of what he had witnessed.

Giving himself a mental shake, he took a hesitant step into the cover of the trees. After speaking to John Atkins his manager at Home Farm and to Phil Greenway, he knew there was no shooting being done today. Both men had understood his request, especially Atkins who had a son missing a leg after the Somme.

With his uncocked rifle hooked over his arm, he trod purposely through the wood. He felt better having the rifle, not that he intended to shoot anything, it was more a case of the familiarity of having a weapon. He'd spent the last four years with a pistol at his waist and his hands felt a little empty without one.

A cock pheasant ran out by his feet, jerking him to a standstill. Instinct made him scan the area then he shook his head to clear his mind. He was on his own estate. There were no Germans here.

He strolled, deliberately making himself relax and breathe normally. He had to master this fear, this irrational dread that he wasn't safe. He was in the middle of Yorkshire for heaven's sake, if he couldn't be safe here then he might as well give up now.

Wood pigeons called from the branches above his head. The cold weather was creeping upon them now. Soon the snow would come, and he'd be housebound, not that he minded that. Unlike most men, it didn't bother him being inside day after day. There was no better place to be when it was snowing than beside a roaring fire reading a good book. He'd have liked to have taken Millie to London for the winter, but her family were coming to stay for Christmas and he knew she was eager to celebrate and be the hostess for the first time to them. In truth he was pleased the house would be full at Christmas. It would help banish previous childhood holidays, which were cold and dreary and no matter what he said or did, he couldn't please his father.

This year would be different. This year he'd have a warm loving family surrounding him. The house, although in turmoil now with redecorating, would shine like a new pin once Millie had finished with it. She'd been working hard all week with the plans for redecorating and overseeing the chimney sweep, who had finally turned up and was working through the house cleaning out the chimneys. She'd hired a few men from the village to strip the walls and start painting and wallpapering. New curtains were arriving every day and he was amazed at how Millie had known exactly what colours to purchase which brightened the house and banish years of neglect and gloom.

He was so proud of his new wife. Millie had been eager to take hold of the running of the house after the dismissal of Mrs Jacobs – a decision he had agreed with, but which had saddened him that such a long-time member of staff had been so dishonest. Yet, he supposed it was hardly surprising when people were left to their own devices they would suit the situation to their own advantage. Both he and Millie had learned a valuable lesson that staff, no matter who they were, needed managing.

He had driven Millie to York to register with an agency for suitable candidates to replace Mrs Jacobs and then they had spent a pleasant day exploring the shops for furniture and wallpaper samples, curtain materials and timber stains before finishing the day with a splendid afternoon tea.

His thoughts distracted, he came upon the narrow stream sooner than expected and knelt to take a drink from the clear running water. As he went to rise, he looked across the stream and stilled. On the opposite bank, propped up against a large oak tree was a rough shelter made of broken branches.

Jeremy cocked the rifle and raised it. 'Who is there? Show yourself!'

Nothing moved from within the shelter.

Glancing at the best place to cross, Jeremy waded into the shallow water of the narrow stream, ignoring the cold water that seeped into his boots and socks.

Army training came to the fore as he crept closer to the broken branches. 'If you're in there, you have two seconds to come out with your hands up!'

With every one of his senses alert, he used the end of the rifle to move aside the branch concealing the entrance. For a moment he couldn't see inside the dimness, but then he saw a form under a coarse dark grey blanket.

'You there. Wake up!' He nudged the shoulder with the rifle, his heart beating fit to burst from his chest.

The body didn't move.

Slowly, tight with tension, Jeremy hunkered down, the rifle pointed to the brown hair just visible on the person. He used the rifle to move aside the blanket and revealed a large man lying on his side facing away from him. He wore a grubby brown suit.

Jeremy roughly nudged the man's shoulder again. 'Wake up.'

When the man didn't move, Jeremy's first thought was that he was dead.

Not wanting to get too close, he knelt at the edge of the entrance and reached in to slip his hand inside the man's jacket. He felt something square resting on the man's stomach and pulled out a small black book. He flipped through the pages. Poetry. Inside the front cover it read.

To my darling grandson, Monty.
Happy birthday,
With love Grandmama

The man groaned, making Jeremy jump.

'Wake up now,' he barked, his grip tightening on the rifle.

Blue eyes flicked open. 'Hel…help…me.' Then he closed his eyes again.

Jeremy sat back and wondered what to do next. He searched the man's pockets again. His fingers touched steel and his stomach dipped when he withdrew two war medals, The British War Medal and the Victory Medal.

Turning the man over so he could see him properly, Jeremy stared at the man's face and the large jagged scar that went from his jaw and down his neck to disappear under his clothes.

Emotion filled him. This man sleeping rough was a returned solider, just as he was. Without thought, Jeremy shrugged off his overcoat and laid it over the man. 'I'll be back, mate. I promise.'

Then running as fast as he could, he ran for Home Farm, which was closer than the house.

~ ~ ~ ~

Millie sat on the window seat in the morning room and read Prue's letter.

Dearest Millie,

I received your latest letter just this morning and thought to write back to you before I go out to dinner at the Bothams with Mama and Papa – Cece is ill in bed with one of her headaches.

I cannot believe the hassle you have endured with that horrid woman, Mrs Jacobs. How happy you must be to have rid of her now. Mama always says good staff are worth their money, but I suppose when you inherit staff you have to find out for yourself who is trustworthy.

I am still having trouble adjusting to you not being here. I know it's been only about seven weeks or so since your wedding, but it feels like YEARS. You always listened to me, whereas Cece has her head in a book all the time or is out doing good works, which makes me look totally selfish when I'd rather go shopping.

I'm so bored – all the time, especially since Grandmama has returned to London. At least she was someone to talk to. Mama says I should look for a husband, and a part of me agrees, but there is no one who interests me.

Do you remember Georgina Radley? We met her a few times at social functions. Her parents lived in that lovely cottage on the Selby Road, and we went there to pick strawberries one summer before the war. Anyway, Georgina has died of the Spanish flu – will it ever go away? Isn't that dreadfully sad? The funeral is tomorrow, and we are all going. The Radleys lost their son when we were young, do you remember? Now they have no children. Mama went to visit them today. I couldn't face it. I wish I was braver at such things like you are, and even Cece, but it upsets me far too much to see others suffering and I can never find anything to say.

Heavens, I must dash, Papa has called saying they are ready to go.

I'll post this in the morning when I go to collect my new hat.

Much love,
Prue – with no new title!

Hearing complaints coming from the other room, Millie folded the letter into her pocket, and went into the parlour to check on the two grumbling under-gardeners who she had instructed to paint another coat of polish on the newly stained floors.

She gave them an encouraging smile. 'It looks very good. Thank you for your hard work.'

'Aye, it's coming on a treat, madam, even though we've not done it before.' The oldest man, called Potters, leaned on his painting mop. 'It'll be finished in an hour.'

'Wonderful. Sir Jeremy and I are grateful to you for doing something inside the house rather than outside. We understand it's not what you are used to, but it saves hiring someone to come from York.'

'Madam! Madam!' Gilly came hurrying into the parlour.

Millie jumped in surprise. 'What is it, Gilly? Why are you in such a hurry and calling so loudly? Seriously who was responsible for your training? That is no way to behave.'

'You must come, madam! Sir Jeremy is calling for you,' the girl panted. 'I was coming from the laundry and saw them drive in on the farm truck.'

'What are you talking about?' Millie asked, following the girl out of the room and into the hall just as Jeremy and several men came in carrying a man on what looked like a door.

'Jeremy?' She was quickly by his side. 'What's happened? Are you hurt?'

'No, no not me. This man needs a doctor, but we've sent one of the lads from Home Farm to cycle into the village to find Doctor Boardman.' Jeremy, holding one side of the door, issued orders for them to take their burden upstairs.

'Who is he? And why have you brought him here?' Millie mounted the stairs behind them.

'There is nowhere else to take him.' Jeremy puffed. 'Which room, Millie?'

'Oh, er… the yellow room is prepared for my parents.'

'That will do for now.' Jeremy and the men disappeared into the bedroom.

Millie wasn't so sure she wanted them in there. It had just been newly painted a warming canary yellow colour. She'd had Sarah and Gilly strip and clean the room for days, so it was smelling fresh and decorated with new bedding and bowls of hot house flowers. She didn't want that man in there and from the state of the grey blanket she'd glimpsed, Jeremy's patient wasn't going to be clean.

She waited by the door as the men transferred the unconscious man from the door to the bed. Each man gave her a nod of respect as they filed out carrying the door between them.

'Jeremy, who is he?' She came closer to the bed and blinked in surprise at the ugly scar running down the man's jaw and neck. 'Do you know him?'

'I found him in the woods, by the stream, sleeping in a makeshift shelter.' From his pockets, Jeremy gave her a little book and two medals. 'He's a returned soldier, Millie,' he said as though that explained everything.

'He might have the Spanish flu, Jeremy. You shouldn't have brought him into our house.'

'He is sick, he needs our help. Where else should I have taken him, to the stables?'

'Don't think me uncaring, for I am not. But if he is contagious, you've risked the entire household.'

'Doctor Boardman will soon tell us.'

'I thought Doctor Boardman was retired?'

'He's all we have for ten miles. He'll come.' Jeremy took a blanket from the wardrobe and laid it gently over the man.

Her husband's compassion melted Millie's heart. Who was she to chastise him for taking care of someone? She glanced at the medals she held and the little black book of poetry.

'He's called Monty.' Jeremy looked down on their visitor.

Millie laid the book and medals on the bedside table. 'When he wakes up I'll ask him if he wants me to contact his family or friends.'

'If he had any of those he wouldn't be sleeping rough in our woods.'

Millie touched Jeremy's arm. 'We can't save every returned solider, darling.'

'No, I know. But imagine how many there are needing help?'

'There are organisations who are doing great work rehoming men, getting them work.'

'His scars will frighten most I should think. I'll offer him a job here.'

'Let us see what he wants to do first, shall we? He might be simply travelling through.'

An hour later, Doctor Boardman sat drinking coffee with Millie and Jeremy in the morning room, the one room that was not spoiled with redecorating and had a roaring fire lit. The house was in no shape for visitors. Millie was embarrassed that the doctor was not being entertained in the drawing room, but it was still empty of furniture as the floor polish dried.

'The man is malnourished and has a slight chest cold, but not the Spanish flu as far as I'm aware. Sleeping out in all weathers has weakened him.' The doctor took another sip of coffee and ate a piece of jam tart. 'If he'd been a smaller, thinner man, I doubt he would have survived.'

'So, he needs rest?' Millie asked.

'Rest, food, shelter.' Doctor Boardman nodded, helping himself to another tart. 'He'll soon be back on his feet.'

'Did he speak to you at all?' Jeremy asked.

'The odd murmur, nothing sensible, poor fellow. Sleep is a great healer, especially in a soft warm bed.'

'I'll go up and sit with him. Thank you, Doctor Boardman.' Jeremy left them, and Millie poured more coffee.

'My husband is determined to make this man well again. Being soldiers they have a common bond.'

'Ah, yes. Men in war tend to stick together when they can. Your husband is a good man and will not see him go without.'

'Jeremy wants to offer this man a position here on the estate.'

'Heart of gold, he has. Not a patch on his father.'

Millie sat straighter. No one spoke of Jeremy's father. 'What was he like?'

'Sir Soames Remington?' Doctor Boardman shrugged. 'He was a man who didn't suffer fools, that was for certain. He had a manner that was abrupt and cold. I wasn't invited here often. Sir Soames wasn't one for entertaining and after his wife died, he became something of a recluse.'

'How very sad.'

'It was how Sir Soames wanted to be. Everyone felt sorry for Jeremy as a child. He grew up in a very sombre household. Sir Soames should have tried harder to be a more involved father. I believe Jeremy enjoyed boarding school though. Then of course he went into the army and when he could he travelled to his mother's vineyard in France and stayed there, or in London. We rarely saw him once he became an adult and didn't have to come home for school holidays.'

'Who could blame him? France and London, even the army would be preferable to a gloomy estate in the middle of Yorkshire with a father who had no time for him.'

'His mother though, she was beautiful.'

'I've seen the painting of her.'

The doctor sipped more coffee. 'Camile, the former Lady Remington would light up any room. She had a presence, you know?'

'She sounds like my sister Prue. She always draws attention.'

'I doubt she could be any prettier than you, my dear.'

Millie smiled. 'We aren't alike at all. I definitely do not light up a room.'

Doctor Boardman gave her a superior look. 'Lady Remington, let me assure you that you have a quiet calming presence that is much more soothing to a person's soul, believe me.'

'Well as long as my husband loves me, that's all I care about.' She paused, wondering whether to mention Jeremy's nightmares.

'You have something to talk to me about, my dear? the older man asked with an inquisitive expression. 'Are you with child?'

'Oh, no. I mean I don't think so, not yet.' She blushed.

'But there is something?'

'Well, it's Jeremy…'

'Oh?' His grey bushy eyebrows rose in question. 'I might be able to help if you tell me.'

'He has dreams, nightmares. Terrible ones really. And last week when we were riding in the woods there were gun shots which scared him dreadfully.'

'It's called shell shock, my lady.'

'Shell shock?' She'd heard the term before.

'It's to be expected. He has gone through a most terrifying experience.'

'But will it go away?'

'In time, I should suppose.' He stretched out his legs, making himself at home. 'I've read medical journals written by doctors who were over there in France.' He shook his head gently. 'Such things they witnessed. Medical science has grown exponentially. I am in awe of the advancement of medicine in the last few years. Of course, war will do that.'

'This shell shock though, are there treatments?'

'There are, yes.' He gave her a grandfatherly look. 'But they are in their infancy, and I would be more inclined to think that Sir Jeremy will return to his normal self in time now he's home and newly married.'

'I hope so.'

'I've read many medical articles about it. Battle fatigue they called in during the war. Terrible business. It's the mind, you see. It's very hard to understand, the mind. Men lost their nerves. Sad business, indeed.'

'I just want him to get better. To stop having these nightmares and jumping at every loud bang.'

'Time. Time will heal. That and your good self. You will see him right, Lady Remington.' The doctor heaved himself to his feet. 'I'll call again tomorrow, but should you need me before then, send a message.'

'Thank you, Doctor Boardman.' Millie saw him out and then went up to the bedroom and their patient.

She smiled at Jeremy who sat beside the bed reading the poetry book. 'Everything is fine in here?'

He gave her a loving smile. 'Yes. He's not woken.'

'I'll instruct Mrs Ellis to set a tray ready for him. Some beef stew and bread and milk will have him on his feet.'

'Has Boardman left?'

'He has. He'll call again tomorrow.' She laid her hand on Jeremy's shoulder. 'I'll sit with him for a time. Go and stretch your legs.'

'Are you sure?'

'Yes.'

'Doctor Boardman has stripped Monty. So, I've given him a wash, best I can. Monty's old suit needs a good clean.'

'Or burning,' Millie interjected, surprised by the ease in which Jeremy spoke of the man.

'Indeed. Anyway, I thought to look in the attics for some old clothes of mine until we can go into York and buy him something new.'

'A good idea. He cannot wear only his underwear while he's here.' She glanced at the man in the bed. 'Did he have nothing else with him?'

'No, not a thing. No luggage or bag.'

'Then he will need clothes.'

'I have plenty of suits, I can spare a couple for him to have. He looks the same height as me.'

'I'm sure he won't mind having too short trouser legs considering the state you found him in.'

Once Jeremy had left her, she settled into his chair and stared at the man. Ignoring the ugly scar, the rest of his features were rather pleasant. Before the wound, he would have been a very handsome man. She jumped suddenly when he opened his eyes. They stared at each other.

Feeling the one to break the silence, Millie leaned forward slightly. 'My husband, Sir Jeremy Remington found you in the woods. I'm Millie, Lady Remington.'

'Monty,' his voice was croaky. 'Thank you.'

'Would you like a drink?' Without waiting for an answer, she filled up a glass from the water jug beside the bed and held it to his lips. The intimate gesture made her blush.

After he'd taken a few sips he rested his head back against the pillows.

'Are you hungry?' She rose. 'I'll arrange for a tray to be brought up.'

'You are kind.' His piercing blue eyes held her still.

'We want you to be well again.'

'Such a burden.' He looked away. 'Forgive me.'

'Is there someone we can notify for you? Someone who can come and see you? Family? Friends?'

'No.' He stared at the wall. 'There is no one.'

'Are you sure?'

'Yes.'

'I will fetch my husband.' Millie walked to the door but paused to glance back at him. Monty had closed his eyes, but a tear seeped out of the corner of his eye.

Chapter Six

Millie stood on the stool and attached the last ornament to the pine Christmas tree, which she had ordered from York. Outside a cold wind blew but as yet no snow had fallen, and she hoped it didn't until her family arrived this afternoon. She was excited to have them here for her first Christmas as a married woman. It was her first Christmas away from home and it saddened her a little that she wouldn't wake up in her old room like she had done all her life, but this sadness was fleeting as the excitement of hosting her family in her own home built.

She had spent hours with Mrs Ellis going over menus and food supplies. Rationing still continued and created its own problems, but with Mrs Ellis's ingenuity, they managed to fill the larder and stores.

The redecorating was finished, and she'd worked long hours getting each room looking fresh and comfortable. Gone were the dark unloved rooms and instead she'd replaced the gloomy atmosphere with light-coloured walls and furnishings, mixing the old precious pieces with recently bought ones.

Gilly and Sarah, no longer under the yoke of Mrs Jacobs proved to be worth their wages as they scrubbed and polished and dusted. Both girls were lighter of spirit and often could be heard humming a tune or having a giggle. Millie much preferred to see them this way than the surly downcast faces they had previously.

She'd instructed the gardeners to grow as many flowers in the greenhouses as they could and where she couldn't have flowers she brought in evergreen branches from the woods to give the rooms a scent of the outside.

Unlike, Jeremy, Millie didn't like being shut up inside all day. Wrapped up warm against the cold, she walked every day in the gardens surrounding the house and sometimes went further across the fields and woods.

Her thoughts drifted to Jeremy as she tidied away the empty ornament boxes to be returned to the attics. Since Monty's arrival last month, Jeremy had spent more time with the homeless soldier than he had with her. They've formed a bond that didn't include her and she had trouble adjusting to sharing her husband.

Recovered from his exposure and malnutrition, Monty now slept in the smaller blue bedroom and had been invited to treat the house as his home. He ate with them and between meals he and Jeremy spent endless hours talking about the war and the future now it was all over. Jeremy drove Monty to York and bought him clothes and personal toiletries. They went into the village and drank pints of ale in The Gold Horn pub and generally couldn't be parted.

Millie knew she shouldn't feel jealous, it was ridiculous to be so, but she couldn't help it. Monty had replaced her. Jeremy chose to spend his time with the other man. With Monty, Jeremy discussed his plans for the estate and Millie simply had to sit there and listen. She wasn't invited when they left the house, she wasn't included in their conversations.

The only good point of having Monty here was that she heard Jeremy laugh more than she ever had. However, when she asked him about his past, he refused to speak of how he ended up in Yorkshire and homeless in their woods. Jeremy told her not to ask.

Monty didn't have to tell them, obviously it was too painful for him to talk about, but because he didn't mention it, Millie wondered more about it than it probably warranted. She truly believed he was hiding something, and she was determined to find out what it was.

She sighed tiredly, having had another night of broken sleep due to Jeremy's restlessness. His nightmares hadn't lessened, but during the day he smiled more, seemed more enthusiastic and for that she was grateful. He no longer spoke of wanting to be in France at the chateau, or if he did, it wasn't to her. She just wished he would involve her more. Before Monty's arrival they had done so much together. It hurt that she was being shut out. She felt alone and unwanted.

Noise on the drive made her look out of the window. 'They're here!' she called though no one was in the room.

She ran out into the hall to the front door before the bell had rung. She ran down the steps to throw herself into her mother's arms.

'How lovely to see you, darling girl.' Mama hugged her tight and then released her, so her grandmama could kiss her cheek.

'I'm so pleased you came, Grandmama. Mama said you might not.'

'As if I'd miss out? I've not got a lot of Christmases left, so I'll be damned if I'll miss this one and spend it alone in London.' She tapped Millie's cheek. 'But your papa's driving leaves a lot to be desired. I'm certain Lionel hit every hole in the road. I'll be black and blue in the morning, you see if I'm not!'

'Millie!' Prue and Cecelia embraced her at the same time, all talking at once.

Finally, her papa came around from the driver's side of the car and held her tight. 'How are you doing, my girl?'

'I'm fine, especially now you're all here.' Millie wiped the tears from her eyes. She didn't realise how much she had missed her family on a daily basis. 'Come inside.'

'How's Rem?' he asked, his expression serious.

'Fine, for the most part.'

'Most part?'

'He still suffers from nightmares, as you know.'

'You look a little pale. Are *you* well?'

'Yes, Papa. I'm well.'

Papa gave her cheek a pat and taking her hand they went inside.

In the hall, Sarah and Gilly took coats, gloves and hats, while Royston and Daisy went down to the car to collect the luggage strapped to the roof.

Millie rang for afternoon tea and ushered everyone into the drawing room and the cheery fire that crackled in the hearth.

'Where is Jeremy?' Mama asked, taking in the room.

'He's due home any minute,' Millie answered, plumping up a cushion for her grandmama's back.

Papa held out his hands to the flames. 'You've made many changes, daughter. I've only been here a few times over the years and it was always a dreary sort of place. It seems more of a home now.'

'Thank you, Papa.'

Mama nodded. 'I agree, Lionel. I never liked coming here, too sombre.' She smiled at Millie. 'I was wondering what changes you would make in time for our visit. I didn't expect so much to have been accomplished. You've done very well, dearest.'

'Thank you, Mama. It was hard work to get it done in time. The tradesmen were very good about it though.' Pleased with their praise, Millie relaxed and as tea trays were brought in, she happily listened to the talk filling the room.

Prue inspected an ornament of a bronze naked lady that sat atop a small side table. 'You'll never guess, Mil, but Frank Bloomingdale married Dorothy Campbell last week. Imagine?' Prue's eyes were wide in surprise. 'I was going to write to you about it, but I thought to wait to tell you in person.'

'The news doesn't upset you, does it?' Cece leaned in close to Millie.

'No, why should it?' Millie poured the tea.

'You always had a soft spot for Frank.' Prue grinned as though she'd spilt a secret.

'Not enough to want to marry him though,' Mama mumbled. 'He is a good catch.'

'Too good for Dorothy Campbell!' Prue declared.

Grandmama accepted a cup of tea from Millie. 'The Campbell family will be overjoyed to have Dorothy off their hands. I'm certain they were worried she'd remain a spinster.'

'Is that so very bad, Grandmama?' Cece asked, teacup and saucer on her lap.

'No, Cecelia, it's not if you have character to carry you through life, but alas Dorothy has no character, has she? Poor girl. A door has more life to it than she does.'

'Frank must have seen something in her then.' Papa selected a sandwich from the tiered stand.

'He saw money,' his wife scoffed.

'Violet,' Papa admonished.

'Well, it's true. The Bloomingdale wealth has disappeared. Frank needed to marry money, and he has done that duty.'

Prue sighed sadly. 'Poor Dorothy to be married for her family money. I would hate that to happen to me.'

Papa laughed. 'I'm not rich enough for you to be the prey for impoverished young men, dear girl, not with three daughters to settle.'

Cece sipped her tea. 'Arnold Botham has gone to New York to find his bride. Apparently, his father has contacts in shipping over there. Wealthy heiresses are falling over themselves to get a British husband with a title.'

Mama tutted. 'He'll have a time of it then, won't he, as the Bothams don't have a title.'

Grandmama selected a macaroon. 'America? How extreme. The drawing rooms of England will soon be filled with American accents and their modern ways. Who wants that?'

'Most titles these days come with crippling debts.' Papa sighed.

'Bah.' Grandmama sniffed with disdain. 'All this talk of money. It's so common.' She peered at Prue. 'You, Prudence Marsh, will marry for love, it's in your nature. You're too impulsive to do anything else.'

'What about me, Grandmama?' Cece inquired.

'You, Cecelia my sweetness, will marry some poor blighted man who needs you desperately.'

At that moment voices were heard in the hall and Jeremy walked in and went to Millie's side to kiss her. 'Forgive my tardiness, I'd meant to be back long before now.'

Jeremy shook Lionel's hand. 'Welcome, old friend.'

'Good to see you, Rem.'

Jeremy kissed the cheeks of all the women. 'How happy I am to have you in my home.' He beckoned Monty further into the room. 'This is my friend, and our guest, Monty Pattison.'

Millie watched her family greet Monty, their polite reactions to his welcome. Prue looked quickly away from his scar, but Cecelia gave him a beaming smile and drew him into conversation.

Grandmama nudged Millie. 'See what I mean?' She nodded towards Cecelia. 'Cece shines the minute there is someone who needs her care.'

Millie's stomach clenched. She didn't want her sister getting close to Monty, not until she knew more about him.

~ ~ ~ ~

'So, if you give your approval, madam, we'll marry in the summer.' Joy radiated out of Daisy like a beacon in the night.

Millie pressed her maid's hands. 'Of course, you have my blessing. I'm very happy for you. Royston is a fine man.'

'He has already spoken with Sir Jeremy and apparently we can have a cottage down the lane near the village for peppercorn rent. We won't be too far away and can do our duties to you both. Will that suit you?'

A short tap on the door heralded Prue into Millie's bedroom. 'Oh, sorry. Didn't mean to interrupt.' She sat on the bed.

Millie smiled, shaking her head at her sister. 'We'll talk more later, Daisy.'

Daisy left the room, taking with her Millie's blue satin evening dress, which needed attention to some of the beading.

'Is everything all right?' Prue asked, tucking a blonde curl behind her ear.

'Yes. Daisy was just informing me that she and Royston are getting married in the summer. She wanted my blessing.'

'Daisy is getting married?' Prue's shoulders slumped. 'Even the lady's maid is getting married before me!'

'I didn't know you were in such a hurry to be wed?'

'Well, I'm not, not really, though it would be nice to even have some suitors taking an interest in me. It's like a veritable desert out there.'

Millie laughed and slipped her arm through Prue's as they left the bedroom. 'You'll meet someone soon enough and probably when you least expect it.'

Prue paused at the top of the stairs. 'I do miss you being at home, Mil. There is simply no one to talk to.'

'I know. I miss you, too. We must meet up more in York, perhaps make it a monthly thing, what do you say to that?'

'Oh, yes, do.' Prue pulled a face. 'Still, it doesn't help me when I want to go to London. Who am I going to go with now? Cece hates doing the things we did. She doesn't like going to Harrods and making fun of the general public who shop there or having tea at the Dorchester so we can show off our best hats. Cece doesn't like going to parties and would rather stay home and *read*. You know what she's like.'

'Take Cousin Agatha with you.'

Prue spluttered. 'Agatha? I'd rather not go at all. She's as dull as dishwater. She's worse than Cece.'

'There you two are,' Papa called up to them from the bottom of the stairs. 'We are walking to Home Farm while the weather holds. Hurry up.'

'Why?' Prue asked as they descended the staircase.

'For fresh air and exercise. Why else?' Papa replied, buttoning up his coat. 'Apparently some new pups have been born to the collie bitch, Jeremy said. I'd like to see them.'

'Where is Jeremy?' Millie asked.

'I'm here, darling.' Jeremy came into the hall with her mother, Monty and Cece trailing behind. All wore outdoor clothes.

'What about Grandmama?'

'She's having a nap,' Mama told them.

'Give us a moment then.' Prue pulled Millie along down the hallway to the boot room. 'I don't like how Cece is spending all her time with Monty. We've been here three days and I doubt she's spent a moment apart from him. She's embarrassing herself.'

Millie shrugged on her coat. 'I'll talk to her.'

'The poor man can't be wanting only Cece to talk to. I overheard him and Papa last night after dinner and he sounded well educated. She must be boring him silly!'

'Yes, Jeremy tells me he is.' Millie put on her hat and slipped her gloves on.

'What else do you know of him?'

'Nothing. At least *I* don't, and Jeremy doesn't inform me of the man's background if he does know it.'

'Why such secrecy?' Prue frowned.

'I don't know, but I'm not happy about it.' Millie gave Prue a look, which she knew her sister understood. 'I really do wish he would leave, but Jeremy won't hear of it.'

'But he can't stay forever, can he?' Prue whispered.

'He can if Jeremy has anything to do with it.'

'But you're newly married. Monty should have the good manners to go.'

Millie shrugged, swallowing down her annoyance of the whole matter.

Prue pulled on her boots. 'Don't worry. I'll make it my business to speak more to this Monty and see what his plans are.'

'Prue,' Millie warned.

'I'll be discreet, trust me.'

Back in the hall, Jeremy took Millie's hand as they all filed out of the house. 'We could have squashed into two cars I'm sure.'

She squeezed his hand, liking that he chose to walk beside her. 'A walk will do us all good. Perhaps later we can—'

'Jeremy,' Monty called him. 'Come and tell Miss Marsh about that book we found in the library yesterday. She doesn't believe me that it was printed in sixteen sixty-eight.'

'I seriously don't believe you. Sixteen sixty-eight?' Cece shook her head.

Jeremy's hand slipped from Millie's as he turned and went to walk with Monty and Cece.

Mama took his place and slipped her arm through Millie's. 'Let them talk of stuffy books and we can chat. Smile, dearest, or everyone will see what's written on your face.'

'I am that readable?'

'To me, yes. You're my daughter.'

Millie smiled sadly and continued walking as Prue and Papa went on ahead. 'What do you want to chat about?'

'Anything you fancy as long as it doesn't involve *books* or *puppies*. I refuse to let your father have one.'

'A book or a puppy?'

Mama's laugh rang out and Millie wondered if there ever was a sound better than her mother's laugh.

At Home Farm while everyone crouched in the stable stall and cuddled the puppies, even her reluctant Mama, Millie hung back and observed Monty as he stood leaning over the stable door. His smile seemed genuine as he watched the puppies crawl over the straw.

'Have you ever had a dog?' Millie asked him.

'No. I'd like to one day though.'

'When you have a home of your own, perhaps?'

'Yes.' He nodded absentmindedly.

'I'm surprised my husband hasn't offered you a cottage on the estate yet, since he seems intent on giving you everything else.' As soon as the words were out of her mouth, she regretted them. At the wounded look in his eyes she knew the barb had hit home. 'Forgive me. That was rude and unkind of me.' She knew she was blushing.

'There is nothing to forgive. You are right. Your husband has been most generous.'

'He is a good man.'

'He is one of the best I've ever met. I value his friendship.'

'As he does yours.' She glanced away, annoyed she had been so petty.

'I am sorry if you feel Sir Jeremy has spent too much time, and money, on me. I did not encourage it.'

She nodded. He was speaking the truth. Jeremy was the one doing all the running in that friendship. He clung to Monty like a lifeline and she was jealous to see it.

'I will leave if it pleases you, and never come back.'

Silence stretched between them as she considered his words.

Letting out a deep sigh, she looked at him. 'That would hurt my husband and I wouldn't hurt him for the world.'

'Millie.' Prue came towards them, giving Monty a dazzling smile. 'You must convince Mama to let Papa have a puppy.' She drew Millie away and Millie was glad she did. Monty made her feel as though she was acting like a petulant child, and perhaps she was, but she couldn't help it. She wanted to be the person Jeremy spent time with, not this returned soldier with a secret past.

Chapter Seven

Jeremy looked at the gathered group of men, chatting affably, the breath misting in the air. Gilly and Sarah handed out small cups of coffee and pieces of Mrs Ellis's shortbread. The sun wasn't long up giving the morning a crisp clear light. Friends and neighbours had joined him, Monty and Lionel on this first game bird shoot since before the war.

'We're ready, sir.' Phil Greenway, his head gamekeeper came to his side, his loyal dog waiting patiently at his feet. 'The beaters are in place.'

'Very good.' Jeremy nodded. 'Gentlemen, shall we make a start?'

After a short ride in the back of the farm truck to the fields surrounding the woodland, they climbed out and spread out in a line. The men became quiet, the dogs eager at their feet.

Jeremy glanced down the line. Monty was next to him and then Lionel on the other side. He cocked his rifle, his stomach fluttering. He looked at the slight rise in front of him, dotted with large bushes of blackberry. Stripped bare of their leaves and fruit they reminded him of the tangled rolls of barbed wire on No Man's Land in France.

He blinked rapidly at a sudden movement in the bush in front of him. His breathing stopped. What was that? A man? Sweat broke out on his forehead and down his spine. There was someone there. Was it an ambush? Had the others seen it? They had to get down, why were they standing up giving the enemy a perfect target?

He knelt on one knee and raised his rifle, hands shaking. Peering into the bush, he wished he had his field glasses with him. How careless to have left them behind. Stupid.

There! Again. More movement. Good God it was the enemy.

'Get down!' he suddenly shouted, his finger on the trigger. He couldn't shoot yet. He must not draw enemy fire until his men were in position.

'Sir.' Monty was instantly beside him. 'Sir. Stand up,' he murmured.

'Don't talk nonsense. They'll see us. Are the men ready?'

'Son.' Lionel placed a hand on his shoulder. 'Rem, come along, my good man. Let us leave this to the others, yes?'

Jeremy frowned, confused. 'Leave? I'm the commanding officer.'

'Sir, we're home, in England.' Monty helped him to stand.

'England?' As though a ghostly veil had been lifted from his face, he noticed the worried look in Monty and Lionel's eyes. Behind them the other men stared, not sure what was going on.

Lionel took a step back and addressed them. 'Gentlemen, my son-in-law is feeling a little under the weather. Mr Pattison and I will take him back to the house. Please stay and enjoy the shoot.'

Jeremy stared back at the bushes – simply blackberry bushes, not barbed wire. There was no enemy on the other side. No one was in danger of being shot or bombed. He didn't have to protect his men. They were back in England.

In a daze, he allowed Lionel and Monty to guide him back to the truck. His shaking grew worse and the shame overwhelmed him. 'Forgive me. I don't know what came over me.'

'There's nothing to forgive, son,' Lionel spoke gruffly and sniffed before giving him a smile. 'Let us indulge in a large breakfast, shall we?'

Jeremy looked at Monty as they climbed into the truck. 'I'm getting worse.'

'It's bound to happen when you're holding a gun again.'

'But it doesn't happen to you though, does it?'

'It's your mind, Rem,' Lionel added. 'You've been through a tough time.'

Jeremy shook his head. 'The war finished over a year ago…'

'It takes time.' Monty held onto the seat as the truck swayed down the track. 'These things can't be rushed.'

Jeremy stared out at the passing fields. How long could he stand being like this? He thought he'd get better after marrying Millie, obviously he'd been wrong. What in the hell was he going to do?

~ ~ ~ ~

Millie sipped her wine, watching the others as they ate and drank. Jeremy at the other end of the table was conversing with Mama, but he looked tired and unhappy.

She knew of his incident at the shoot that morning. Papa had been so upset to see first-hand how affected Jeremy still was about the war. He hadn't realised the post trauma was as bad as it was. For the rest of the day, Jeremy had been quiet and withdrawn, disappearing into his study. She had gone to him, but he had dismissed her concerns with a wave of his hand, saying that it wouldn't happen again. However, neither of them had that control over his reactions and they knew it.

When she spoke to Monty about it, he had less to say and would have stayed in the study with Jeremy, but Cece and Prue requested him to drive them into York for afternoon tea. Millie had stayed home and tried not to let Jeremy's dismissive behaviour affect her.

Grandmama forked up some potato. 'Mr Pattison, you are from Kent, I believe?'

All eyes looked at Monty, and Millie held her breath. Grandmama was the one person who could wheedle information out of the most closed mouth.

Monty wiped his mouth with a napkin. 'Yes, madam, that is true.'

'Lovely area of the country. Lots of sunshine. Are you near the sea?'

'No, madam, but it doesn't take long to reach it.'

'Swimming in the ocean is a most joyous activity.' Grandmama sipped her wine, a distant gaze in her eyes. 'I once swam in the Mediterranean with a young Italian man, called Mateo. Handsome as the devil he was. He painted me.' Grandmama frowned. 'I never did see the finished result. Perhaps that was a good thing, it might have been terrible and then I would have had to lie and say how wonderful he was.' Grandmama grinned cheekily. 'He was terribly good at other things, mind you.'

'Mama!' Mama gasped, and Millie and her sisters giggled.

Grandmama frowned. 'Oh shush, daughter, I wasn't going to be vulgar. I'll leave that for my memoirs.'

'Memoirs?' Mama stared, appalled. 'You're not writing your life history, are you?'

'I might. I have a few scribbles. And why shouldn't I? I've lived a very full and interesting life. Far more than you have, I must say. I have seen and done so much why shouldn't I leave my stories behind for others to enjoy?'

'That depends on your version of enjoyment. I hardly think people will want to know about your ramblings across Europe as a young woman,' scoffed Mama.

'I disagree,' Papa put in. 'I think Adeline's adventures would be most entertaining.'

'Thank you, Lionel, and indeed they are. I've climbed the pyramids of Egypt, sailed down the Nile, snake charmed in Marrakesh, danced naked under the stars in Salzburg—'

'Mama! That is enough!'

Grandmama shook her head in disappointment. 'Daughter, you are truly a puritan. I don't know where you get that from for your father and I were not so restrictive in our ways.'

'Did you spend long in Austria, madam?' Monty asked. 'I once was going to travel to Vienna…' Suddenly he stopped and gazed down at his plate.

Millie watched him play with his food, the look on his face was unreadable, as though he was shutting down any emotion. She wished Grandmama had prodded him more on his past instead of talking about her adventures.

Grandmama sipped more wine. 'Austria is beautiful in the summer. When I left Salzburg, we headed to Italy. We, my cousins and I, followed the sunshine and spent a year and a half travelling. Our parents despaired of us ever returning home to England.'

'I want to travel,' Prue said wistfully.

'And so you should,' Grandmama replied. 'Everyone should travel.'

Mama's eyebrows rose. 'I think not, Prudence. Not unless you have a husband beside you.'

'What nonsense, Violet,' Grandmama snapped. 'Let the girl go if she wants to. All she needs is a good maid and a friend or two.'

'Do not give her any ideas, Mama. The world is a different place now as to when you were travelling. It's not safe.'

'You do talk nonsense, daughter.' Grandmama huffed. 'Do you think the world is only fearful now? The world will always be dangerous no matter where you are. The girls should be out there broadening their minds by experiencing different cultures.'

'Can we talk of something else, please?' Mama sighed. 'I'm tired of hearing the same argument.'

Millie indicated to Gilly to clear the plates. 'Dessert is apple pie and custard as I know it's Papa's favourite.'

Papa swelled with pride. 'What a wonderful daughter you are.'

Cece chuckled. 'I'd like to think we are all your wonderful daughters, Papa?'

'Of course, of course.'

Jeremy smiled at Millie. 'I might be biased, and I mean no disrespect you Cece or Prue, but I do believe I picked the best of the bunch.'

Everyone laughed, and Prue threw her napkin at Jeremy.

Millie relaxed a little as Jeremy winked at her. Whatever bad mood he was in earlier had disappeared. His tender loving gaze from the other end of the table melted her and she smiled in response.

'I propose we play charades,' Prue announced and received answering groans.

'You always act for too long, Prue,' Cece complained. 'You never make it simple. It's like we have to watch a complete play by you to get the answer. Let us do something else.'

'Oh, you are a spoilsport, Cece,' Prue scoffed.

'Let us play hide and seek.' Cece clapped her hands. 'We've not played that here before and we'll have so many new hiding places to find.'

'Oh yes, let us play that,' Prue agreed. 'Jeremy, you're counting first.'

'Why me?' he asked with a laugh.

'Because you live here and will know all the best hiding places and we'll never find you.'

After the meal, Grandmama sat with a book and a glass of port in the drawing room with Mama, who declared she couldn't possibly play a child's game. However, laughingly, Papa said he'd make the numbers up.

Jeremy started counting by the front door as the others scattered around the house to hide.

Millie went along the corridor to the boot room, thinking perhaps Jeremy would go straight upstairs to search. A large cupboard which held a paraphernalia of outdoor things stood by the door leading outside and she slipped inside the dark interior, trying not to disturb the fishing rods, nets and old boots.

She pushed aside some ancient musty coats and squealed when Monty stared at her. 'I'm sorry. I thought no one would have got in here yet. I'll find somewhere else.'

At that moment, they heard Jeremy call that he was finished counting.

'Get in and close the door, hurry,' Monty whispered.

Embarrassed, Millie squished in beside him. She was deeply conscious of his closeness, the soft breathing. She remained as still as possible, hardly daring to take a breath. What if Jeremy found them together like this? Her stomach clenched as Monty moved his hand, it touched her skirt.

'Sorry,' he whispered.

She swallowed, not knowing what to do. She was acutely aware of his body. She closed her eyes, remembering when she was sixteen. They'd had a party for her birthday and later they'd played this game. She'd hid in a wardrobe in one of the bedrooms and Frank Bloomingdale had suddenly joined her. Within moments he was kissing her, and she was kissing him back. The darkness and secrecy had heightened her senses and she could have stayed in that wardrobe and kissed Frank for hours, but Cece had found them and sprang them apart. That had been her first kiss, proper adult kisses that had tingled her skin and clenched her stomach. Every party afterwards, she and Frank would kiss when playing hide and seek.

Is that what Monty expected? Is that what everyone did playing this game and just not her and Frank?

She bit her lip with indecision. Should she go or stay? What would he think if she just fled? Would he wonder the reason? What was her reason? She didn't like the man. She didn't want him in her home and was insanely jealous of his relationship with Jeremy, but as a person, he seemed… nice.

'Lady Remington,' Monty murmured.

'Shush!' she whispered harshly, not wanting him to speak. She strained to hear any footsteps. Hoping against hope that Jeremy wouldn't open the cupboard door and see them together. She had to get out.

With a quick glance at Monty, seeing only his shadowy profile, she flung the door open and hurried out of the room. She'd never play hide and seek again.

~ ~ ~ ~

Millie woke with a jerk as something hit her face hard. In the bed beside her, Jeremy mumbled and flung his arms about. She ducked as another hand swept by her face.

'Get down!' Jeremy yelled, his legs tangled in the blankets. 'Do you obey orders, soldier?' he scorned loudly.

'Jeremy.' Millie reached out to him, but he threw her away.

'Keep your heads down, men. They're coming over the top!'

'Jeremy!' She knelt up on the bed as he tried to flee. 'Wake up.'

'Bombs!' Jeremy screeched, hurting Millie's ears.

'There aren't any bombs, my darling.'

The bedroom door opened, and Monty hurried in, tying his dressing gown around him.

'Sir!' He held Jeremy's shoulders in a tight grip. 'Sir. It's over. We won. It's all over.'

Slowly, dazed, Jeremy shoulders sagged, and he blinked rapidly, coming back to them. 'Good God.'

Monty released him. 'Everything is just fine, sir.'

'Yes, yes.' He stared at Monty. 'I'm fine.'

'Of course, you are, sir.' Monty relaxed his grip.

Jeremy turned to Millie, his eyes widening in alarm. 'Darling, I'm so sorry.'

'I know you are.' She smiled in reassurance, wishing she could take this torment from him.

'You're face!' Jeremy stared at the red welt on her cheek. 'God Almighty. I've hit you.'

'It doesn't hurt,' she lied, not wanting to touch where he'd smacked her one.

'I've hit you again. I can't believe it. Sweetheart, please forgive me.'

'There's nothing to forgive. You aren't in control when you're asleep.'

Head bowed in shame, Jeremy left the bed. 'This can't continue. Look what I've done to her, Monty.'

'Sir, it was an accident. You weren't striking her, you were fighting a battle. You didn't know it was Lady Remington.'

'That doesn't excuse it.'

Millie reached for her dressing gown from the end of the bed and put it on. 'Jeremy, please come back to bed. I am totally fine, I promise you.'

Jeremy stood shaking his head, reaching for his own dressing gown. 'No, I can't bear the thought that once again you've been hit because of me and these stupid nightmares.'

'You aren't aware of it. You're not in control.' Millie climbed from the bed. 'Monty, could you leave us please?'

'Of course.'

'No.' Jeremy stepped towards the door. 'I need a drink. I can't sleep now. You go back to bed, darling. Monty will keep me company for a while.'

Millie froze. 'I can keep you company. Allow Monty to go back to bed.'

Jeremy glanced away. 'No, I'll not keep you awake any longer, my love. It's the middle of the night. Us men will relight the fire downstairs and sip whiskey and talk of nonsense like we usually do. I'd feel better knowing you were warm in our bed and sleeping.' He left the room without waiting for her to answer, and after a bashful look at her, Monty followed him out.

The winter cold filtered through her dressing gown and bare feet. Close to tears, Millie got back into bed and huddled down into the blankets. She tried not to feel alone, or inconsequential, but she did.

Yet again Jeremy had shut her out and preferred Monty's company. Why? Why couldn't he share this torment with her? He said she would heal him, but how could she do that when he continually pushed her away?

She touched her sore cheek, blinking back tears. What was she going to do?

~ ~ ~ ~

Jeremy stood by the fireplace, one elbow resting on the mantlepiece watching Millie. She glowed as she handed out Christmas presents to her family. Today was the happiest he'd seen her, surrounded by her loving family and hosting a successful Christmas

Day. While she bubbled with happiness, he felt sad and confused. He hoped he hid it well. Nothing was to spoil the day for Millie.

He knew she'd been nervous that today would go well — that people ate their fill, liked their presents and generally created a happy atmosphere. She had pulled it off.

Snow had threatened after breakfast, but they managed to drive to the village church for Christmas service that morning. After spending time chatting to villagers and estate staff, they'd hurried home cold and ready for the feast Mrs Ellis and her team had worked hard to prepare. The dining room looked festive and welcoming after the cold church.

Now, as snow fell outside, putting off visitors from calling, Jeremy smiled as Prue squealed with delight over another present she'd opened, a peacock blue silk scarf. His wife had excellent taste.

Jeremy went behind the Christmas tree and pulled out a huge box, which he slid gently towards Millie. 'Merry Christmas, my love,' he said softly, enjoying her surprise.

'Another present? You have spoilt me, Jeremy.'

'It's the one thing I want to do often.'

She carefully ripped open the wrapping paper and gasped. 'A gramophone!'

Prue and Cece jumped up just as excited.

'What records did you get?' Prue inspected the present as happy as though he'd bought it for her. 'Oh, do set it up, Jeremy. We can listen to it all night.'

'I thought Cece was to play the piano tonight, that's tradition,' Papa grumbled. 'I don't want to listen to that thing.'

'Be quiet, my dear.' Mama laughed. 'Let the girls have their fun. I'll beat you at cards instead.'

'Yes, let us listen to this music for a change,' Grandmama approved. 'What a splendid present, Jeremy. Very thoughtful.'

'We can dance all night and Cece won't get tired fingers.' Prue grinned.

As the others talked music, Jeremy knelt beside Millie. 'Are you happy with this present?'

'Very much. I was delighted with the beautiful carved desk you had commissioned to be made for me.'

He took her hand and kissed it, knowing the desk meant a lot to her as it was the first piece of furniture in the house that was truly hers. He'd seen the tears gathered in her eyes as he unveiled it to her after breakfast.

'I want you to be happy,' he whispered. 'I know I'm not the easiest person to live with. You have put up with a lot in such a short time.'

Her expression became loving and she cupped his cheek in her soft hand. 'I love you…'

There was hesitation in her voice and his heart flipped. 'But?'

She shook her head. 'But nothing.' She kissed him quickly and rose from the chair. 'Shall we push back the chairs and play the gramophone?'

Soon the room was full of music and laughter as Prue and Monty danced energetically with Cece partnering Millie. Jeremy sat in the corner next to Grandmama Adeline and she gave him a wise smile.

'How often do you have them?' she asked.

'Pardon?' He wasn't sure he heard her correctly.

'Your nightmares.'

'Millie told you?'

'I heard the commotion the other night. I don't sleep well at night.' As Adeline spoke she watched the dancers, not giving away anything to anyone.

'They started in the trenches towards the end of the war.'

'You need professional help.'

'I know.' He wiped his hand over his face, the guilt and the shame hung heavy on him.

She glanced at him. 'I'll give you the name of a fine doctor in London, a personal friend. We'll get you right again.' She patted his hand. 'And if we don't I doubt you'll be the first madman in the family.'

He jerked his head round to stare at her but when she chuckled, he saw the joke and laughed with her. 'Poor Millie. To be saddled with me. Perhaps I shouldn't have married her. I was being selfish.'

Serious once more, Adeline sighed. 'You give her no credit, son. Millie is stronger than you think. But she's unhappy. I can tell.' Adeline nodded towards Monty dancing with Cece. '*He* isn't your wife. Though he spends more time with you than Millie does.'

'No, I know, but he understands what we soldiers went through. He knows my dreams, the horrors we suffered. Millie, in fact, no civilian will ever understand it.'

'No, we don't and won't, naturally.' She gave Jeremy a steely look. 'But try to explain to her. It'll help you both. If you keep pushing her away, you'll end up too far apart and may never come together again.'

'I love her enormously.'

'I know.' Adeline gave his arm a little pat. 'The loving bit fades though if you don't build on it.'

'Come on, brother-in-law, I insist you dance!' Prue hurried over to them and pulled him up from the chair. She dragged him into the middle of the other dancers. He smiled at Millie, but she turned away and with a sinking heart he knew Adeline was right. Despite her smiles today, she wasn't happy, and he was the cause of it.

~ ~ ~ ~

'Did you have a good day, Daisy?' Millie enquired as she undressed and got ready for bed. It was the wee hours, after two o'clock in the morning and the house was only just now quieting down.

'I did, madam.'

'The staff enjoyed their party in the village hall?'

'We did. It was good of you and Sir Jeremy to let us have the rest of the day off after the Christmas meal was finished. Did you manage your supper without any problems?'

'We did. My sisters and I brought everything up from the kitchen that Mrs Ellis had left prepared for us. It was a simple case of putting it out in the dining room and everyone helped themselves. We even took the trays back down and washed the plates up.'

'You didn't!' Daisy gaped at her.

'We did.' Millie took out her earrings. 'I hated to think of the kitchen staff coming in and seeing the mess after their party.'

'That's so thoughtful, madam.'

'Well, we are very capable of washing a few plates and bowls. If our papa had allowed us to work during the war, we'd have seen and done much worse.' It still irked her that she'd been denied permission to volunteer as a nurse and go to France. If she had, perhaps she'd understand Jeremy's reticence to talk about what he'd seen and done, or he may think that he *could* talk to her if she had seen some of it herself. It was all very frustrating.

'Mrs Ellis got a bit weepy, too much sherry I think, when we sang songs she kept thinking of her brother who was killed in the war. He was a very good singer apparently.'

'How sad for her.' Millie thought again how much the war had affected so many people.

After a quick wash, she slipped on her nightgown and brushed her hair while Daisy hung up her dress. 'Don't come in too early in the morning, Daisy. I doubt I'll be up at the normal time.'

They both glanced at the little gold clock on the mantle as it chimed half past the hour of two.

'I think breakfast will be late.' Daisy gathered up the used towel and underclothes. 'Do you need anything else, madam?'

'No, thank you. Goodnight.' Millie yawned and climbed into bed just as Jeremy walked in.

'Goodnight, Daisy.' He held the door open for her.

'Goodnight, sir.'

He closed the door after her and began to undress. 'I've sent Dobson to bed. The house is all locked up, fireguards up.'

She watched him unbutton his shirt and felt the familiar tingle of attraction.

'I have something for you.'

'You do?' She frowned, puzzled. 'What is it?'

He disappeared into his dressing room and came back out with a long velvet box. Sitting on the bed, he gave it to her. 'I couldn't resist this.'

'Jeremy! You've already given me such lovely presents.'

'Well, the gramophone wasn't very personal and I'm certain Prue will try and sneak it into the motor car when they leave.'

Millie laughed. 'We'll search her luggage.' She opened the box and stared at the sapphire and diamond necklace that sparkled in the lamp light. 'It's so beautiful.'

'Not as beautiful as my wife.'

She took the necklace out of the box and held the heavy coldness of it in her hands. 'I can't wait to wear it somewhere.'

'Wear it now.'

'But—'

'Wear only that.' Desire flared in his eyes and her stomach dipped in response.

She pulled off her nightgown and then handed the necklace to him. She shivered as he hung the necklace on her bare skin and then he kissed her shoulder.

Resting her head back against him, she gave him full access to her breasts as his hands encircled them, his fingers playing gently with her nipples.

'You are over dressed, husband.'

'You're right.' He stood and took off the rest of his clothes and then joined her in the bed.

She cupped his face in her hands and kissed him passionately, wanting him so much it was like a physical ache.

Jeremy groaned, his body tight and hard and she revelled in the power she had to make him feel that way, to want her so much. She closed her eyes as his whispered words of adoration accompanied his tender hands as they caressed her. Her heart swelled with love.

In bed she felt it was the only time she had him to herself. It was their oasis; the one place she knew she had his full attention. It's where no one could come between them, including Monty.

Chapter Eight

'What do you mean, you're leaving?' Millie's teacup clattered back to its saucer.

Jeremy came to sit beside her at the dining table, breakfast forgotten. 'Adeline gave me a doctor's name and address in London. A doctor who treats men like me. She has met him at social gatherings and heard great things about him and his treatments.'

'Grandmama never mentioned this to me.' She wished her family were still here, but they had left yesterday morning to return home, the holiday over.

'No. She knew it was my place to do so.'

Millie sat very still. 'Then I'll come with you.'

'No, my darling. I need you to stay here.'

'Why? Surely I can be at the London townhouse while you are being treated?'

'I won't be treated in London, that's just where this doctor's offices are. He'll send me away, further south, Plymouth, I believe.'

'Plymouth?'

'Yes.' He rubbed his hand over his face, tiredly. 'It's a type of asylum.'

'Asylum?' Millie stared, then bit her lip, trying not to react too surprised by this sudden news, but she felt winded by it.

'For returned soldiers who have shell shock, men like me.'

Her mind went in different directions. She wanted to beg him to take her with him but knew that wasn't possible. 'Are you sure you want to do this?'

'I don't think I have a choice, do I? I can't keep putting us through this. My nightmares… I hurt you…'

'You don't mean it. I don't blame you.'

'I know you don't, but if there is some cure, something which will ease this mental torture, then I must try it. I'd rather like to live the rest of my life without jumping at every loud bang or crash. I have fields of game birds that I can't bring myself to shoot. How do I face friends when they ask me why I'm not holding another shoot? How do I tell them that when I raise my rifle I don't think of pheasants, but instead I'm expecting a German attack? That the enemy are hiding in the bushes, not birds. It brings me out in a cold sweat just thinking about it.' He sighed. 'Then there are the nightmares, the lashing out at you. It floors me, Millie, that I have struck you. I can't live with it. You are my most precious wife and I am hurting you.'

She gripped his hand. 'Of course, you must go. We must do whatever it takes to make you well again.'

'You know that nothing else would part me from you, don't you?' The worried look in his eyes melted her heart.

'Yes, I know. I'll be waiting here for you to come home.'

'I am eager to go.' Jeremy glanced around the room. 'Perhaps this doctor will give me reason to feel comfortable in this place, too.'

Millie touched his cheek gently. 'I understand your reluctance to feel at home here and if this house is part of the problem then we'll move to London, or anywhere you want to.'

He strode to the window. 'I can't feel at peace here and believe me, I have tried, really I have. I don't know if it is because of my head, the war, or because I see my father's disapproval in every room. I hear his condescending voice echoing in the halls.'

'Oh, Jeremy. Why haven't you mentioned this to me before?'

'I thought your new decorations in some of the rooms would remove the shadows of the past, but it hasn't. I see my father in the gardens – he thought them a waste of time and money. He had my mother's rose bushes ripped up and replaced with practical plants like bay trees, which the kitchen could use. I see him in the stables, cursing the grooms for some small misdemeanour. I see him upstairs as I go past his bedroom door.'

She went to him. 'Then let us sell the estate.'

'Sell it?' He grimaced. 'The whole country is still reeling from the war. Who has the money to buy estates such as these any more?'

'Then we'll rent it out.'

'And go where?'

'There's the London townhouse.'

'You want to live in London, the middle of the city?'

'I will live anywhere as long as we are together.'

'But you'll be so much further away from your family.'

She raised her eyebrows at him. 'A day's train ride, that is all. I'm sure we'll all survive that. Besides Grandmama spends more time in London now. She says it's easier for an old woman to live in town rather in the country. She doesn't have to go far to see people. So, I'd not be lonely. I'll make friends and

Prue and Cece will never be off the doorstep. Prue loves London.'

'It's something to think about.'

'I'm not attached to this house and neither are you. It makes sense for us to go somewhere else.'

'We'll discuss it in more detail when I return.' He kept staring out the window. 'I'll catch the London train from York tonight. Monty will drive me to the station.'

Her jaw clenched at the mention of that man's name. 'Is he going to London with you?'

'No. I want him to oversee things here. There's a lot to do on the estate. I've a list as long as my arm, and Monty can make a start on it. Much was ignored during the war and left to ruin. Most of the boundary walls and hedges need repairing, cottages and barns need new roof shingles. The woodland needs thinning and replanting. Then there are the sheep breeding programmes which have been a half-hearted job in the last few years. John Soames and Phil Greenway need someone they can turn to when these projects start, and Monty is the man for the job. We need to hire more men, which I'm eager to do. So many returned soldiers are without jobs. I'd like to support them if I can.'

A swift flare of anger ignited in her chest. 'I can see to all that. What else do I have to do without you here?'

'Monty is my agent. He has a job to do, let him do it. You have enough with running the house. You'll have to be my secretary as well. I leave you in full control of all my correspondence.'

She couldn't answer him. He had already distanced himself from everything. She gathered up her courage and it was easier to do this with a touch of anger. 'You've been giving this some thought then. It's not a decision you've just made. You discussed it with Monty, I take it?'

Jeremy turned to her. 'Darling, I know you aren't fond of Monty, but he's a good man.'

'I wouldn't know. He's a stranger. A stranger living in my home.'

'Then now will be the chance for you two to get to know one another.'

Stepping away, she shrugged. 'I see no need to really. As a mere worker surely he should occupy a cottage in the village?'

'Millie! He is my friend.'

'But not mine, Jeremy! You've just inflicted him on me!'

A cold expression came over his face. 'I see.'

'Do you?' she scoffed. 'Within our first week of living here we've had Monty Pattison sharing our lives. Did you ask me what my thoughts were about that? You made him your land agent without any information or proof of who he was, just his say so.'

'I trust my judgement in this.'

'Really? Tell me how many other land agents do you know that live in the main house?'

'He's in a back room that was unused anyway. He has become my friend. He is educated and comes from Kent and—'

'He was homeless living in the woods. What other *gentleman* does that? Why isn't he living in Kent? Yorkshire is a long way from there. Has he told you everything about himself?'

'No, Millie, not everything, but enough. He doesn't know everything about me.'

'*You* aren't living in *his* home.'

'What reason do you have to hate him so much? Monty has given you no cause for you to feel this strongly.'

'I cannot understand why you aren't as concerned as me. You are happy to leave me with this man, whose past I know nothing about. Don't you find that odd?'

Jeremy ran a hand through his hair. 'I trust him.'

'I don't.'

'Then trust me!'

'How can I?'

He gave her a wounded look. 'You don't trust me.'

'No, not your judgement about him, not at this moment.'

'Because of my nightmares?' A muscle clenched in his jaw. 'Or my shattered nerves, is that it?'

Millie folded her arms. 'Can you honestly say that you are thinking clearly right now? You've brought a stranger into our home and made him a part of your life without even consulting me.'

'He isn't a bad man.'

'How can you possibly be sure of that?'

He sighed heavily. 'I'll ask him to move out. I just assumed he would keep you company while I was gone. Obviously, I have that wrong.'

'Thank you, but I don't need his company.'

'I'll go and pack.' Jeremy walked to the door but hesitated on turning the handle. 'You do realise Monty and Cece have promised to exchange letters? I wouldn't be surprised if this man you want to banish will soon be your brother-in-law.' He closed the door softly behind him.

Alarmed, Millie hurried to the morning room, which she used as her personal office and sitting at the desk Jeremy had bought her for Christmas, she took paper and pen and started writing.

Dear Prue,

Jeremy has just told me that Cece and Monty Pattison are to be exchanging letters. I am certain you'll be as distressed by this news as I am. Something must be done. We cannot allow Cecelia to be involved with a man who we know nothing about.

Forgive my brevity, but I wanted to write to you about this situation as soon as I heard. I will do some investigation from this end, and I implore you to do the same from your end. You know me well enough that I would never normally interfere in business that has nothing to do with me. However, Monty Pattison refuses to divulge his past and he could be anyone! Do we want this stranger in our family?

Much love, your devoted sister,
Millie.

Thankfully, as Jeremy's luggage was loaded into his car, Monty sat in the driving seat and didn't come into the house.

Millie stood in the hall. A deep unhappiness filled her as she helped Jeremy don his coat and hat. She bit her lip to stop herself from crying.

'I'll write as often as I can. I'm not sure what the rules will be.' Jeremy buttoned up his coat.

'We must put in a telephone, that would make things easier. What do you think?' She tried to think of practical issues. 'Shall I look into the cost of it?'

'Yes. I did think of it a few weeks ago. I said to Monty that…' He stopped, a guilty look on his face.

Millie straightened, ignoring the sharp stab of jealously that once more Monty had been the one he discussed things with. 'You'd best hurry. You don't want to miss your train. The melted snow might make the roads difficult.'

He suddenly took her in his arms and held her tight. 'I love you. You do believe that, don't you? I'm doing this for the both of us.'

'Yes, I know. I love you, too.' She buried her head into his shoulder, wishing with all her heart that her marriage was a normal one and her husband who she adored wasn't leaving her.

~ ~ ~ ~

Millie sat at Jeremy's desk in his study. Outside a harsh February wind was blowing a gale. She was tired of winter and longed for the long warm days of summer. In front of her ledgers and correspondence was spread out over the desk. So many letters arrived each day. Jeremy was chairman of a great many organisations and each one wrote to him often with invitations to meetings or new proposals that needed his consideration. With each one she wrote back stating his apologies but at present he was away and would contact them once he was home again.

Her pen paused, she wondered when he would be home. Although he'd only been gone for five weeks, it felt like the longest five weeks of her life. She kept busy each day, the house and estate needed her attention, and then there were the invitations from the wives from neighbouring estates to luncheons and dinners, most of which she refused. However, she couldn't refuse them all and sometimes she felt the need to spend an hour away from the house and simply talk to other people who had conversations that didn't include running estates but were more on the subject of fashion and the latest gossip. Never had she thought she would miss those types of chats, but she did. There were times when she didn't want to write cheques or deal with tradesmen but instead wanted to choose a new hat or feel the latest silk samples from the dressmaker.

Some days she drove herself into York, eager to be lost amongst the crowds of sightseers and shoppers. She'd take tea and then walk the cobbled streets happy to window-shop. Other times she'd meet her mother and sisters and they would spend afternoons at the milliners ordering new hats or visiting family friends she'd not seen since before her wedding.

As always, being with her family lifted her spirits and although they knew about Jeremy and his place at the asylum, they didn't speak of it unless she brought it up. They seemed intent on making her laugh every time she was in their company and she loved them all the more for it. Afterwards she often thought about how it would feel if she and Jeremy did move to London and she wouldn't have these days with her mother and sisters.

Rising from the desk, she searched out Jeremy's latest letter and reread it for the tenth time.

Dearest Millie,

My darling, I have a short time in which to write to you for activities are planned for this afternoon. At the moment the specialist doctors here feel I need a complete break from my life, and instead they encourage me, and the other return soldiers, to talk of the war.

One doctor, a kind older man – he served in the Boer War – said that to unburden one's soul is sometimes the only medicine needed. How true that is remains to be seen. We are invited to unburden ourselves at every opportunity. I find it difficult to speak as freely as some of the other patients here, but I'm becoming much better at it in recent days.

The house, I say house, but it is rather more like a hospital, overlooks the sea. It used to be a spa in the last century, so I'm told.

We are some miles from Plymouth, and not encouraged to visit there, or leave the grounds at all. However, we have access to a secluded beach, which is reached by a winding little track down the side of a cliff. I walk there most days, in all weathers. I like the serenity the ocean brings. Perhaps I was a sailor in another life? There is an abundance of birdlife at the beach. I watched the birds for hours, wheeling and diving overhead. It looks so carefree up there.

The days go by in tolerable repetition. We wake up, wash, eat, partake in some physical activity, then eat again, in the afternoons we have discussions, sometimes in groups, sometimes one-to-one. If the weather is fine we work in the gardens, or walk to the beach, if the weather is bad we play cards or read. Royston is my constant companion. I think he likes it here though, for it is similar to being in the army again, surrounded by men, organised by rules.

I, however, just wish to be with you.

I miss you terribly, but I do feel better in myself, be assured of that. Believe me there are so many men here in a worse situation than me. I feel a little bit of a fraud. One man, Denis, cries every night, but during the day he is extremely happy and chatty. Another man plays the piano all day, he refuses to talk to anyone, but his music is beautiful. There are men here who shake constantly or hurt themselves. It's a pathetic sight to see grown men babbling like babies. The worst cases are in a different wing to us, and we rarely see them. Those poor men are given experimental treatments, electric shocks and such. If one was to ignore that area, you could happily believe you were on holiday at a wonderful hotel. We eat well and are treated with the utmost respect as though we are guests, not patients.

For the rest of us, our treatment is varying. We are encouraged to game shoot in the surrounding fields, imagine that? As yet I have not taken them up on the offer, but I feel I will have to as part of my healing. Aside from the shoots, we have 'meetings' which make us face similar situations as we did in France. It is to help us rationalise what we saw and did during the war. All terribly useful I'm sure and I can't argue the idea of it as I've not suffered one nightmare since arriving here. Can you believe that, for I barely do!

Another fact I've learned is that officers out-number all other ranks in this type of suffering. We, us officers, felt the strain of sending men under our charge over the top and into battle – or as they put it – into the slaughter. Which we did, often…

I must go, my darling, for the gong has been sounded and I don't want to be late.

Please be assured that I am not unhappy here. I feel it is doing me good and we must take strength from that.

I'll write again soon.

Your loving husband,
Jeremy.

Millie gently ran her finger over Jeremy's writing. He said he wasn't unhappy, yet she felt he wasn't happy either. His tone seemed to be of indifference. Selfishly she wanted him home, but none of his letters so far indicated a time when that would happen. She wanted him to be cured, obviously, but how long would that take?

'Madam?'

Millie looked at Gilly, who stood at the door expectantly. 'Oh, forgive me, Gilly, I didn't hear you.'

'Mr Pattison is here. He's in the drawing room.'

'Thank you.' Millie folded away Jeremy's letter and thrust it into her pocket. She wiped a hand over her forehead, feeling a little tired and unwell. Like Jeremy she felt indifferent to everything today. Perhaps she needed to go to bed earlier, but sleep was proving difficult to come by since Jeremy left.

Entering the drawing room, she found Monty standing by the fireplace as Jeremy used to do so often. It annoyed her. 'You wished to see me?'

'Good day, my lady.'

Millie stiffened. Why did he have to always make her feel in the wrong. And the way he uttered, *'my lady'* made her feel as though they lived in a royal palace. She wasn't a queen, for God's sake. Why couldn't he simply call her madam as everyone else did?

'I haven't disturbed you from something important, have I?'

'Just ledgers and paperwork.' She hadn't seen him for over a week, despite his requests for a meeting. 'Time doesn't seem to be my own lately.'

'I know I should have waited for you to have a free moment, but I needed to talk to you.'

'Is there a problem?' She walked further into the room, but suddenly the furniture was spinning, and she was falling.

'Millie!'

She came around, lying on the floor and Monty cradling her head. She went to sit up, but he held her down.

'No, my lady, please remain where you are. Gilly is getting you some water. I've sent for the doctor.'

'Heavens, I don't need a doctor, Monty.' Embarrassed she ignored his protests and sat up.

He helped her to the sofa. 'I think it is best you are checked over.'

Gilly came hurrying in carrying a damp cloth and a glass of water. 'Oh, madam. How do you feel?'

'I'm fine, truly.'

Monty adjusted a cushion behind her back. 'Hopefully Doctor Boardman will not take long in attending.'

'I really don't need him.' Millie hated the fussing.

'Have you eaten today?' Monty asked.

'I had toast and tea at breakfast.''

He glanced at the clock. 'It's gone after two, my lady.'

'That explains it then. I've not had enough to eat or drink today.' She glanced away from him, wishing he wasn't there. 'Perhaps we should cancel Doctor Boardman's visit, poor man. He is in retirement, you know. We can't have him trudging up the drive for such a minor thing.'

'I'm sure he'd be delighted to have any excuse to come to Remington Court.'

She smiled, knowing he spoke the truth. Doctor Boardman needed no prodding to come and have a cup of tea and taste the delicious cakes Mrs Ellis provided.

They heard the front door knocker sound.

'That was rather quick.' Monty straightened and adjusted the cuffs of his shirt beneath his jacket.

Sarah stood in the doorway. 'Madam, you have a visitor, a Captain Isaacs. He's come to see Sir Jeremy,' she announced anxiously.

'Oh dear. What terrible timing.' Millie patted her hair into place, her curls no doubt were a riot about her head. 'Show him in, Sarah, please.'

'Would you like me to leave?' Monty asked.

'No, for should Doctor Boardman arrive I'll need you to chat with Stephen, if that's all right with you?'

'Certainly.' He bowed his head.

'Millie, Lady Rem, you look magnificent.' Captain Stephen Isaacs strolled in like a breath of fresh air.

Millie had only met him at her wedding, but he had left a lasting impression as someone full of life, always joking and laughing, living every day with supreme gusto. She had liked him in the first instant.

'Captain Isaacs!' She hugged him too tightly to be proper, but she didn't care. He was a link to Jeremy. She blinked back silly tears. 'I'm so happy you have come.'

'Well, who could ask for a nicer welcome than that? I believe at your wedding I begged you to call me Stephen?' Stephen smiled, his dark hair, over long than was allowed for the army swept into his eyes and he pushed it away with a flick of his fingers.

'Stephen, this is Monty Pattison, Jeremy's land agent. Monty this is Captain Stephen Isaacs, Jeremy's *closest* friend.' She felt nasty for saying that, but it was the truth. Monty couldn't think he was Jeremy's *only* friend!

'Indeed! I have heard about you most favourably in letters from Rem.' Isaacs shook Monty's hand. 'Good to meet you at last.'

Millie turned to Sarah who remained standing in the doorway. 'Tea, please, Sarah.' She smiled at the two men in front of her. 'Please sit down.'

'Where is the dashing captain, Lady Rem?' Stephen asked, sitting by the fire. 'I know I've arrived unannounced, but I thought to surprise him, and you. I hope you don't mind?'

'No, not at all. You are always welcome here, Stephen.'

'I'm on my way home to Oxfordshire after traveling to Scarborough to visit my sick grandmother. Sadly, she passed away last week, and her funeral was yesterday. I felt after all that I must stop and see you both, for Jeremy wouldn't forgive me if I was in the district and not pay a call.'

'I'm so sorry to hear about your grandmother,' Millie said.

'She was eighty-five, a grand age for anybody.' Stephen shrugged. 'But she was a good old egg and loved me well as grandmothers often do.'

'Jeremy isn't here, I'm sorry.' Millie felt awful. 'Where is he?'

Millie glanced at Monty and sighed. 'He's in Plymouth.'

'Plymouth? Good Lord, whatever for?'

At that moment, the front door knocker sounded again. Millie groaned for it meant Doctor Boardman. She looked at Monty.

Monty leaned forward to Stephen. 'Lady Remington fainted just before you arrived. The doctor is here to make sure she is fine.'

Stephen looked aghast. 'I say! You should have said right at the start. Here I am waffling along. I will go and leave you in peace.'

'Nonsense. I'm perfectly well. I insist you stay!'

Sarah brought in the tea tray and Gilly brought in Doctor Boardman, who being a large, affable man, full of bonhomie instantly commanded the room.

Introductions were made and then the kind old doctor whisked Millie off to the bedroom.

'Now then, Lady Remington, tell me what happened.' Boardman placed his bag on the bed and opened it.

'I fainted, Doctor, that is all. I am perfectly fine now. I didn't have enough to eat today, only breakfast. My fault entirely.'

'Tsk, tsk, my lady. Food and drink are a vital part of living, especially as someone as busy as you are. Nevertheless, let us have a look at you and then we can go from there.'

Millie sat on the bed. 'There is no need, I assure you.'

'Let me be the judge of that.' He smiled.

Chapter Nine

Millie sat at the head of the dining table, sipping a glass of white wine. She smiled when appropriate and added to the conversation when needed. However, Doctor Boardman, Monty and Stephen were content to control the majority of the talking and she was thankful for it. Even Monty's presence didn't penetrate the fog that was surrounding her mind at the moment.

After his examination, Doctor Boardman had declared her to be pregnant.

With child.

Likely at least three months.

The child would be due in the height of summer – a July baby.

She couldn't think straight.

She was carrying a baby. How had she not known? Shouldn't she have felt different? Her hand went to her flat stomach. Shouldn't she have a bigger stomach by now? She had no clue. Her first thought was to write to Jeremy and tell him. But would that help or hinder him? Would the thought of her being alone here and pregnant hamper his progress in Plymouth? Could the prospect of becoming a father be too much for him to cope with on top of everything else? Was she to burden him further?

On their honeymoon they had talked of children and Jeremy mentioned he wanted a whole tribe of them, for being an only child was something he didn't want his child to go through.

But what would he think now? His mind was tortured. How would he deal with the news that a baby was about to enter their lives? Would the responsibility be too much?

What if he didn't want a baby feeling the way he was? What if he didn't return from Plymouth for a year or so? How could she manage without Jeremy?

Her breathing quickened. Sweat broke out on her forehead. She'd be alone with a baby. Alone with a baby in this house that she didn't even like. This wasn't her home. She tried to make it so, but it didn't have the love as her family home of Elm House.

She'd have to talk to her mother. She'd drive over and see her. Mama's wise counsel would settle her. She longed to see her mama, to hear her calm voice.

'Lady Rem?' Stephen touched her hand where it lay beside her plate. 'You look very pensive.'

She summoned a bright smile. 'I just wish Jeremy was here. He would have enjoyed this dinner tonight.'

Stephen grinned. 'Indeed, he would have. What conversations we'd have shared. I have missed him a great deal.'

'You'll stay for a few days and not only for tonight, won't you?' she asked, suddenly desperate for him to remain in the house. He was a connection to Jeremy and more importantly she liked his company.

'Ah, I would like nothing better, Lady Rem, but I must report back to my barracks by tomorrow.'

'Jeremy mentioned that you had decided to remain in the army.'

'Yes, well, it's all I know. I'd joined up before the war, so I might as well stay in it now no one is shooting at me.' He laughed.

'Perhaps when you next have leave you will come and stay with us? Jeremy would like that and so would I.'

'Nothing would give me more pleasure.'

'Shall we go into the drawing room and be comfortable?'

They left Sarah and Gilly to clear away and decamped into the drawing room before the roaring fire.

After an hour, Doctor Boardman said his goodbyes, leaving Monty and Stephen drinking brandy, while Millie enjoyed a cup of tea, though she walked him to the door.

'Now, although I am retired, I am at your beck and call, Lady Remington, especially when I am invited to enjoy such a wonderful meal.'

'You are welcome here even without a medical reason. Thank you for coming and allowing the estate to call on your services, despite your retirement. We will try not to depend on you too much.'

'I don't mind it at all. York is a long way away when there's an emergency.' He shrugged on his coat. 'I do suggest you register with the midwives in York and at the hospital but should the little one be in a rush I am not far away.'

Panic filled her. She had no idea about being pregnant or babies or what she was meant to do. 'I have time to do all that, don't I?'

'Indeed, you do, don't worry.' He smiled sympathetically. 'Now, I had best get Tippy home for she'll be wanting a meal of hay.'

Thankfully, she knew that Tippy was his pony. She waved goodbye to him as he pulled his big body into his little trap and told his pony to walk on.

Millie re-entered the drawing room and picked up her cup of tea.

'So, now the good doctor has left us,' Stephen leaned forward in the winged back chair by the fire, 'I want to know all that has happened with Jeremy. Monty filled me in a little earlier when you were with the doctor, but Lady Rem, I implore you to tell me everything.'

'What can I say?' She shrugged her shoulders. 'Jeremy suffers cruelly. Such terrible dreams that transport him back into the trenches. Nothing seems to help him.'

Monty nodded. 'He's so remorseful when he lashes out during his dreams and Lady Remington cops the brunt of it.'

'He doesn't mean to do it!' Millie snapped at Monty.

Stephen sighed deeply and sipped his brandy. 'Poor Rem, and poor you. I never expected him to be tormented so deeply, but it is hardly surprising.'

'Oh? Why?' Concerned, Millie gave him her full attention.

'Rem, like me, being an officer, had full responsibility of the men. They were ours, body and soul. Their lives were in our hands to wield and use as needed. You understand that, don't you, Monty?'

'I do,' Monty answered, staring into his glass.

Stephen gazed into the fire. 'How do I describe it to you?'

'In any way you can. I would like to know what you all went through.'

'Words don't do it justice, you understand?'

'I appreciate that, but anything will help.'

'Poor Rem,' Stephen repeated, sipping his drink. 'He took such responsibly too intensely. Every decision, every order that was sent down the line to us had to be followed, no matter how ridiculous they seemed. There were times when we didn't understand the commands at all, or we felt they were unnecessary, and it was made worse when we had to order men, some so young they weren't even shaving… we had to order them to their deaths. Rem always led from the front…'

Millie held her breath. 'He was in the thick of it.'

'Naturally. It is the way he's made.'

Monty shifted in his chair. 'It was the waiting that was the worst.'

Stephen snorted. 'God yes. Waiting for that word, that whistle that sent us over the top. Rem was always there, urging the men on, helping them up the fire step—'

'Fire step?' Millie interrupted.

'The step built along the trench that men stood on to fire from over the sandbags.'

'Oh, I see.'

'We'd send them under the hanging communication wires and over the sandbags into No Man's Land and to certain death, or at very least a horrible wound.'

Monty had a faraway look in his eyes as his fingers gently touched the scar on his jaw and neck. 'The guilt of surviving a battle was sometimes so heady you wanted to scream and shout or drink yourself senseless. You didn't do any of that, of course. You simply waited for the next order, which hopefully was one that had you coming out of the lines and into some French village where you could spend some money on a drink and a woman.'

Stephen nodded. 'It wasn't always the battles that demanded so much from a man. Trench raids were the most feared amongst all soldiers.'

'Trench raids?' Millie murmured.

'Yes, a wonderful suggestion by the generals that in the quiet times between battles, a select group of men would risk everything to venture into the enemy's trenches to gather intelligence, or prisoners, if we were lucky, and that sort of thing.' Stephen sipped again. 'Rem was very good at it. He had the superior mind that knew just how to handle these trench raids without loss of life. Only, once you do something successfully you were asked repeatedly to keep doing it. He was a victim of his own success.'

Stephen bent to add another piece of wood to the fire. 'Rem was a fine officer, but more than that he was one of those unique soldiers who knew how to read the war. Often, he was requested to go back out of the lines to speak to those who rolled the dice. At first, he went willingly, eager to tell them how we were faring, but he soon realised that those in command weren't listening to him. After that, he stopped reporting back, simply sent a runner with a message.'

'He did well not to be demoted,' Monty said. 'Some of the commanders I met would have happily taken his commission.'

Stephen nodded. 'True. There were some right bastards in high command. Forgive my language, Lady Rem.'

'So, he wasn't taken seriously, when asked for his advice?'

'Not always, no.' Stephen settled back into his chair. 'The times we were not in battle, most men slept, relaxed, played cards, wrote letters home, you know? But not Rem. He seemed to be on his own personal crusade, always thinking about the next battle, the next orders. The man never slept. It doesn't surprise me in the least that he has nightmares. I would imagine most of us do at times, but with Rem being so intense, it makes sense that his dreams are powerful enough to cause him havoc.'

Shaken by the disclosure, Millie added more tea to her cup. 'Will Jeremy recover though? Will he be afflicted like this forever?' She looked at Stephen. 'You were an officer and you don't suffer as Jeremy does, do you?'

'No, I don't. I haven't the answers. I wish I did. Perhaps it comes down to how personally you took the war, the decisions we had no control over. I actually didn't care.' Stephen frowned. 'I don't mean to sound unfeeling, but unlike Rem, I took nothing to heart as he did. The orders sent down to us were followed. I didn't ask why, I didn't see the end results. I just followed the orders I was given. Rem wasn't like me. He argued the actions, he thought about the consequences. To him the men mattered more than anything. They were not fodder for German machine guns. It became an obsession to him to keep the men safe.'

'He cared too much,' Millie murmured. She felt as though she was learning more about the man she married but also becoming more distant from him. She had married a man she didn't really know, not deep down inside, not what was in his head. She'd happily married the idea of being in love and being married to a handsome wealthy man of good social standing and pedigree.

'And look where it has got him.' Stephen swore under his breath. 'He can't let go. He's haunted.'

Monty offered a cigarette to Stephen who shook his head. 'He told me that writing letters home to the families of men that had died was agonising. I wouldn't envy him that task.'

'It wasn't fun,' Stephen added. 'Each letter was hard to write. How do you tell a mother or wife that their man has died? You were writing words that would destroy a family.'

'Such a terrible task,' Millie murmured. She couldn't imagine writing such letters of sadness.

'What amazed me more than anything was that Rem has returned here.'

'Here? To England?' Millie stared at him, surprised. 'To marry me, you mean?'

'On, no, I don't mean that. I knew how much he wanted to have you for his wife. He didn't speak of you much, and when he did it was only to me. Rem wouldn't talk about the future a lot, but when he did, he was full of such devotion. I've never seen a man want a woman as much as Rem wanted you.'

Millie's heart swelled with love.

'But he also knew it would mean living here, and…' Stephen's expression was apologetic, 'and he hated this house.'

'Because of his father?'

'Yes, the man was a cold fish. Not evil, just uncaring. He didn't allow anyone to speak of Rem's mother. He sent Rem away to school as soon as possible from a small age. I came here for a few days in one of our school holidays and good God it was like being in prison. Hideous dark rooms, cold that cut through your bones, servants creeping about like ghosts. I couldn't wait to get away.' Stephen looked about him. 'But you have made wonderful changes, Lady Rem. The place is much lighter, warmer.'

'But does Jeremy see those changes or does he still hate the place and the memories it holds?' She felt a hollowness inside. 'When we married, he said that he didn't want to take me away from my family and selfishly I thought living here at Remington Court would be perfect, as we'd have my family close by and it'd be a new start for him, too. We could wipe away the past.' She gazed into the fire. 'New wallpaper and painted rooms aren't enough though, are they? I know he would rather be at the London townhouse.'

'Or the chateau.'

'Yes,' she agreed. 'The chateau holds his heart, but it's been through a war and he didn't want us to start our married life in such a place.'

'I agree with him.' Monty nodded. 'War-torn Northern France would not be the best place to take the woman you loved.' His eyes softened as he gazed at her.

She turned away towards the fire and rubbed her forehead in frustration. 'Living here is making him worse, isn't it? I am making the problem worse, aren't I?'

'We don't know that, my lady.' Monty's soft voice was too much.

Feeling sick, she jerked to her feet. 'Thank you, both of you, for sharing the war with me. I think I will go to bed. Goodnight.' She fled from the room before she vomited.

~ ~ ~ ~

Millie pulled the Napier to a stop in the driveway of her parents' home, Elm Court, on the outskirts of York. Usually she enjoyed driving, relishing in the freedom it afforded her. However, not today. It'd been a terrible drive with rain starting half way on the journey and it was one time she wished she had a chauffeur. Her shoulders ached with the tension of concentrating on driving on muddy roads and peering through a splattered windscreen.

She hurried up the stairs and like magic the front door opened as Forbes, the family butler, welcomed her inside.

'Are my parents at home?' she asked, shaking the rain from her skirt.

'Your mother is, my lady, but your father is still in York.' Forbes took her driving gloves and coat. 'Tea, Lady Remington?'

'Thank you, that would be wonderful after such a drive.' Millie headed into the drawing room and found it empty. She heard voices coming from the conservatory. In a glass room full of lush plants and thick cushioned chairs, Millie found her mama and Cecelia looking over *The Lady* magazine.

'Is there anything interesting in it?' Millie asked, smiling at their surprise at seeing her.

'Darling girl! What are you doing here?' Mama embraced her.

'I thought to come and see you.'

'Are you lonely out there in the wilds of the country?' Cece asked, full of concern, giving her cheek a kiss. 'Are you missing Jeremy terribly?'

'Yes, naturally.'

'Have you heard much from him?'

Millie sat at the table. 'He writes and tells me about everything he's doing and what it is like. He doesn't seem unhappy.'

'He'll be missing you enormously, poor man,' Mama declared.

'I hope so.' Millie gave a little smile. 'I would hate to think he's not missing me at all.'

'You need to keep busy,' Mama instructed, folding the magazine away.

'I do try, Mama.'

'The Ashton Home for Women and Children could do with another patron, if you've a mind. I was speaking to Mrs Victoria Ashton only yesterday. She and her husband, Joseph are getting on in years, but they are still so busy with their work. I believe they are in their late seventies and still they barely have a minute to themselves. Such good people. York should be proud of them.'

'Indeed, I have met Doctor and Mrs Ashton many times. They are nice people.' Millie felt a lecture coming on from Mama about doing good works. 'I do a lot for the village and the Remington Court staff and estate. Trust me, there are nights when I and awake until the small hours answering letters and requests and planning events and repairs and all sorts of things.'

'Yes, I know you do. Much more than Soames ever did. Don't be like him and ignore the people who depend on you,' Mama advised, reaching for the bell for tea.

'Don't ring it. Forbes has already asked me.'

'Oh good.' Mama settled herself and gave Millie a direct look. 'As I was saying you need to join more societies. I barely have time to myself and that's the way I like it. I cannot imagine how some women do nothing all day. Just now Cece and I were trawling the advertisements for staff. The young girls come and go now with such relentless regularity. I simply don't have time for it. I've had to rearrange my afternoon appointments to read these advertisements and make a shortlist of suitable applicants. Cece will write to them and organise the interviews this afternoon.'

'Why aren't the staff staying?'

'They earned more in the factories during the war and have become used to those good wages. How is a family to compete?' Mama scoffed. 'Do you find it the same at Remington Court?'

'No, not really. We've a skeleton staff anyway. I've not be in the mind to employ more. I don't feel at home there yet. We make do with Sarah and Gilly in the house and then Mrs Ellis has her girls. It is enough for now with just Jeremy and I. We haven't done much entertaining and if we do we hire women from the village to help out.'

'Well, I believe the girls should be grateful to even have a position offered to them. The factories are hiring the men again and the women are back in the home. The single girls need to realise the war is over and take whatever position they are offered.'

'You've used agencies in the past to find staff, why don't you continue to do that?' Millie asked.

A discreet cough made them turn towards Forbes.

'Yes, Forbes?' Mama sighed. 'Please don't inform me I have another visitor. I've quite had my fill today.' She shook her head at Millie. 'Three different ladies called this morning. Three! I've done nothing but drink tea and commit small talk.'

Forbes coughed again. 'Madam, Mr Marsh has arrived home, but he has gone upstairs to lie down. He sends his apologies.'

'Gone to lie down?' Mama stood up, a look of confusion on her face. 'What do you mean gone to lie down?' She stared at Millie and Cece as though they had the answers. 'Is he ill? I can't remember the last time your papa was ill.' Her face lost all its colour.

'Go up and see to him, Mama.' Millie stood as did Cece and they all went into the drawing room and through into the hall.

'We'll wait down here.' Millie held Cece back when she would have followed their mother upstairs.

'It'll be a trifling little cold, you'll see.' Mama stormed up the stairs. 'As if I have time for this!'

'Come, Cece.' Millie rubbed her sister's arm compassionately. 'Forbes, the tea, please?'

'I'll find out what the hold up is, my lady.' Forbes's expression was thunderous at the lateness of the maid as he went down the hallway.

'Should we not call for a doctor?' Cece wrung her hands, dithering at the bottom of the stairs. 'Papa is never ill.'

'Papa wouldn't want a fuss.' Millie ushered her sister back into the drawing room and went to the window. Rain lashed the pane, flattening the plants in the garden. 'I might have to spend the night, Cece. I don't fancy driving back in this weather.'

'Did you bring a bag?'

'No. I should have. I don't know where my mind is some days. Though I did tell Mrs Ellis and Daisy that I might stay over if it became too late to return home, yet I didn't bring a change of clothes with me. How silly.'

'Never mind, you can borrow a blouse and skirt from me.'

Millie smiled her thanks and wondered if she could still fit into Cece's clothes. Had her waist thickened since she and Cece had worn each other's clothes back when she was unmarried? Did she look pregnant?

The thought went from her mind as Mama entered the drawing room wearing an anxious expression. 'He's feeling a little unwell. He's not sure why.'

'Should we call Doctor Morris?' Cece was beside Mama's side instantly.

'Your papa says no, that he just needs a nap and he's sure he'll be fine. But he looked ghastly.'

Sally, the parlourmaid, entered carrying a tea tray while Forbes hovered by the door.

'I think I'll sit with him for a bit.' Mama took a step then faltered. 'Forbes, perhaps send a note to Doctor Morris and see if he'll call by when he has a moment free.'

'I'll get Thomas to cycle there now, madam.'

'Yes, very good.'

Alone with Cece, Millie poured the tea. 'Where's Prue?'

'Gone to London with Grandmama.'

'You didn't want to go, too?'

'No. I promised Agatha I'd help her sort out Uncle Edmund's library at Crabapple Cottage.'

'How is Uncle Edmund?' Millie asked, making a mental note that she must write to her father's brother soon, and Agatha as well.

'He is getting older and more quieter every time I see him.' Cece jumped as thunder rolled overhead.

'I barely managed to say two words to him at my wedding, I was so busy.'

'He'd have preferred that. Poor Agatha. I don't know how she copes with living there.' Cece half-heartedly ate a biscuit. 'Prue irritates me no end but at least there is noise in this house when she is here.'

'Agatha has grown accustomed to it.' Millie munched on the treacle oat squares that she loved so much. She must get the recipe from Mrs Hood, the cook and give it to Mrs Ellis. 'Why are you sorting out Uncle Edmund's library? I would have thought he'd not want anyone to touch his precious books.'

'It's becoming overcrowded and a serious danger. He has piles and stacks of tomes rising so high that if they toppled over they'd kill someone or fall in the fireplace and burn the house down! Agatha made Uncle understand that it needed sorting. So that's what we are doing. I go over every morning and spend a few hours cataloguing and boxing the books to store in the loft.'

'Our cousin would relish the company,' Millie murmured thinking of her shy cousin. Agatha was an only child born late to Uncle Edmund and Aunt Nell. Sadly, Aunt Nell had died when Agatha was only nine years old. Agatha had grown up in a quiet house with only an old governess to look after her and a studious father who spent more time reading his books than with his only child. As a consequence, Agatha adored coming to the Marsh house whenever she could and being amongst the fun-loving cousins.

Cece took another biscuit. 'I don't mind helping at all. I always feel sorry for Agatha, as though she got the short straw in the family. Look at us, we've had most wonderful lives with loving parents and Grandmama and all the benefits that come from Papa being so successful at business. Whereas Agatha lost her mother young, her father being only an English professor meant they didn't live as… lavishly as we have done.'

'Yes, I agree. Poor Agatha. I shall invite her to Remington Court.' Millie suddenly had an idea. 'Why don't both you and Agatha come to Remington Court next week and stay a few days, or longer if you want?'

Cece's face lit up. 'Oh, yes, can we? That would be wonderful.'

Too late Millie thought of Cece's fondness of Monty.

The evening was spent quietly, Papa stayed in bed, an unheard of phenomenon. The doctor had called and seen Papa and said it was exhaustion and perhaps a slight chest infection and Papa would be right as rain in a day or two.

Mama, full of concern that her robust husband had gone to bed in the middle of the day, picked at the delicious dinner as though it was no more than scraps from the bin.

Cece and Millie tried to keep her spirits up, but she made mumbled replies showing no interest in joining in any conversation.

'I will go up, I think, girls.' Mama scraped back her chair. She gave each daughter a kiss and left the room.

'Papa will hate that he's making Mama miserable,' Cece said as they left the table, no longer hungry and ordered coffee to have in the library.

Millie ran her hand along the rows and rows of book spines as she had done since she was a child. She loved this room. It was always warm and welcoming with a huge blazing fire in the winters and facing south had the sun all day in the summer. Although the staff would beg her to close the shutters to keep out the sunlight so as not to spoil the furniture and books, she would refuse and curl up on the cushioned window seats and read for hours.

Millie yawned as Forbes brought in the coffee tray and set it out for them. 'You can lock the house up for the night, Forbes. Mama has already gone up and Miss Cecelia and I will retire shortly.'

'Very good, my lady.'

Left alone, Cece giggled. 'I still can't get used to you being called Millie, Lady Remington.'

'Nor can I. It's been five months since the wedding and it still feels as though they are talking to someone else.'

'Are you happy, Mill?' Cece added milk to their coffees and a lump of sugar each. 'I mean really happy? You have no regrets?'

Millie accepted the cup and stirred it. 'I am. I love Jeremy terribly. Obviously, his shell shock problems have made things a trifle difficult. He is ashamed and feels guilty about it, but I assure him that it doesn't change how I feel about him.'

'And marriage… all of it… is satisfactory?' Cece had an odd look in her eyes.

'Yes. Why? What do you mean?'

'Are there… I mean.' She blushed as easily as Millie did. It was only Prue who didn't blush.

Millie looked at her over the rim of her coffee cup. 'Are you talking about what happens in the bedroom?'

Cece blinked rapidly. 'Well, I say!'

Laughing so much she had to put the cup down, Millie found she couldn't be serious. 'It is wonderful, Cece, I promise you.'

'It is?'

'Well, yes. I wouldn't lie to you. I'm telling you the truth. Jeremy and I love each other very much and when you feel like that you want… well, you want them to touch you… everywhere.'

'Heavens. I can't imagine.' Cece was nearly as red as her hair.

'Nor could I until we kissed, properly kissed, then suddenly it all made sense.'

'It did?'

'Yes.'

'So, it's better than you feared?'

'Yes. There is nothing you need to fear about it. As long as you are with the man you love.' Millie sighed, thinking of Jeremy and missing his arms around her. 'I feel a little lost without him now.'

'That's so lovely. I'm happy for you, Mill, truly I am.'

'I can imagine that not every marriage is like ours. I'm sure those couples who marry without love must find it difficult and strange.' She shuddered. 'I couldn't imagine having *sex* with someone I didn't love as much as I love Jeremy.'

'Yet a great many people marry and are not in love.'

'I wonder how they manage it?'

'Maybe they have separate bedrooms and take lovers.' Cece grinned. 'I could see Prue doing that.'

Millie laughed. 'Yes, very much. She will probably find some rich old man who lives in a grand castle but has no teeth and smells of old goats.'

Cece leaned forward. 'And she takes a young lover like an underfootman.'

'No, it'd be a younger handsome son of a poor clergyman.'

'Or the vicar himself!'

'Cece!' Millie nearly spilt her coffee as they laughed.

Mama's frantic yells rent the air.

For a moment, Millie and Cece simply gaped at one another. They'd never heard their mother yell in their lives.

As if jerked by an invisible string, they both ran out into the hall and up the stairs, skidding to a halt at the doorway of their parents' bedroom.

'Mama?' Millie opened the door, Cece pressing against her back.

'Get the doctor! Hurry!' Mama's anxious cries lifted the hairs on the back of Millie's neck.

Millie pushed Cece back into the corridor. 'Go, Cece, go get Forbes, quickly now.'

With Cece hurrying downstairs, Millie stepped into the room. Mama sat beside the bed holding Papa's hand, telling him help was on the way and he would be fine. Millie forced herself to look at her darling papa, who's whole left side had drooped alarmingly. He was deathly still, but breathing.

Chapter Ten

Millie sat at her mother's writing desk with half her attention on the door and anyone passing by it in case they needed her.

Picking up the pen, she paused, gathering her thoughts, then began to write.

Darling Jeremy.

It is with a heavy heart that I write to you from my parents' house. I was here visiting them yesterday when Papa returned from town feeling unwell. Later he had an episode, which Doctor Morris declared to be a stroke. It breaks my heart to see Papa like this. The whole left side of him has drooped. Mama is beside herself, and Cece and I are trying to help in any way we can but there is nothing any of us can do but wait and hope he gets better. Doctor Morris says that sometimes stroke sufferers return to normal, with little side effects while others never regain control of the damaged side. So, we wait and see how Papa responds. He is weak and not communicative and sleeps a lot.

Prue and Grandmama are expected at any moment. I sent a telegram to them last night and they are catching this morning's train from London.

Please don't feel the need to leave Plymouth. Your treatment and recovery are most important and there is nothing you can do here but sit and wait as we are doing and that would be a waste of your time when you could be getting better in Plymouth. I am fine. Worried, naturally, but holding it together for Mama's sake. I've never seen Mama so quiet and tormented as she is. She's not left Papa's side and stayed awake all night talking to him even though he was sedated.

I've spent today clearing Mama and Papa's diaries and informing Papa's business associates of his condition. I will stay here for a few more days until Papa is more himself and Mama doesn't need me. Cece has been marvellous, a natural nurse Doctor Morris said. She's better at it than me, perhaps it was fate that Papa stopped me from going to France during the war and training as a nurse. I think I am more the organiser and feel most at use overseeing the staff and house for Mama.

Doctor Morris says that once Papa is stable enough to move, then he believes Papa could do with being somewhere warm to help him recover. Mama insists on going to Italy, and staying in a friend's villa, but whether Papa is strong enough for such a journey I do not know.

You'll be interested to know that Stephen Isaacs called at Remington Court to see you and he was dismayed to hear that you had gone to Plymouth. He stayed one night, and we talked a great deal. He told me a lot of what you both went through during the war. Don't be cross at him for telling me as I asked him to, and I am glad I did. I understand a bit more of what you went through now. Stephen says he will write to you next week. He may even come down and see you if he can get leave again so soon. Fingers crossed that he does.

I hope you are continuing to do well with your treatments and you are feeling better in yourself.

I hear the door, which should be Prue and Grandmama's arrival. I'll send this letter in the last post.
I love and miss you terribly.
Your loving wife,
Millie. Xx

As she wrote on the envelope she heard Prue's voice high in concern and Grandmama's quieter tones. Thinking Cece to be upstairs, Millie rose from the desk and headed to the hall.

'Millie!' Prue, dressed in a duck-egg blue dress and matching coat, looked stylish and elegant. She gave her bag to Forbes and rushed to Millie and embraced her tightly with tears in her eyes. 'How is he?'

'Still the same,' Millie answered, before hugging Grandmama. 'No change. Doctor Morris sedated him last night and today Papa has been quiet and dozing.'

'Where is Mama?' Prue stepped towards the staircase. 'Can I go up?'

'Yes, go up. Papa might be awake and Mama and Cece are with him.' Millie gave Forbes her letter. 'Can you post this for me, please?'

'Certainly, Lady Remington. Shall I arrange for some tea, or would you prefer an early meal?'

'Grandmama are you hungry?'

'I'm famished,' Prue said from the top of the stairs, 'but a sandwich will do.'

'I agree.' Grandmama nodded. 'Sandwiches are just what we need. What they pass for food on that train is deplorable. Pigswill it is, and I'll never think differently, but we were in such a rush we didn't have time to collect a hamper. Forbes, feed us well, if you please.'

'Very good, madam.' Forbes bowed and left them.

'Apart from the food, how are you, Grandmama?' Millie asked, taking her arm as they walked into the drawing room.

'Sad, my dear. Lionel is the last person I expected to suffer from such an affliction, poor man. He's always been as healthy as an ox for as long as I've known him.' Grandmama unpinned her hat, took it off and patted her grey hair into place. 'And you, my dear?'

'I'm fine.'

'Of course, you are. Totally dependable, you are. You must be a great comfort to your mother.' Grandmama sat in the chair closest to the fire. She scrutinised Millie. 'Are you wearing Cecelia's clothes?'

Millie glanced down at the green silk blouse and narrow navy skirt. 'Yes. I didn't bring a change of clothes.'

'You should always leave a trunk of clothes here as I do. Saves a lot of bother.'

'I will do that.'

'And Jeremy?'

'He's fine, doing well in Plymouth.'

'That letter you gave to Forbes, was it to him?'

Millie smiled. 'Acute as always. You never miss a thing, do you?'

'My dear, I've made it my life's work to *never* miss a trick. Sharp eyes equals a sharp wit.' Grandmama straightened out the coffee-coloured dress she wore. 'You've not asked him to come home, have you?'

'No. There is no point. Jeremy can't help Papa.'

'No, and although he could give you comfort, that would be selfish of you and detrimental to his own issues.'

'I agree.'

'Good girl. I knew you would be sensible.'

They looked up as Prue walked in, dabbing her eyes. 'I can't bear to see him like that.'

'Stop weeping, girl. Who will that benefit?' Grandmama snapped but held out her hand to take the sting out of her words. 'Come by the fire and warm yourself.'

'Mama is so brave.' Prue sniffled.

'What is there to be brave about?' Grandmama frowned. 'She is a woman faced with a difficult time and so she will get on with it. As if any daughter of mine would go to pieces?' Grandmama frowned at the notion. 'Lionel needs her to be strong, not in a fit of hysterics.'

'I know, but not everyone is as solid as you and Mama,' Prue said.

'The women in this family are. I refuse to have anything else. I couldn't be doing with nervy little ninnies.'

'Like Uncle Hugo's wife?' Prue grinned. 'Aunt Daphne tries your patience, doesn't she?'

Grandmama groaned. 'Lord above, why my son chose such a scatterbrained mouse I'll never know. I'm extremely grateful he had the good sense to be posted out to India and I don't have to socialise with her. She's an embarrassment to the family.'

Millie felt sorry for their Aunt Daphne, who they used to make fun of as children for she was easy to scare and easy to tears. 'I miss Uncle Hugo though. He was always such fun.'

'Indeed.' Grandmama stared into the flames. 'The last five years he's been in India have been difficult for me. Your grandfather would be proud of him though, India is not a stress-free assignment. Unrest in India is growing worse.'

'You went there on your honeymoon, didn't you?' Millie asked.

'Yes. What a splendid time we had,' Grandmama said dreamily. 'Such heat made everything so… intense. Spices filled the air, and the women jingled with every movement from all the bangles they wore. Your grandfather and I rode elephants up into the mountains, such lush jungle, sweeping valleys and exotic animals I've never seen since.'

'I want to travel,' Prue announced. 'I want to see the world.'

'Not everything in the world is worth seeing, dear girl.' Grandmama sighed. 'I, too, would like to do a little bit more exploring before I'm in my coffin.'

'Grandmama, don't speak of such things, especially not now,' Millie admonished.

'Slip of the tongue.' She waved her hand airily.

Forbes came in carrying a basket of logs. 'Ladies, a light meal is waiting for you in the dining room.' He added more wood to the fire.

'I shall go fetch Mama,' Millie said, rising. 'I doubt she's eaten today.'

'She's no good to Lionel if she is weak from hunger,' Grandmama tutted.

Millie hurried up to her parents' room and quietly went in. Mama and Cece were sitting on either side of the bed. Papa seemed to be sleeping. They both looked at her expectantly.

'Will you come down and have something to eat, Mama?'

'No, I'll not leave him.'

Cece stood. 'Mama, you cannot go all day without food. Papa would be most displeased with you.'

As if he was listening, Papa opened his eyes and waved his good right hand.

'Dearest.' Mama leaned forward. 'What do you need, Lionel?'

He made a noise that they couldn't understand. He closed his eyes. 'Ee-eat,' he mumbled

'There, you heard him, he said eat, and so you will,' Millie told her Mama. 'I will stay with Papa. Go down and have a rest and speak to Grandmama.'

'Very well.' Mama rose, giving a lingering stare at her husband and headed for the door. 'I won't be long, my dear.'

Sitting on the chair her mother just vacated, Millie smiled at her darling papa. 'You've just got me for a while, will I do?'

He smiled lopsidedly and nodded. 'G-good.'

Millie squeezed his hand. 'What a shame I can't sing to you, Papa.' She chuckled as he snorted. 'You always say I have the voice of a cat whose tail has been caught in a door.'

He tried to laugh and instead dribbled down his chin.

Millie jumped up to wipe it with a handkerchief from the bedside cabinet. She smiled at him, but the smile faltered when she saw the anguish in his eyes. 'You'll be better soon, Papa. You have to believe that.'

His right hand squeezed hers.

Emotion clogged her throat. Her poor darling Papa. 'I love you. We all love you.'

He nodded.

She glanced at the newspaper beside the bed. 'Shall I read to you?'

He nodded again, and she picked up the newspaper. She read aloud the first article her gaze fell on. 'The Prime Minister, Mr Lloyd George has visited Birmingham to receive the freedom of the city. Apparently, the Prime Minister spoke of the recent Paris Conference and made a firm declaration of what Germany has to do in regards to disarmament and reparation…'

~ ~ ~ ~

Millie pulled the Napier to a stop in front of the house and closed her tired eyes. She'd driven home from York through hard rain but as she grew closer to Remington Court the sun had come out and near blinded her. She didn't know which one she preferred. She sighed and opened the car door. The gravel drive crunched under her feet, they'd not had any rain here. Movement caught her eye. Two men were climbing over the roof. From around the side of the house, Monty came with another man, both deep in conversation. The sight annoyed her. Monty looked so comfortable in his role, as though he was the owner of the house. After being with her family, returning here alone emphasised how much she didn't want to come back. This place was tolerable when Jeremy was here but without him, she was beginning to hate the house as much as he did.

Monty looked up and waved, but she hurried into the house without acknowledging their presence.

'Lady Remington! Welcome home.' Sarah came out of the drawing room, carrying a dying bouquet of flowers.

The sight of the flowers depressed her further. 'Thank you. I'm home for a few days, Sarah. Tell Mrs Ellis I'll speak to her in an hour. I'd like a bath drawn, please.'

'Yes, madam.'

Rubbing the strain from her shoulders, Millie walked into the morning room and straight to her desk where a large pile of mail waited for her.

Millie had stayed for another week with her parents, then with a heavy heart decided this morning to return home to Remington Court. She wanted to drive back to her parents' house in a few days, but she needed to put plans in place with her staff to allow her to be away again. She also needed new clothes. Cece's slim skirts and dresses were too tight. Millie needed to visit the dressmaker in York and have a new wardrobe ordered.

'Lady Remington.' Monty came into the morning room as she sat sorting out all the correspondence that had arrived in her absence.

'Good afternoon, Monty.' She didn't want to see or speak to him, and after going through the pile of letters and not seeing one from Jeremy she was in a bad mood.

'It is good to see you home, my lady.' He stood just inside the doorway. 'I was most sorry to read the telegram that your father was ill. How is he?'

'He is confined to his bed and his whole left side has… fallen. A stroke.'

'A terrible tragedy.'

'He's not dead, Monty. He will recover.'

'Of course.'

'Has everything been all right here?' She sorted the letters into piles of importance.

'The roofers are here inspecting the tiles.'

'Was that prearranged?' She couldn't remember a roof inspection being on the list of jobs needed doing.

'No, it wasn't, but I thought it prudent.'

'Really? Surely there are a number of other duties my husband thought to be more important for you to carry out?'

'Sir Jeremy mentioned the roof but yes there were things he listed that he thought needed to be priorities. However—'

'If my husband thought the roof wasn't a priority then I fail to see why you should engage roofers to come and inspect the roof.'

'Lady Remington, Sir Jeremy left me in charge and—'

'It is an expense we can do without at the moment. Sir Jeremy wasn't thinking correctly when he placed you in this position.'

A muscle clenched in his jaw. 'You think he made a mistake?'

'You have no qualifications to run the estate. My husband took pity on you being out of work.'

'Lady Rem—'

'I do not have the time or the inclination to further this conversation.' She turned her back on him. 'Please excuse me. I need to change.'

She waited until she heard his footsteps recede before she sat down at the desk. Why did that man rub her up the wrong way? Everyone else liked him yet his mere existence on the estate made her blood boil. It was irrational. She hated the way she acted the minute he was near. He made her rude and nasty. She had to control it.

Sarah stood in the doorway. 'Madam, your bath is ready.'

'Thank you.' Millie went upstairs to her bedroom to find the full bath situated before the blazing fire.

Despite the homely impression, it was still strange to walk in and not feel Jeremy's presence, but he hadn't time to put his stamp on the room. There was nothing that was his lying about. His clothes were hung in the dressing room and any personal toiletries had gone with him to Plymouth. At a glance no one would think a married couple occupied the room. Like the rest of the house it was simply a well-decorated room but lacking love.

Daisy entered the room, carrying fresh towels and another jug of hot water. 'Madam! I'm so pleased you're back. How is everyone back home, and poor Mr Marsh?'

'Apart from Papa, everyone is well.' Millie undressed, feeling ridiculously teary. She wished she'd stayed with her mama now.

'Oh, madam. Don't cry.' Daisy stood beside her and gently touched her arm. 'He'll be better in no time. Mr Marsh is a strong fellow.'

'Yes, I know, but it's been awfully difficult, Daisy.' Millie climbed into the warm water and relaxed back against the bath.

'It would be, madam.' Daisy soaped up a cloth and handed it to Millie. 'Will Sir Jeremy be coming back as well?'

'No.' Millie glanced at Daisy while she washed her body. 'You are missing Royston?'

'Yes, very much, and I know he needed to accompany Sir Jeremy, but it's been weeks…'

'We both miss our men,' Millie agreed. 'Sir Jeremy isn't ready to return home yet. I don't want him leaving Plymouth before he's fully well again.'

'Even though he is to be a father?' Daisy asked, pouring the jug of hot water into the bath.

'How do you know?'

'I know your cycle, madam, and look at your tiny bump when usually you're reed thin, and I should know for haven't I been your lady's maid for five years?'

Millie sighed and glanced down at the slightest swell of her stomach which only days ago was satisfyingly flat. 'Yes, I never thought of that.'

'No one knows at all?'

'No, and I want to keep it that way. So please don't write to Royston and tell him. Sir Jeremy needs to concentrate on what he is doing. I don't need to burden him. I know you want Royston home as soon as possible but I'm sorry, Daisy, even for you, I won't bring them back before he's ready.'

'I understand.'

'But I am returning to my parents' house in a couple of days and you will come with me. You'll be able to see your family.'

'Oh, wonderful. Thank you, madam.' Daisy sobered instantly. 'I don't mean it's wonderful that Mr Marsh is unwell, I didn't mean that.'

'I know you didn't.' Millie washed her hair. 'Now tell me what's been happening here.'

'Not a lot. Mr Pattison has been dreadfully busy. Mrs Ellis adores him.'

Millie's jaw tightened at the mention of Monty.

Daisy rinsed Millie's hair. 'Mrs Ellis says the estate has never been so cared for.'

'Indeed?' Millie climbed out of the bath and wrapped a thick dressing gown around her as Daisy wrapped another one around her hair.

'Oh yes, madam. He has whipped everyone into shape. Mr Greenway believes Mr Pattison is still in the army giving orders, but lots of work has been done. Then, when Sarah mentioned in the kitchen that the attic bedrooms she and Gilly sleep in were full of damp and the minute it rains they need buckets to collect the drips in, he went straight into action and went up into the attic roof and found the problem.'

Millie spun to face her. 'There's rain coming into the house?'

'Aye, madam. Broken tiles it is. He insisted on employing roofers to come and fix it, which they did today. Mr Pattison said water damage was an important issue that needed attention straight away. It was his day off yesterday, but he spent it crawling in the roof to assess the damage.'

'Bugger.' Millie groaned and whipped the towel from her hair. She'd treated Monty abominably over the damn roofers and it was all necessary! What must he think of her?

Daisy's eyes widened at the language.

'Forgive me, Daisy.' Millie rubbed her forehead. 'I will have to apologise to Mr Pattison. I suppose the polite thing to do would be to invite him to dinner.'

'I think he would like that. He seems a lonely sort of fellow.' Daisy collected the towels.

'And I need some of my clothes altering until new ones arrive. Can you sort some out, please?'

'Why don't you wear that blue silk with the low waist for dinner?' Daisy went into the wardrobe and brought out a long blue silk dress with black beading at the neckline. 'This one was very generous in the waist when it was made. You could wear it for a few weeks yet. You have a purple and red two-toned silk as well. You know the one with the scalloped hem?'

Millie donned underwear. 'Yes, they will do for now. I'll wear that blue one tonight. What about the day dresses?'

'I'll sort through them while you dine, madam.'

'Thank you. I'll need several to be packed.'

Collecting the jug, towels and worn clothes, Daisy nodded. 'Of course, madam.'

A couple of hours later, Millie entered the drawing room feeling anxious. The blazing fire was welcoming but the thought of spending the evening with Monty was unsettling. Yet, she had been in the wrong about the roof and needed to make amends.

Alone in the room, she wished Remington Court had a butler for a butler could be relied upon to make small talk when there was no one else in the room. There was no one to pour her a drink either with Jeremy gone. She must send out enquiries for a butler. Sarah, as good as she was, didn't portray the quality of service found in a well-schooled butler.

'Lady Remington.' Monty bowed from the doorway.

She turned, her stomach clenching. 'Come in.'

'I came in via the kitchen as I needed to speak to Mrs Ellis.'

'Would you like a drink?'

'Allow me. Sherry?'

'Please.'

She watched him at the drink's cabinet pouring the sherry. He wore a new suit, his dark hair slicked back, and his shoes were polished to a high shine.

He smiled as he brought her over the crystal glass and she detected his nervousness. He smelled of soap and was cleanly shaven as though he'd taken extreme care to be very presentable tonight. She could not deny he was a handsome man, and understood why Cece had become attached to him.

Millie took a deep breath. 'I feel I owe you an apology, Monty. In fact, I do owe you an apology. I was too quick to judge your actions today concerning the roof. I didn't have all the facts. I apologise for thinking you had gone beyond your duties without speaking to either myself or Sir Jeremy. I hope you can forgive me?'

'There is nothing to forgive, Lady Remington.' His smile was fleeting, his eyes held a wariness in them. 'Your first duty is to this house and unnecessary expenditure must be closely monitored. I understand that.'

'Still, I was wrong to simply assume…' She looked away, embarrassed and sat down. 'You have every right to be annoyed with me. My husband said I should trust you, and so I must.'

'Trust has to be earned, I know that.'

A slight knock interrupted them as Sarah announced dinner was ready.

In the dining room the long table was set for only two at one end. It looked sad to see the tablecloth folded so small and the simple settings seemed incongruous to the length of the table which fitted twelve chairs. She hadn't thought that when Jeremy was home, for the two of them often dined with friends and neighbours, and as always Monty took a seat since Jeremy found him.

Millie sat at the end of the table, her normal place and smiled at Monty as he sat to her right. She needed to relax in his company. Jeremy would want her to make friends with him and for his sake she should try.

'It seems strange to not have Sir Jeremy here with us,' Monty said as though reading her thoughts.

'I agree.'

'You must miss him dreadfully.'

'I cannot even put into words how much.' Millie nodded to Sarah and Gilly who served the first course of carrot and coriander soup.

'I do, too.' Monty poured their wine. 'Your husband was the first person, since I left the army, who actually treated me with genuine friendship.'

Millie sipped her wine feeling uncomfortable at her own lack of sympathy. 'Jeremy is a good man.'

'There is nothing I would not do for him. That's the honest truth. He has given me a home, a job and a sense of wellbeing that I thought I would never have again. When he found me I was ready to die. I was actually impatient for it to happen.' He touched his jaw and neck. 'I wished that the machine gun that did this to me had killed me. I had nothing to live for.'

'How did you become to be in such a state? Have you no family?' She couldn't help but ask the burning questions she'd wanted to ask since Jeremy found him.

Monty held his spoon over the soup, his gaze not leaving hers. 'You want to know my story?'

'I think I have the right to know since you're living on my estate.'

He nodded. 'Sir Jeremy knows it, but I asked him not to speak of it to anyone.'

'I am his *wife*, not just *anyone*.' Millie felt the same anger rise again she always felt with Monty. 'You've created secrets between us.'

'Forgive me, I didn't wish to cause—'

Urgent knocking on the front door and the ringing of the bell interrupted them.

Millie frowned as Sarah left to answer it. She glanced at the clock. At eight o'clock it was late for callers. 'Who could that be?'

Sarah returned and with her was Jonas, her papa's chauffer.

Millie's heart leapt in her chest. She jerked to her feet. 'Jonas?'

'I'm sorry to disturb you, Lady Remington.'

'What's happened?'

'I've been sent for you, my lady.'

'My father?'

'He's taken a turn for the worst, I'm afraid. Can you leave immediately, my lady?'

'Yes. Absolutely.' Millie looked wildly about, not knowing what to do first.

Monty placed his hand on hers. 'I will see to everything. I'll have Daisy follow on in the morning with your luggage. Go now and think only of your father.'

She nodded and rushed from the room. In the hall, Sarah had her warmest coat and gloves ready for her.

Millie swiftly went out into the night and climbed into the back of her father's Bentley.

Chapter Eleven

She was too late.

By the time Jonas pulled the car to a stop in front of the house and Millie ran into the hall, the gentle sobbing which greeted her spoke of the passing of her beloved papa. Prue, Cece and Grandmama sat in the drawing room grieving.

In the bedroom, Millie joined Mama, who sat by the bed, her hand on her husband's. The room was lit by candles only, none of the electric lighting that Papa was so proud to have installed. The soft glow created a calming atmosphere, which she knew, was Mama's doing. To have hysterics and wailing would be totally undignified.

Papa appeared to be sleeping, but he looked so much younger than how he'd looked when Millie left just that morning.

'Come and say goodbye, dearest.' Mama spoke without emotion, her gaze not leaving Papa's face.

'He seems so much at peace,' Millie whispered. She bent and kissed Papa on the forehead.

'I feel he'd be terribly angry.'

Millie glanced at her. 'Angry?'

'To have left us. Nothing would ever make him want to leave us. We were his life, his girls.' Mama swallowed. 'He wasn't ready to go, I know that. We should have had years left.'

'He loved us very much.'

'Yes. And he was the love of my life. How will I go on without him?' Mama's voice broke on the last word and she quickly sat straighter, fighting the pain.

'What do you need me to do, Mama?'

'The funeral needs organising. In the morning there will be much to do. That's why I wanted tonight alone with him, our last night together.'

Millie rose went around the bed and kissed Mama's cheek. 'Leave everything to me.'

'Thank you, dear girl.' Mama squeezed her hand. 'What would I do without you? It's always you who I can depend on, Millie. You are my strength.'

~ ~ ~ ~

Darling Jeremy,

I hope this letter finds you well. I am sorry it's been several days since my last letter and I received your telegram, thank you. I'm pleased you listened to me regarding not returning for Papa's funeral. As much as I wanted to see you, I can't tell you how much, but my efforts were focused on supporting Mama and the girls and if you had been with me, I feel I wouldn't have done that as well as I did. Mama needed me greatly and being the eldest it was my responsibility to help her and my sisters, even Grandmama, who also suffers.

However, I am back at Remington Court now. I arrived last night and hand on heart I am rather glad to be away from such misery which invades my former home. Never have I experienced my delightful old home in anything but happiness and laughter, music and fun. But it resembles nothing of that now. Papa's presence is missing and gone with him is the essence of what was 'home'.

I've been away for over three weeks and felt I needed to return to check on things here, though Monty has done a magnificent job of keeping everything running smoothly. He even attended the funeral, which was good of him.

When I left I felt guilty, but I needed a little space. Organising the funeral and the wake afterwards was a strain I don't care to repeat. Mama was a tower of strength, of course, but underneath I feel she is also as fragile as glass. She sits quietly for hours, sometimes gently crying and at other times staring into space. Grandmama has taken her and my sisters to London for a change of scenery. Mama didn't want to go, but Grandmama refused to listen to her arguments as to why she had to stay in Yorkshire. I think it is a good decision and Mama needed to be out of the house for a time, just as I did.

Papa's funeral was well supported. A great many people attended the church service. So many people came that they spilled out into the churchyard, and despite the rain, they all stood there under umbrellas until the end. Isn't it strange how it is only funerals and weddings when we meet up with people who at any other time we don't see? I saw so many acquaintances that I knew as a child and it was a delight to see them, but on such an occasion! Why do we leave it so long between gatherings?

Millie put the pen down and wiped her sore eyes. She was terribly tired. The last three weeks had been the most trying of her life. She ached to have Jeremy's arms around her. She had to be strong, and put him first, so he would come home well and restored, but the toll of being on her own was beginning to wear her down.

She turned hearing footsteps and wasn't surprised to see Monty come into the room.

'Welcome home, Lady Remington.'

'Thank you, Monty. I spoke to Mrs Ellis this morning and she said all is well here?'

'Yes, madam, that is true. Nothing of any great importance happened.'

'Thank you for keeping the estate running so smoothly while I was away. I am grateful.'

He gave her a sad smile. 'It was my pleasure. I think at such a time the last thing you needed was to worry about what was happening here.'

She glanced down at the letter. 'I was just writing to my husband. Is there anything I need to tell him?'

'Only that we are managing in his absence.' Monty rubbed his scar. 'I have written to him myself recently, reassuring him that the estate was fine.'

She nodded, suddenly feeling out of place and lonely. For the first time in weeks she didn't have a grieving family to give her undivided attention to and she felt as though Remington Court didn't really need her either and she was at a loss as to what to do.

'The sun has a little warmth in it today for the first time this week. I do like the month of March when spring arrives. I was wondering if you would care to take a walk around the gardens? Sir Jeremy said you had plans to create a formal garden on the west side of the house.'

She remembered saying that to Jeremy one night while they lay in bed after making love. She'd talked of re-establishing the beautiful flowerbeds in honour of his late mother and he had said it was a wonderful idea. Jeremy had promised to help her design it. She wanted to do it with Jeremy, not Monty. Why did it have to be Monty who was here and not the man she loved?

'Perhaps another day.' She picked up her letter. 'I have much to do being my first day home.'

'Very well. I'll be at Home Farm today should you need me.'

'Thank you.' She turned from him, dismissing him. 'Good day, Monty.'

~ ~ ~ ~

Jeremy lay shaking and panting, his mind coming back to reality and receding from the chaos of the battlefield. He opened his eyes and in the gloom of the night, he made out the simple furnishings of the bedroom he'd been assigned in the retreat.

'Sir!' Royston came rushing into the room, his dressing gown undone over his pyjamas.

'Sorry, Royston.' Jeremy sat up and swung his legs over the side of the bed. 'Did I make much noise?'

'No, sir. I heard you as I was awake reading. Being in the next room has its advantages.' Royston lit the gas lamp beside the bed.

Jeremy put his head in his hands. 'It's been weeks since I had a nightmare. I thought I had been cured of them.'

'But, sir, we've been here for three months and look how many you've had in that time? A great many less than you had at home. That's such an improvement.'

'I think it was thinking of home that triggered it.'

'How so?'

'I was reading Millie's letter before I fell asleep. She has returned to Remington Court after the funeral.'

'Sad business.' Royston went to the alcove and lit the gas burner of the camp stove to boil the kettle for a cup of tea. It was a familiar job he'd done all through the war. 'Mr Marsh was a decent man.'

'He was indeed. A true friend of mine for years and one I shall miss more than I can say.' Jeremy paced the room. 'I should have gone to the funeral. Why did I stay here?'

'Lady Remington implored you to stay here and continue your treatment. Mr Marsh would have wanted you to as well.'

'But what about what *I* want?' Jeremy snapped, then groaned. 'That sounded so selfish of me. Bugger it all!' Frustrated he stared at his wedding photo he'd put on the narrow mantlepiece above the fire. He gazed at Millie's beautiful face, radiating such love and happiness. Since that day he'd not given her much reason to be so happy.

'You being well is all Lady Remington wishes for, no matter how long it takes. My Daisy has told me so in her letters.'

'But I miss her. So many times I have fought the urge to get on the next train home.'

'Are you ready though, sir? And if you're not, would all this have been a waste of time if you leave now?' Royston brewed the tea.

Jeremy sighed, feeling torn.

Royston passed him the cup. 'Haven't the doctors said you're recovering faster than they expected? And that you might only need a couple more months of being here?'

'Yes.' Jeremy thought of all the conversations he'd had with the specialist over the last months. Some days he felt rejuvenated, ready to face the future, then other days he sunk into a pit of gloom, remembering all he'd seen and done. On top of that was the thought of returning to Remington Court. He closed his eyes at the anxiety that built in his chest every time he thought of his father's house.

'Are you feeling tired, sir?'

'Yes. I think I'll sleep now, thank you, Royston.'

'Very good, sir. I'll see you in the morning.' Royston left him.

Jeremy climbed back into bed and turned off the gas lamp. In the darkness he lay staring up at the ceiling, his body aching for Millie, but she was hundreds of miles away in Yorkshire, at the one place he would be happy to never see again. Could they sell the estate, or even rent it out as Millie suggested? He didn't care what happened to the house he was born in, it could burn to the ground for all he cared. However, now her father had died, her mother and sisters would need her more than ever. It would be selfish of him to take her away from Yorkshire, and he'd caused her more than enough misery already.

He thought of Chateau Dumont, his mother's family's home in Northern France. The sun always seemed to shine at Chateau Dumont. In the summer the rolling fields of vines shimmered liked a sea of green. To him, Chateau Dumont was home. It was where he spent many summers as a young man learning the craft of making champagne under his uncle Louis's tutelage and the only place where he felt a sense of home and family.

As he drifted into a half-sleep he saw his father standing at his bedside, crying silently, a glass of whisky in his hand like he always had.

'She loved you more than me, and I hate you for it. I wish you had died and not her. She was mine before you came along!'

'Papa?'

With one hand, his father wrapped his fingers around his neck and squeezed. Jeremy jerked at the pain, the lack of air. He flayed his arms, trying to break the iron grip that held his throat.

'Papa!'

Suddenly his father stepped back, drank some of the whisky and stumbled from the room.

~ ~ ~ ~

Millie turned in front of the full-length mirror to see the back of the evening dress. 'I like it, Daisy.'

'It falls nicely, madam.' Daisy bent and twitched the back of the skirt into place better. 'I like the colour too.'

'It's so much shorter than my other dresses.'

'It's the fashion, madam. Showing the ankles is the new thing.' Daisy untied another box.

Millie swirled, liking the freedom of movement. The shimmering aqua colour caught the sunlight coming through the bedroom window. 'Did the matching shoes arrive as well?'

Daisy trawled through the numerous boxes on the bed. 'Yes, here they are.'

Millie slipped off the shimmering sheath of silk and laid it on the bed. Standing in her shift, she picked up a day dress of soft cream and tan stripes with a drop waist and deep pockets. 'The pockets are amazing.'

She held up a dusty pink dress with silver buttons angling down the side of the skirt. 'I'll need to have new boots and shoes since they'll be seen all the time, like those we saw in the catalogue.'

'Double-buttoned boots in different colours.' Daisy nodded.

'This one is very nice.' Millie held against her a deep blue walking dress with wide lapels edged in white piping that was also on the cuffs. 'Again, the drop waist will hide my condition for a little longer.'

Daisy gave a cheeky smile. 'I very much doubt it, madam.'

'Really?' Millie stared at her reflection and smoothed the satin of her shift over her little bump, which in the last month had grown rounder. She'd still not officially told anyone yet. Daisy knew, of course, and the staff glanced at her stomach sometimes, but she'd not publicly announced her pregnancy. Why she didn't know. Perhaps because she hadn't written to Jeremy yet and told him and she wanted him to be the first person she said the words out loud to.

However, Monty often gave her reason to suspect that he had guessed. He was very courteous as always, and on the rare occasions they were together he would hover as though he expected her to faint again.

As she dressed in a pale shimmering satin of pale gold that felt cool and wonderful against her skin, she wondered where Monty was now. Last week he'd come to her to ask for permission to have a week off, as he needed to go south for personal reasons. She had allowed him to go and not enquired as to why he needed to, but questions burned inside her head.

Since that night her Papa died when she and Monty had dined, and he was about to tell her his past, she had not felt inclined to approach the subject again, as much as she wanted to know his secrets.

In the month since Monty offered to walk in the gardens with her and help her design the flowerbeds, she had kept busy and the times she had to meet with him were minimal and all business was completed as fast as possible. She had successfully put him in his place. He lived in a cottage in the village and had an office in an outbuilding by the stables.

There was no reason for them to spend any time together that wasn't concerning the estate. She didn't want Monty's friendship and she certainly didn't want Jeremy returning and spending all his time with Monty again. The man was an employee, a member of staff, and any ideas he had that he was more than that needed to be squashed. She'd been foolish to invite him for dinner, but that mistake wouldn't happen again. She was polite in his company but not friendly and that's how she liked it to be.

'That's beautiful, madam,' Daisy said, coming out of the dressing room where she'd gone to put away the new shoes.

'Yes. It's a new favourite.' Millie undressed again, and suddenly tired, she donned her sensible skirt of navy that Daisy had altered and a loose shirt of lemon and white pinstripe.

The April weather had arrived warm and promised heat of the coming summer. Outside the birds chirped loudly in the trees and, in the distance, lambs frolicked beside their mothers.

Millie glanced at the other boxes and dresses she'd not tried on. 'I'll check the rest later, Daisy. I feel the need for fresh air.'

'Aye, madam, it's a lovely day out there.'

Walking down the stairs, Millie thought she heard a car on the drive and sighed. She wasn't in the mood for visitors. She spent most days making calls to various friends and acquaintances in the village and other estates. It was her way of keeping occupied. Being out of the house made her feel less lonely, but it was exhausting paying so many calls and involving herself in the village. Today she had wanted a day to relax, perhaps read a book, or finally draw the garden designs.

Sarah answered the door but soon stepped back as like as human whirlwind, Prue, Cece and Agatha rushed in and as soon as they saw Millie on the stairs they squealed and ran to embrace her.

'Heavens, I never expected you!' Millie gushed, so happy to see them.

'It was a spur of the moment thing really.' Prue unpinned her hat as they went into the drawing room. 'We were at a loose end and thought to come here for something to do.'

'Gracious, Prue, you do flatter me!' Millie grinned.

'You don't mind, do you?' Cece looked worried. 'I told Prue we should send a telegram first.'

'Nonsense, as if Millie would want us to ask permission to come and stay. She's our sister not an acquaintance.' Prue smiled lovingly at Millie. 'You'd have us here anytime, wouldn't you?'

'Of course.'

'Told you!' Prue tutted at Cece.

Millie rang for tea. 'How's Mama? Why did she not join you?'

Prue preened in front of the large mirror that hung above the side table along the wall. 'She's at home and wanted peace, or so she said, and sent us off with kisses and a firm push.' Prue laughed.

'She's worried you're on your own too much,' Cece added.

'But now Mama will be on her own?'

'Grandmama is with her. She's closed up the townhouse in Mayfair for the summer and is staying with Mama,' Cece said.

'London is too hot in the summer anyway.' Prue finished patting her hair into place and sat back down.

'How long are you staying for?'

'Until you are tired of us,' Prue answered.

Cece smiled. 'Probably not long then.'

'And how are you, Agatha?' Millie asked her quiet cousin. 'And Uncle?'

'Papa is well, though Uncle Lionel's death has hit him hard. He hadn't expected that, for Uncle Lionel was always so energetic, unlike Papa.'

They were all quiet at that.

Agatha smoothed down her grey skirt. 'I wasn't sure I should come, but Cece and Prue insisted as Papa has a friend staying from Oxford.'

'You're allowed to have a few days away from the house, Aggie.' Prue shook her head in frustration. 'You take being a dutiful daughter too far, it's boring. I think Uncle will be glad of the break from you, really I do.'

'Prue!' Millie admonished.

'Well, it's true.' Prue waved her hand dismissively. 'The poor man has his friend staying and they would not want Aggie to hover over them like a nursemaid.'

'I wouldn't!' Agatha argued, blushing.

'You would, and you know it.' Prue tossed her head. 'You need a husband and a nursery full of children.'

Agatha squirmed. 'I hardly think so. You're a fine one to talk, anyway. Where is your husband and children?'

Prue's blue eyes widened. 'Good lord, Aggie, there is some spirit in you after all!'

Sarah knocked and entered the room.

Prue frowned. 'Really, Millie have you not engaged a butler yet?'

'No, I haven't.' Millie dismissed her sister's censure. 'Sarah, we would like tea, please. Also, please arrange for three bedrooms to be made up for my sisters and cousin.'

'Yes, madam.'

'Do not scuff my luggage, it's new,' Prue added. She turned to Millie 'I bought it in London. Oh, and I went to a new seamstress when I was there. I had heard from one of Grandmama's friends that in the East End there where a great many new fabric shops and for a fee, a seamstress would create beautiful dresses for next to nothing.'

'You took advantage of poor people!' Cece scoffed.

Prue glared at her. 'I did not. Those people were grateful for my custom, I can assure you of that.'

'You'd have made them work by candlelight for hours and hours in squalid rooms. I've seen it. It's shameful.' Cece shook her head.

'How is it? That is their jobs, it's what they do.' Angry, Prue glared at Cece.

'It's called exploitation! If you read a book or newspaper for once in your life, you'd know about it.'

'Oh, be quiet, Cece. I don't know who you are trying to impress with all this new way thinking. You're not running the country.'

'And you are the reason why woman have struggled to get the vote!'

'We've got it now, haven't we?'

'No, we haven't, only women over the age of thirty and who have property or a university education. We, as in you and I, have nothing, no say.'

Prue waved her away. 'You are boring me now. Stop this infernal preaching.'

The anger and frustration was clear on Cece's furious face. 'One day you will find that not everything in life is easy, trust me on that.'

'I think that is enough of that now. If this is how you've been behaving I can understand why Mama wanted rid of you both.' Millie stood as Gilly brought in a tea tray.

'Oh my!' Agatha stared at Millie's stomach. 'I'm sorry, Millie I wasn't aware you were with child. No one told me. Congratulations!'

Millie stilled, the teapot hovering over the first cup.

'What are you talking about?' Prue demanded then peered at Millie. She reached out and touched Millie's round stomach, which the loose blouse didn't hide as well as she'd hoped. 'My God, it's true!'

'Oh, Millie!' Cece cried and jumped up to hug her.

'Why didn't you tell us?' Prue accused. 'I'm extremely annoyed you have kept this from us!'

'Because I only found out just before Papa died and well… Jeremy isn't home and…'

'Do you not think that this kind of news would be so welcomed right now?' Prue's eyes filled with tears. 'Mama will be so happy. It'll give her something to look forward too. Really, Millie it was most selfish of you to keep this to yourself.'

'Hush, Prue,' Cece snapped. 'It's Millie's news to tell when she is ready to.'

'And what about the rest of the family? Can we not have something to be happy about after the tragedy we have just suffered.'

'I was going to tell you,' Millie said, taken aback by Prue's words.

'When? When the child was celebrating its first birthday?'

'Why are you being so horrid?' Cece barked at Prue.

'I'm sorry.' Suddenly Millie burst into tears, which surprised her as much as it did the others.

The women crowded around her, unsure what to do and full of apologies and crying as well.

Prue pushed Cece out of the way and pulled Millie into a tight hold. 'I'm so sorry, Mill. You know I love you more than anything and I'd never hurt you. I'm a nasty person who doesn't deserve such a lovely sister as you. I'm so sorry.' She sniffed in a most unladylike way. 'I didn't mean any of what I said, I'm just so excited to be an aunt. It's the most wonderful news, I can't believe it!' Prue wiped her eyes and her tears left streaks down her powdered cheeks.

Millie wiped her own eyes, wondering why she was so emotional. 'I'm fine, truly, and you've nothing to be sorry for. I know you didn't mean it. You are just you, which means you speak before you think. You've always been the same.'

'I'll try harder, I promise I will.'

Cece grunted. 'I doubt that will ever happen.'

'Shut up, Cece.' Prue sniffled more quietly, then she brightened. 'Imagine! If the baby is a girl I can take her shopping.'

'And if it's a boy?' Agatha smiled, her expression full of relief that the sisters had calmed down.

'Oh, I do hope it's a boy.' Prue chuckled. 'We need a boy in this family.'

'How Papa would have loved to have a grandson,' Cece said.

Millie concentrated on handing the cup and saucers around. For the first time she actually believed that it was all real. She would be a mother! Soon there would be a little baby needing her. The thought terrified her. Yet it also filled her with a strange sense of wonder. Sometimes she felt a flutter as the baby moved within her, but she tried not to think about it or let it affect her in any way. To deny that a baby was growing inside her had made her feel more in control. However, now her sisters had brought it to the fore of her mind, she couldn't reject the reality any more.

She had to tell Jeremy. She needed her husband home.

Chapter Twelve

'What have you found out about him?' Prue asked Millie, indicating Monty.

Millie glanced down the grassy bank where Monty and Cece were walking along the trickling stream. She'd not wanted him to join them on their picnic but Cece had invited him before Millie could say anything. 'Nothing. I only speak to him regarding the estate, nothing more.' She raised an eyebrow at Prue. 'I tasked you with that chore.'

'I know, but it went clean from my mind when Papa died. We did no entertaining while in London either, so I had no opportunity to ask discreet questions at dinner tables.'

'That's understandable.' Millie took a bite of treacle tart and brushed away the crumbs.

'Cece is too obvious.' Prue dabbed at her mouth. 'Monty can be in no doubt of her feelings.'

Agatha sat up to join in the conversation. She'd been lying on the blanket reading a book. 'Monty is a nice man, though, isn't he?'

'Well yes…' Millie admitted reluctantly.

'Sir Jeremy wouldn't employ him if he thought him unsuitable.' Agatha closed the book. 'I mean, Cece is in no danger from him?'

Prue's eyes narrowed. 'Why do you say that?'

Millie's heart squeezed. 'Do you know something we don't, Aggie?'

'Tell us!' Prue demanded.

Agatha brushed off her skirt. 'Cece spoke to me in confidence.'

Prue looked fit to burst. 'I swear if you don't tell me, Agatha I'll never speak to you again or invite you to another event as long as I live!'

'Prue, calm down.' Millie sighed at her dramatic sister. 'Aggie, what do you know? We are only concerned for Cece and wouldn't want her to get hurt.'

'Cece came into my room last night. We spoke about Monty. They'd been out riding all day—'

'All day?' Millie quizzed. 'While we went shopping in York, Cece stayed home and went riding?'

'She told us she had a headache!' Prue glared at Millie. 'She lied to us!'

Agatha held up her hand to calm them. 'She simply wanted to spend some quality time alone with him, that's what she told me.'

'She tells you more than she tells anyone.'

Agatha held her book to her chest. 'She trusts me and I'm breaking her confidence by telling you. She will hate me.'

'I will hate you more if you keep things from us,' Prue snapped.

'She said we've been here at Remington Court for over a week and snatching ten minutes at a time with Mr Pattison wasn't enough.'

'Have they been writing to each other?' Millie could barely contain her anger. Monty was behind this, she was sure of it.

'Yes, and she has fallen in love with him.' Agatha shrugged as though it wasn't a problem at all. 'She meets him every day. It's very romantic, isn't it?'

Millie groaned. 'That's not what I wanted to happen at all! We don't know his background.'

'Why is she being so silly!' Prue fumed. 'A land agent as a husband! Why is she choosing someone so poor? She can do so much better than him.'

'Love doesn't know the difference between rich and poor, Prue,' Agatha argued.

'Oh, be quiet, Agatha. Not everything is as rosy as in your stupid books.'

Millie packed away their picnic. 'I'll not have it. She's making a fool of herself over someone we know nothing about. I knew trouble would come from him. I warned Jeremy!'

'I don't see what the fuss is all about?' Agatha frowned. 'Surely if he is a decent person that's all that matters?'

Prue knelt up to help pack away. 'Except he was a homeless ex-soldier with a secret past that he is unwilling to divulge to anyone but Jeremy. Which means he only has this position that Jeremy gave him in which to support Cece! Papa would be livid.'

'She can do so much better than Monty Pattison.' As Millie went to stand, a sharp pain stabbed her in the stomach. She groaned and pitched forward onto her hands.

'Millie!' Prue held her. 'What is it?'

'I don't know…' Another pain hit her hard in the groin, sucking the breath from her body.

Agatha wrung her hands. 'It can't be the baby she's not due until July. Doctor Boardman confirmed it again when he checked Millie a few days ago. He was telling me when he stayed for dinner that he's delivered two babies this week alone, but he's got a few months before Millie's baby arrives.'

'Shut up, Agatha!' Prue snapped.

'I need the doctor.' Millie puffed as another pain encircled her body like a vice. 'Something is wrong.'

Prue stood and screamed for Cece.

Millie, on her hands and knees, felt a gush of wetness between her legs.

'Oh my God!' Prue cried.

Millie sat on her side and stared at the pool of blood covering her dress. She started to shake. 'Prue!'

Prue knelt beside her and held her shoulders. 'It's all right. You're going to be fine,' she said sternly, as though her sheer force of will would make everything better.

Cece and Monty rushed to them and in one swift movement, Monty picked Millie up and started hurrying up to the house.

'Send for Doctor Boardman!' he shouted.

Millie felt light-headed. Dizzily, everything blurred except the pain that rolled down her body in waves. 'Monty? I don't want to die, or my baby.'

'You won't, my lady. I've got you and won't let anything happen to you.'

Her head dropped against his chest and she knew no more.

~ ~ ~ ~

Jeremy laughed at a fellow ex-soldier who had just run into the waves and shrieked like a little girl as the coldness hit him.

'Are you off in, sir?' Royston asked, spreading out a towel on the sand.

'No, it looks too chilly for me.' Jeremy held his shoes and socks, enjoying the feel of the cool wet sand between his toes.

Around him a group of patients from the retreat sat relaxing on the sand, others were walking along the beach, smoking and chatting.

'There's talk of starting a game of cricket.' Royston rolled up his trouser legs.

'Last game I played was in Flanders, do you remember?' Jeremy sat down on the other towel and stared out to sea. 'We'd been pulled out of the front line and sent back to have a couple of days rest.'

'That was in the last summer of the war, yes, I remember. Didn't you score fifty?'

'Fifty-eight.' Jeremy smiled. 'Got caught behind.'

'Dodgy decision.'

'You should know, you were the bloody umpire!' Jeremy pushed Royston's arm in jest.

'I couldn't let you score a century, the men would have had my guts for garters! There was a lot of money riding on that game.'

Jeremy laughed, relaxing back on his elbows. In the last few days he'd felt the best he had since before the war.

Royston lay back on the towel. 'You weren't expected to play in that game, as you'd not joined in any other time. Then suddenly you were striding out to the wicket and the men were shouting at the unfairness of it. They knew you were a good cricketer at university. Someone even said you could have played for England.'

'I was never that good.' Jeremy grinned, remembering the good times playing cricket before the war started.

'Rumours are a wonderful thing, especially for the other side's confidence.'

'And the wagers.'

'Definitely for the wagers.'

Their laughter was cut short as Cyril, a young attendant from the retreat came running down the beach shouting Jeremy's name.

Jeremy jumped to his feet, his blood ran cold at the urgency of the boy's shouting. 'Here! What's happened?'

'A telegram, sir.' Out of breath the boy thrust the telegram at Jeremy.

Jeremy scanned the note.

'What is it, sir?' Royston stood beside him.

'It's from Prue, Millie is ill.' He thought his heart would stop.

'Come.' Royston scooped up the towels and together they ran up the beach.

'She's ill, Royston.' Jeremy couldn't believe it. 'Millie must be bad for Prue to send for me.'

'We'll get home as soon as we can.'

My darling Millie needs me. It was all he thought as he pounded up the stairs to the road above, his head whirling with unanswered questions.

~ ~ ~ ~

Millie sat on a cushioned chair and stared out of the bedroom window. Daisy was fussing about tidying the already neat as a pin room. Sarah had left a tea tray, which Millie had ignored. Where her sisters and Agatha were she didn't know.

'There now,' Daisy said. 'Shall I get you anything, madam? A book, or the newspapers?'

'No, thank you.' Millie continued to stare out of the window, watching the scattering of fluffy white clouds shift across the blue sky. She'd watched the clouds the entire drive back from the hospital in York.

At least this car ride she remembered, unlike the one going to the hospital, which she couldn't recall at all.

The last five days were a haze.

All she knew was that her baby was dead.

'I'll leave you to rest, madam, but I'll not be far away if you need me.' Daisy gave a timid smile.

Millie didn't comment. She didn't need anything or anyone. She was a shell, an empty shell. She was a nothing. Not a wife, for her husband wasn't here, she wasn't a mother, for her baby wasn't here.

She squashed down the emotion that kept trying to build inside her. She didn't want to cry, or even feel. What would that achieve? Grandmama always said crying was a waste of energy and time. She was right. Crying wouldn't bring back her baby, or Jeremy.

Millie threw the blanket off her knees that Daisy had placed over her. She wasn't cold, or an invalid. Outside the sunshine beckoned. Perhaps she could go for a walk? No. If she left the bedroom everyone would fuss over her again.

She'd had enough of fussing. At the hospital, it had been doctors, nurses, her sisters and Mama fussing over her. Only Grandmama had been quiet. Just a presence sitting beside her bed, not saying anything, just holding her hand. Words weren't needed. What could words do anyway? Words don't heal bodies. Words don't heal broken hearts.

She heard the door open, but she didn't turn around. She didn't care who stood there. When a hand touched her shoulder she stiffened, bracing herself for the sympathetic voices she'd come to hate. She didn't want sympathy. She wanted to be left alone.

'Millie.'

Startled by the familiar voice, Millie's stomach flipped as Jeremy crouched down beside her chair. She stared at him. He looked older. Grey was liberally threaded through his dark hair now. He was unshaven, his stubble giving him a wilder look that she strangely found attractive. She'd never seen him with anything but a smooth face.

'I came as soon as I received the telegram yesterday. We missed several connecting trains and had long waits at stations, but I got here as soon as I could.'

'You shouldn't have left Plymouth.'

'I couldn't have stayed knowing you were ill.'

'It was a wasted journey.'

'Don't tell me that. It's been a hell of a journey. Monty collected Royston and me from the train station in York. I'd managed to send a telegram from London and although we missed our train, we managed to get several others and slowly make our way north. Monty, not knowing our arrival time, waited five hours at York Station.'

Monty.

That familiar clenching of her stomach at his name made her clench her fists. Jeremy had just walked in the house and already Monty was the focus of his conversation. She didn't care Monty had waited for hours at the train station, or that Jeremy's journey had been long and tedious.

She took a deep breath to calm herself. 'What have you been told?'

'Everything.' He seemed uneasy. 'Why didn't you tell me about the baby?'

'I was going to.'

'When?' Anguish altered his tone. 'You were six month's pregnant. I don't understand why you didn't tell me.'

'Because I felt you needed to concentrate on getting better. You didn't need distractions.'

'Distractions?' His eyes widened. 'Being told I was to be a father wouldn't have been a distraction, it would have been a joyous occasion!'

'I thought it would bring you home before you were ready. I apologise if I have done the wrong thing. I was only thinking of you.'

'Millie,' his voice softened.

'You should go back to Plymouth.'

'I'm not going back.' He stood and went to the window. 'I'm done with being there.'

'Are you cured?' A flicker of hope sparked in her chest.

'As much as I ever will be. I won't know until I begin living normally again.'

'So, you might not be? Which means all those months of being away were for nothing?'

'I don't know, Millie. Only time will tell. I'd like to think not. The doctors say I need to cope in any way that I can. To draw on my experiences in Plymouth to manage how I'm feeling, to prevent the attacks, or episodes, from occurring.'

'I'm feeling tired.' She stood and walked to the bed. 'I might have a nap.'

'Yes, of course. Can I get you anything?'

'No, thank you,' her voice wavered. She desperately wanted him to hold her, but he'd made no move to touch her and she wouldn't go to him.

'I'll come up in a little while then.'

When he'd left the room, Millie curled up into a ball on the bed. Fighting the tightness in her chest, she closed her eyes and willed sleep to come, for when asleep she wasn't hurting.

~ ~ ~ ~

Jeremy swirled the whisky around in his glass. He'd rejected the girls and Monty's invitation to go riding with them and give Millie peace in which to rest. He had wanted to stay close to her, but she had not come out of the bedroom. Therefore, he'd spent the afternoon going through accounts and correspondence in his study. After a couple of hours his head was throbbing, and he'd made no progress. It seemed Millie had kept it all under control anyway.

Millie.

The one person he loved more than any other was now so distant from him, he didn't think he'd survive it. When he'd gone into the bedroom all he'd wanted to do was hold her, to try and share with her the grief she was suffering, but he couldn't. She'd stiffened at his touch. She'd shown no degree of warmth towards him.

But then what did he expect?

She had gone through a dreadful ordeal and he'd not been here to help her. She was grieving for a baby he'd only found out about and whom he had no feelings for. He'd not seen Millie with a pregnant belly, or felt the baby kick against his hand, nor had he held her as she went into premature labour. He'd not been here. How could he share something he wasn't a part of? She deserved to blame him. He blamed himself.

He drank the last of his drink, wondering if he should stay downstairs or go up and see Millie. He was relieved when the girls came into the room preventing him from making a decision.

'Jeremy, there you are!' Prue sighed dramatically as Prue does and flopped onto the sofa. 'Jonas just dropped off a note. Mama and Grandmama will arrive in the morning. They would have come back with us from the hospital, but Mama had to cancel a few things and pack some clothes first.'

'I'm sure Millie will be happy to see them.'

Cece dithered by the door. 'I was going to play the piano, as Millie enjoys listening to me play, but maybe she's still sleeping?'

'I shall go up and find out.' Prue went to stand.

'No, I'll do it.' Jeremy left the room and headed upstairs to his bedroom. His head felt fit to burst while his heart was beating twice as fast as normal. Would Millie talk to him?

He opened the door and found the bedroom empty. Surprised, he went into the dressing room and found her at the wardrobe wearing her shift and stockings. 'Millie? What are you doing?'

Her large eyes turned to him, and he knew her smile was forced because there was no warmth in it. 'I'm selecting a dress to wear for dinner.'

'Are you well enough?

'I'm not ill, Jeremy. I was pregnant. Now I'm not.'

He cringed at her cold words. 'You need to rest. You lost a lot of blood.'

She winced. 'I have been resting and it's been days since… Anyway, it's time to return to normal life.'

'Millie, it's too soon.'

'How would you know, Jeremy? Are you a doctor? Do you know how I'm feeling?'

'No, I don't, but I would if you talked to me about it. The one thing I have learned from Plymouth is that bottling everything up inside doesn't help you.'

'What do you think to this one?' She pulled out a forest green silk dress with a drop waist that would conceal the slight bump she still had.

'It's a very nice dress.'

'Nice?' Her laugh was brittle. 'Nice will have to do then.'

'Millie.'

'What Jeremy?' She stared at him as though she hated him. 'Why don't you go down and be with the others while I get ready? I'm certain *Monty* has much to discuss with you.'

'This isn't like you.'

She chuckled. 'How could *you* possibly know? We were mere strangers when we married, and had what… three months of marriage, which was shared with another who had your attention more than I did, and then suddenly you were gone. So, you don't know anything about *me*, nor I about you!'

'What are you saying?' He had a dreaded feeling of losing control of everything that mattered to him. 'Millie, please…'

A knock interrupted them as Daisy came in. 'Sorry, madam, time got away from us.' Daisy turned to Jeremy. 'Forgive us, sir.'

'Where's Royston?' he asked, not that he cared, he just didn't want to stand there like a fool.

'In your dressing room, sir.' Daisy hurried to Millie's side. 'The green, madam?'

Millie turned from Jeremy, clearly dismissing him. With a heavy step, he left the dressing room.

Chapter Thirteen

Millie strolled the cobbled streets of York, looking uninterestingly into the shop windows. The warm sun of late May banished any stray clouds and brought out the sightseers and shoppers. A small boy ran past yelling at his sibling who was chasing him.

Her baby had been a boy. That's what they told her, though she'd not seen him. He'd been bundled away the moment he was born.

She shook her head, dismissing the memories of that awful day six weeks ago. Six weeks was all it was.

Six weeks of being lost and alone in a house she'd come to hate as much as Jeremy did. It felt longer than a month and a half. It felt like six months or six years. How long could she cope living as they were? Jeremy slept in another room. They barely talked and the pain of that cut her in half.

It was worse now her family had gone home. With her sisters and Agatha there she could pretend all was well. With Mama and Grandmama whose personalities dominated any room they entered, Millie could slink into the background and keep the focus from her. During the clear spring days, she'd gone for walks with the others, or on shopping sprees. She'd sent invitations out to neighbouring estates and friends for dinner parties and garden lunches. She'd become good at never being in a room alone with Jeremy.

But now her family had departed, she had to look for other ways to keep busy. She still took long walks, only this time alone. She visited the village every day, calling in to see the elderly, the shopkeepers and even helped at the school.

Could she spend the rest of her life in such a way though? Her marriage was broken, as was her heart. She didn't have the answers, didn't know what to do.

The churches throughout York chimed four o'clock, and she knew she should drive home before it became any later, but the thought of returning to Remington Court filled her with dread. Monty ate with them again, and she found she preferred it. Anything was better than the forced polite chat between her and Jeremy, or the silence, which was even worse. But with Monty at the table, she could let the men talk while she picked at her meal, drank her wine and retired to bed early to read.

With a long sigh, she left the busy streets of York and walked to where she'd left the Napier near the Minster. As she reached the towering grandness of the Minster, she paused to allow a funeral procession go by. The weeping women and solemn men reminded her of her own papa's passing. She missed him greatly. She missed his wise head and his comforting embraces. Her papa had always had time to listen to his girls' woes no matter how trivial they'd been. What would he say now, about her situation? She'd married one of his best friends – a man he trusted and respected.

Impulsively she followed the mourners inside the Minster intending to sit at a back pew, but as she noticed people quietly weeping and taking their places she suddenly felt an intruder. This was their grief, their loved one, not hers.

Shocked by her insensitivity, Millie fled from the Minster and ran down a cobbled lane to behind a building where the Napier was parked. Feeling foolish, and close to tears she climbed in and set off for Remington Court.

When she pulled the car to a stop in front of the house, she sat with her head on the steering wheel, not wanting to go inside.

A tap on the window scared her.

Monty leaned forward. 'Lady Remington? Are you all right?'

She gathered her bag and climbed out. 'I'm fine.'

'You look pale.' He followed her inside.

'I'm fine.' She'd made a decision. 'Where's my husband?' She needed to find Jeremy. A rising panic urged her to search the drawing room, the dining and morning rooms.

'Lady Remington, please, wait.' Monty hurried behind her.

'Where is he?' She had to find Jeremy.

'He's gone.'

'Gone?' As though a bucket of ice-cold water had been thrown over her she skidded to a stop in the middle of the hall. 'Gone where?'

'He packed a bag and caught the train to London. He said he'd left you a note.'

'I had the car. How did he get to the train station?'

'I took him in the farm truck.'

She swallowed back the lump in her throat and instead held on to the growing anger building in her chest. '*You* took him?'

'Yes.'

'You! It's always you, isn't it? Getting involved, always in the way. Ever since you arrived here you have been involved in our lives, whether I wanted it or not. You wormed your way into Jeremy's affections, made him depend on you! Why can't you just leave! Go on, get out. Leave here! I don't want you in this house or near my husband. *Get out!*' She screamed, wanting to hit him, or smash something, anything that would take away the pain inside her.

'Millie, please.' Monty looked stricken.

'Did you not hear me! I said get out!' She lashed at him, striking him across the face. The slap sounded loud and her palm stung. She stood rigid, mortified that she'd hit another person.

'Oh God!' She stumbled, then ran from the room and out through the French doors onto the terrace. She dashed across it, wanting to escape, but she lost her footing on the first step down to the lawn and collapsed onto the stone steps. She sobbed as though she'd never stop.

A raging agony shook her body. She couldn't breath as she cried the hardest she'd ever cried. Wave after wave of grief flowed out of her. She cried for Papa, her unseen baby and her damaged marriage. It was as though a dam had broken and she was shattering into a million pieces.

Eventually, she quietened, her shoulders shuddering, nose running, and her eyes swollen and sore.

She felt his presence before she heard or saw him.

Monty sat down on the step beside her. He handed her a white handkerchief, folded and pressed.

After she'd blown her nose and wiped her eyes, she still didn't look at him, but stared at a lazy bumblebee as it buzzed over the buds of the yellow roses bordering the terrace.

Monty held out an envelope with her name on it.

Carefully, as though each movement would end her, she opened the envelope and pulled out the piece of paper.

Dearest darling Millie,

I'm going away for a time to the London townhouse. My being at Remington Court isn't helping either of us. I see the misery in your eyes and the great attempts you endure to not be in my company.

I never wanted this to be our life.

I have loved you for a long time, but I see now that I didn't know what love really was. There has to be communication, trust, respect and attraction to build a love between two people. I have failed in building on those attributes. I am to blame, I know this. I thought I knew best when clearly, I didn't. My issues made me withdraw from you, and when I learned that I needed to open up to you, it was too late, and you had suffered too much without me.

I don't know how to repair the damage done.

What I do know is that Remington Court can never feel like home to me. I have tried to feel comfortable here, but it won't work and it's part of the problem. There are too many ghosts, and now added to that is the failure of my marriage to the woman I adore.

I will not stand in your way regarding a divorce. I will wait to hear from your solicitor.

You are a truly wonderful person, and for what it's worth I love you more than you'll ever know, and that's why I'm letting you go.

Jeremy.

Millie sobbed. The ache so intense she thought she'd die from it. He had left her. He blamed himself solely when she was also guilty. She had turned from him. Instead of sharing her grief over their lost baby she had shunned him, blamed him for not being with her.

Putting a hand over her mouth to suppress any more sobs, she gave the note to Monty to read.

'I thought as much.'

'You did?'

'I'm not deaf nor dumb, my lady.' He hung his hands between his knees. 'I've been in torment watching you both drift further apart. You were such a special couple. A handsomer couple I've never seen. You are beautiful, and he is handsome. The love he has for you was difficult for me to see.'

She glanced at him for the first time since he had joined her on the steps. 'Why?'

'Because it reminded me of me.' His smile was sad and didn't reach his eyes.

'How so?'

'You've also had a low opinion of me, haven't you?'

She swallowed and sat up straighter.

'You don't have to deny it, for I know it's true. You thought I was a homeless stranger who'd come into your world and took your husband from you.'

'I admit that, yes. I hated you for it.' She had no reason to hide the fact for he knew the truth.

'I know. If I had been stronger I would have left here and gone on my way, but I couldn't.'

'Why?' She peered at him through stinging eyes. 'Do you love my husband?' There, she'd said the sentence she'd been longing to utter for months.

'No, Lady Remington. I am not one of those type of men.'

She wasn't sure if she believed him.

'I promise you I don't. I think Sir Jeremy is a fine man, but only as a friend.'

She nodded, partly reassured.

'Believe me, I am attracted to women only.'

She wanted to ask about Cece but refrained. She didn't have the brain power to think straight at this moment, and considering that her husband had just left her, it wasn't important.

'You want to know my past, so I will tell you.' He stretched and rubbed his neck as though he had a physical ache there.

Suddenly she didn't care. What did any of it matter? 'You don't have to.'

'I want to tell you. Enough time has gone by for me to speak of it without the sharp pain of it. I am the Honourable Montague Francis Titus Pattison. I am the fourth son of the Earl of Conclurde.'

'No!' Millie gasped. She could tell by the look in his eyes that he wasn't lying to her.

'I was born at Holden Park in East Sussex, not far from Tunbridge Wells. Do you know of it?'

'No, I don't,' she said quietly.

'My parents are dead. My eldest brother was killed at Mons. My second brother and heir, Philip has been declared bankrupt and Holden Park was recently sold.' He looked out over the garden. 'Before the war I was engaged to be married. Beatrix wrote regularly to me, and when I was wounded she came to visit me at the hospital in France and then in London where I was having more surgery. I was looking forward to a wedding when I had fully recovered.' He touched his scars. 'Beatrix knew the extent of my injuries, though she'd only ever seen my bandages and not the ugly truth of what was beneath them. When I was released from hospital and sent home, I was told that Beatrix was at Holden Park, which surprised me. I went in search of her and found her in the conservatory with my other brother Donald. Beatrix screamed when she saw me.' Monty shook his head, his eyes bleak. 'I looked like a monster in her eyes.'

Millie stayed quiet, allowing Monty to finish his story.

'The week before I showed up, Beatrix had married Donald. The news devastated me as you can imagine. I couldn't take it in that the woman I loved for years had married my brother. There were arguments, tears and accusations. I behaved ungentlemanly. I punched Donald, shouted at Philip, drank too much. My injuries and scars pained me and I took too much medicine to dull the ache. Every day I played with the thought of shooting myself in the head.'

He stood up abruptly but didn't walk away. 'A week after my arrival, Beatrix was found hanging by a rope in the barn. She'd left a note saying she was sorry and couldn't take the heartbreak of what she'd done in hurting me and putting brother against brother.'

'Oh my.' Millie stood also. 'Monty…'

'I left the same day. I simply walked down the drive and kept walking. I had nothing.'

She touched his arm.

'The family fortune has gone. Death duties when my father and brother died bankrupted us. The family wealth had never been great, we were one of those impoverished aristocratic families for a century or more, then the death duties finished us off.' Monty went down the steps.

Millie followed him.

'I didn't want to live.' He shrugged resignedly. 'When Jeremy found me, I had given up.' He looked at her sadly. 'I am the son of an earl, and a brother to one, yet I have nothing only this position Jeremy gave me, which I am qualified for by the way.' He gave a small smile.

'You are?'

'Four years of studying at Cambridge and a degree in Botany and Agriculture. I can write to my old tutors and get them to confirm it, if you want?' He grinned.

She smiled slightly, feeling rebuked and embarrassed. She had given Monty such a hard time. He was a good man, a gentleman, the son of an earl who'd fought for his country and she had treated him as if he'd been worse than a criminal. He had gone through so much, his injuries, his surgeries and the death of the woman he loved. 'Please, forgive me? How you must hate me.'

'Not at all. I admire you greatly.'

'I'm not worthy of your admiration.'

'You are too hard on yourself.'

'I've driven my husband away.'

'You've been through a great deal. The whole situation has been extremely difficult for you both.'

'We all have.'

They began walking across the lawn as the setting sun created a shimmering golden light over the garden and fields. Each lost in their own thoughts, silence stretched between them for several minutes.

Reaching a gate that led into the sheep fields, Millie paused, and rested her arms on top of the rail. 'Do you have feelings for Cece, or is it too soon after Beatrix?'

'I honestly don't know. Your sister is charming and honest. What you see is what you get. I feel… safe with her. She sees past my scars.'

'Cece would never hurt you.'

'No.'

'But you don't love her.'

'I don't know. I believe I could though. But it might be difficult, as I think I'm half in love with you, too.'

She gaped at him.

'Forgive me, I should have remained quiet.' He held up his hands. 'Don't worry, I know you love your husband and he you. But I can't help what is in my heart.'

'Monty.'

'That day in the cupboard when we were playing hide and seek. All I wanted to do was kiss you.'

'Monty…'

'Say nothing. I don't want you to say anything at all. This is all on my part and I am a total bastard for having feelings for my friend's wife, especially after all Jeremy has done for me. I should have been stronger.' He ran his hand through his hair. 'I'm not making any sense.'

'I'm sorry.' And she was. Terribly sorry that he cared for her. She was also a little frightened that perhaps she could return those feelings should she and Jeremy be apart for any longer.

'Don't be. You've nothing to be sorry for. I shouldn't have let my feelings control me, but I can't help it. I think you are wonderful.'

That he was genuine stirred her heart even more and she scrambled to think clearly. This could easily get out of hand. 'What about Cece? I'm rather certain she might be in love with you.'

He wiped his hand over his face tiredly. 'Then I am a lucky man to have a lovely person like Cece to love me.'

'But?'

'But what? I don't know what to do about Cece.'

'There is time.' Millie turned her back on the fields. 'Time for you to forget about me. All I ask is that you don't lead Cece on to think there might be a future between you if there isn't one. I wouldn't like to see her heart broken. We both know the feeling is rather hideous.'

'I won't do that to her.' He sighed a deep sigh. 'As you say, I just need more time.'

'Shall we go in for a drink?' Millie walked towards the house.

'And Jeremy?'

Millie hesitated. 'I love him. I don't want to lose him. I will fight for our marriage.'

'Good. You both deserve happiness.'

'And tomorrow I'll travel to London to see him.'

His eyes widened in surprise. 'Excellent idea.'

'Tonight though, you and I have to make some plans.'

He stopped and stared at her. 'We do?'

'Yes.' For the first time in a long time, Millie smiled, and it felt great to do so. 'I'm taking Jeremy to the chateau in France, and I need you to take care of Remington Court for us for the foreseeable future.'

Chapter Fourteen

Millie paid the taxi and alighted onto the Kensington street lined with five storey pale-stoned townhouses. Four steps led up to the black-painted front door and it was opened before she made it to the top.

A butler, she knew to be called, Hemmingway stood in impressive black and bowed. 'Lady Remington.'

Shocked that he knew who she was, Millie paused. 'How did you know it was me? I didn't send word beforehand.'

Hemmingway allowed a tiny smile to show as he stepped back for her to enter. 'Training, madam. The staff and I have studied your wedding picture since the day it was sent down by Sir Remington to be framed and hung in the drawing room. So, we would know you instantly.' He flicked his fingers to a youth also dressed all in black and he went running outside to collect Millie's luggage.

'Very clever.' Millie took off her gloves. 'Is my husband at home?'

'No, my lady. He is walking in the park.'

'Which park, do you know?'

'Kensington Palace Gardens, madam. He has gone there every day.'

Millie pulled her gloves back on at his nod. 'In that case, I'll go and see if I can find him.'

She headed up the street towards Kensington High Street, which was busy with traffic. She waited for a break in the horse and carts, the omnibuses, the motorised taxis and private cars and crossed the street with other pedestrians.

London always delighted her with its frantic pace, and hustle and bustle of commerce. It was so different to York and stranger still to the quietness of the Yorkshire countryside. However, after a week or two of putting up with the crush of crowds and the noise, she was usually glad to be heading north again. But not this time. From here they would go to France. She simply had to convince Jeremy it was the right thing to do, too.

Kensington Palace Gardens were enormous, and she wondered how she thought she'd ever find him, but since the sun was shining and the birds were twittering in the trees, she kept walking, enjoying the surroundings, delighting in the squirrels which ran up and down the trees in search of titbits and nuts. Nannies called after their little charges while they pushed large black prams. Millie shied away from looking at the babies inside and instead crossed the grass away from the impressive red-bricked Kensington Palace and made for the lake, or The Long Water as it was called.

She combed the people strolling along beside the water, searching for a man alone. There were several. Some older men were chatting together on a bench, and further along a man walked his little dog.

Millie kept walking, eyes scanning for her husband. She wondered why she wasn't nervous, but instead her stomach was a pit of excitement. She wanted to run, to smile, to laugh and tell the people she was passing that everything was going to be all right. Inside her heart she knew it.

Then she saw him.

He was leaning against an enormous tree, watching children play with boats at the edge of the lake. Her heart somersaulted at the sight of him. The stoop of his shoulders spoke of his forlorn mood.

Not knowing she was coming, Millie was able to stride up alongside of him before he was aware of her. His trilby hat was set low over his eyes, and although the day was warm he had a coat over his suit. He looked sad, lonely. Alone.

'Jeremy.'

He spun around surprise evident on his face. 'Millie! What are you doing here? Is everything all right?'

'I've come to see you.' She took a step closer. 'We have things to discuss.'

He nodded, shutting down again. 'The divorce.'

'No. Chateau Dumont.'

'The chateau? What do you mean? Have you received word from France? Has something happened?'

'Do you love me, Jeremy?'

Taken aback by the question, he gave her a long look. 'You know I do.'

'And I love you.'

'You do?' He didn't sound convinced.

'Unequivocally.'

His shoulders sagged. 'But…'

'There are no buts. I've left Monty in charge at Remington Court and we are moving to France.'

'We are?' Astonishment widened his eyes. She could see the play of emotions across his face from bewilderment to hope.

'I think it is high time you showed me your mother's estate, and it's about time I sampled some of the chateau's champagne.' She smiled to ease the tension.

'But the region has been through a war. I told you before our wedding the whole area was under German occupation.'

'And I'm sure they are rebuilding, as we should be, too. Isn't it what you most want, to live at the chateau?'

'It is, yes, that and you.'

'Well, you have me, so let us do the next bit.'

'Millie it is a huge undertaking, the vineyard is broken and—'

'I don't mind broken things.' She smiled to show him that she meant him as well and he gave a slow smile in return.

'The estate is not truly fit for you to live in.'

'Let me make that judgement. I'm much tougher than you realise.'

'I have come to know that, believe me. I thought I had to take care of you, but instead it has been the other way around and I feel…'

'What? Less of a man?'

'Perhaps, yes.'

'I won't listen to you talk like that, Jeremy. You suffer the effects of a bloody war because you cared too much. That is not a weakness in my eyes and never will be. I'm proud of you. From what Stephen told me you took the burden of war onto your own shoulders and continued to do that when you found Monty.'

'I'm sorry I put Monty before you.' He gazed down at the ground. 'I felt that he was one man I could save, when over the years there have been so many I couldn't save.'

'Yes, I understand that now.'

'My priorities were not in the correct order and I'm sorry for the hurt I caused you.'

Her heart swelled with love. 'I can't be angry with you for caring too much. I was, don't get me wrong, I was furious with you and I hated Monty, but I'm over that now because we are going to France and we are starting again.'

'Are you sure the chateau is where you want to live? I can't live with you making more sacrifices for me, Millie. It's not right.'

'Until I get there we won't know if I can live there, but I'm willing to give it a try for you, for our marriage and ultimately for me. Because if you are happy and our marriage thrives then I'll be happy too and that's all I want. I don't expect it to be easy, but I thought we should give it a go.' She held out her hand. 'Will you show me Chateau Dumont?'

'Yes, of course.' He took her hand and gripped it firmly. 'I don't know what to say.'

'You don't have to say anything.' She smiled.

'But what of your family?'

'They will cope without me.' She knew they would not like the idea of her moving to a country that had just suffered a war, but that wasn't her concern.

'The chateau is a wreck.'

'Then we will rebuild it.'

He gave her a long look, his eyes full of love. 'Can we fix our marriage?'

'I think so, yes. It won't be easy, but I know I don't want it to end.'

'Neither do I, but I didn't know what to do. I thought coming to London and giving you space from me would help you make another kind of life without me.'

'I don't want another any kind of life without you.'

'The baby…'

'There will be others. The doctors said in the hospital I could have more.' She gazed tenderly at him. 'I didn't handle it well.'

'Don't apologise, please. I was the one who should have shouldered that burden with you and I didn't.'

'I should have told you that I was pregnant.'

'I wish you had, but I understand why you didn't.'

'I need you to kiss me, Jeremy,' she whispered achingly.

He gathered her into his arms and crushed her against him. His mouth was soft and tentative, then grew urgent.

After a moment, and fighting the urge to kiss him more passionately, she pulled away and grinned at him. 'We are in a public place, Sir Remington.'

He laughed and looked around at the playing children and the odd person walking by. 'Then let us leave here quickly.'

Arm in arm, they strolled back along the paths of the park towards the street. The noise of the traffic was an assault on her ears after the quietness of the estate.

Millie noticed a cab coming along the street and stuck her hand out to stop it. She turned to Jeremy. 'Let us book the tickets for the ferry. I want go to the chateau as soon as possible.'

'We will, my darling, but first we are going back to the house and we are locking our bedroom door and staying in bed for hours.'

'In the middle of the afternoon?'

He gave her a devilish wink. 'Yes, in the middle of the afternoon, and all night if we wish!'

~ ~ ~ ~

Millie woke and stretched, feeling the weight of Jeremy's arm over her waist. Outside the window, Paris was waking up to a new day. She gazed at Jeremy asleep beside her and felt the familiar attraction rise in her. They had made love every day since she arrived in London, cementing the bond, the closeness between them. It would take time to repair their marriage, but it certainly was on to a good start.

Slipping from the bed, Millie smiled as Jeremy sighed in his sleep and rolled over. She went to the desk by the window and looked out on the street below. A man on a bicycle rode past, waving hello to a woman who walked along the pavement with her tiny dog, even at this time of the morning she appeared elegant and sophisticated and she reminded Millie of Prue.

Taking pen to paper she began a letter to Prue.

Dearest Prue,

We have safely arrived in Paris.

We only stayed in London a few days before experiencing a pleasant crossing of the English Channel by ferry to Calais. We then caught the train to Paris. The hotel we are staying in is on a street just off from the Champs-Élysées. A delightful place and the staff are most friendly. I think they are eager for custom and nothing is too much trouble. We shall stay here for a few more days, but we are both wanting to get to the chateau and start our life there.

Paris is a little different to the one we visited a year before the war. I think we were too young then to take advantage of the beauty of Paris and all it had to offer. The public gardens are in full spring bloom and the weather has been glorious. I seem to remember we didn't visit many couture establishments, and those we did gave more attention to Mama and Grandmama than us. However, the ones I visited yesterday were delightful and you would have loved being with me and discussing the styles and fabrics. I've ordered a new wardrobe for the autumn and winter – my first fully Parisian selection of winter clothes. Are you terribly jealous? I can't wait to see them when they arrive. Hopefully by then Daisy will be with me once more. Jeremy and I decided to allow Daisy and Royston to stay at Remington Court for a few months to get married and have some time together before they travelled out to us. Royston has been so devoted to Jeremy for six years, that he deserves a break now.

So, for the meantime, Jeremy is my lady's maid and I'm his batman. It is funny to see him wrestle with my numerous buttons and hooks and eyes on my dresses. While in London I got my hair cut short, it is a riot of curls and very much easier for me to take care of without Daisy's help.

Last evening, we met up with Jeremy's elderly business partner, Monsieur John Baudin at his offices along Rue Royale. Monsieur Baudin was so pleased to see us. I found him very handsome with perfect English. He is tall with silver hair and a short-clipped beard and has a charm that makes everyone feel they are special to him. Jeremy said the man speaks seven languages, which is indispensable when you are in the export trade. The poor man did find it hard selling the chateau's champagne during the war, but business has picked up again in Europe, though not so much in America. The Temperance Movement there is gaining sway and alcohol is seen to be the work of the devil apparently!

We are dinning with Monsieur and his wife tonight and I have bought a most gorgeous dress in soft gold silk. It cost a fortune considering it is but a slip of a thing. Paris fashion is not like that in England. The skirt hems are a good four inches shorter here. I will send you some magazines to show you. Oh, and I'll enclose a headband for you, so you can see what is all the rage here. I've bought several in different colours. They have adornments, feathers, beads, and tassels. I'll also send you copies of the weekly magazine, Le Petit Echo de la Mode, for you to read and to look at the latest fashions. I've put several in the post for Cece, too.

I have done much shopping for you all, but none yet for the chateau until I see it and assess what it needs. Jeremy has warned me that the estate was under German occupation for many years and when he visited briefly before we were married he saw that it was in terrible shape. I believe I will have a challenge on my hands getting it right again.

Jeremy has bought a new car, since we left the Napier at Remington Court. This one is an Italian made Fiat Tipo-501, which instantly became his pride and joy and was promptly nicknamed, Tippy. It's blue in colour with brown leather interior. I've never seen Jeremy so happy as he was when we walked out of the hotel and the driver parked it on the street.

I know you must all be wondering how we are faring, and I can assure you we are both well. I am fully recovered, and Jeremy is doing much better, too. He's only had one dream and that was on our last night in London. We dare presume he is cured but there is a definite lift of his head since arriving in France, which pleases me enormously.

'What are you doing, woman?' Jeremy asked lazily from the bed.

She turned and grinned at him. 'Writing to Prue.'

'Bugger Prue. Come here and please your husband. He has needs.' He winked saucily.

She laughed and left the desk to climb in beside him.

In one swift movement he pulled her satin nightgown over her head and was kissing her neck. 'I can't get enough of you,' he whispered.

'That's all I need to hear!' She took his face between her hands and kissed him passionately.

His hands roamed over her naked body, cupping her bottom and pulling her closer against him. He was hard and demanding and she sighed with pleasure that after the difficult times they'd experienced, they could still find a profound desire with one another.

'I love you so much, Millie,' he murmured, his lips nibbling her nipples. 'You make me so very happy.'

His soft words touched her to the core. She brought his head up to kiss him ardently. 'We are not to be parted ever again. Promise me.'

'I can easily promise you that.' He deepened the kiss and nudged her legs apart. She welcomed him fully, loving the feel of him as they become joined as one.

~ ~ ~ ~

A few days later, Millie was second guessing her hastiness to see the chateau as she climbed from the motorcar and stared at the ruined estate and buildings.

With his business meetings done, and Millie's shopping completed, they'd packed the Fiat — Tippy, left Paris and headed north-east towards Épernay. The warm weather of early June lifted their spirits, but as they made their way closer to the Champagne region, the effects of years of war started to show.

Bombing and trenches became a familiar blot on the landscape, burnt and ruined buildings featured in every town and village they passed through the closer they got to the Chateau Dumont.

When late in the evening Jeremy slowed Tippy and turned down a dusty dirt lane, Millie was thankful they were close. On either side of the road mangled vineyards went for as far as she could see. Grass had been allowed to grow high between the rows of vines, not that it mattered when the vines themselves were shattered and torn, the once neat rows lay broken and cut up.

'Do these vines belong to you?'

'To us, yes.' Jeremy glanced at the passing vines. 'We can rebuild, but it will take time.'

Jeremy slowed the motor car at two large wrought iron gates which were closed to them and she hastily climbed out to open them and let Jeremy drive through. She noted the peeling black paint, but also admired the crest of arms belonging to the Dumonts.

The dirt drive wound through a short avenue of trees before opening out into a spacious area of overgrown lawn and there, in the last rays of the evening sun, stood Chateau Dumont.

Standing beside the car, Millie stared at the pale-stoned chateau, with its two turret towers at each end. Between the towers, Millie counted two floors and dormer windows in the roof. The ground floor was dominated by impressive wooden doors with two enormous windows on either side. The storey above held five large windows.

It took a moment for her to acknowledge that the chateau originally would have been stunning, but it no longer held that claim. The war had ravaged it.

Many of the windows were cracked or missing entirely. The roof had collapsed in the corner near the right tower, and many slate shingles were broken and had slipped down to land in the rusted gutters, some of which were hanging free from the building.

Weeds and an unkempt garden dominated the area in front of the house. The circular water fountain was empty of water and the bronze statue of three naked women offering their hands up to the heavens where missing a great many body parts.

'I did warn you, my love.' Jeremy came to stand beside her, gazing at the chateau with a mixture of love and sadness.

'You did.' She swallowed. The enormity of the job ahead was daunting, and she dreaded to think what inside looked like.

'Come, let us go in.'

The front doors were made of thick wood studded with black iron. It took Jeremy a few attempts to get it open.

'Is it locked?' Millie wondered when the doors failed to budge.

'It shouldn't be. Pascal should be here. I did send a telegram announcing our arrival would be today.' Jeremy stepped back.

'Does Pascal live here on the estate?'

'Yes.' Jeremy peered in through the window on the right of the door. 'He has a cottage by the stables.'

'Perhaps we should go find him?'

'Monsieur Remington!'

They turned as a short square-shaped man hurried around the corner of the chateau.

'Here he is.' Jeremy walked to meet him and shook his hand. 'Pascal, my friend.'

'I did not hear you!' Pascal said in heavily accented English.

'This is my wife, Millie, Lady Remington.' Jeremy made the introductions.

'Ahh, *belle madam*!' Pascal took Millie's hand and bowed over it. She liked him instantly.

He then broke into a fast-paced discussion in French, which lost Millie completely.

Jeremy nodded and rubbed his chin. 'Oui. Oui.'

'What is it, Jeremy?' Millie looked from one man to the other. It sounded serious whatever it was.

'The stables, which I'll show you tomorrow, is built on three sides. Apparently, there was a wild storm here last week and one side of the stable wing collapsed. It had been damaged extensively with bombing and the storm finished it off.'

'Oh dear.'

Jeremy took her arm as Pascal produced a large iron key and opened one of the two doors. 'That is not all. A bomb was found in the fields.'

'A bomb?'

'Yes. It hadn't exploded. The French army were here yesterday and took it away.'

'Good lord. Are there any more?'

Jeremy shrugged. 'No one can tell. There is so much rubble and damage, there could be another buried, or maybe not. I've told Pascal to not have anyone go near that part of the stables until it is secure.'

Millie followed Jeremy into the entrance hall and stopped. In front of her was a sweeping wooden staircase going up to a landing then two wings of stairs went to each side of the hall.

The entrance was wide with a parquet floor. The walls were painted green, but time had faded the colour and dust and cracks in the walls gave it a neglected unloved appeal.

'Come into the drawing room.' Jeremy ushered her off to the right where she took in another large room, made light by the two tall windows but which again had old world grandeur sadly depleted. A huge dirty fireplace dominated the room, the smoke stains blackening the chimney breast above it. All the paintings were striped from the walls, as were the curtains, and even the chandelier. The room was bare, dirty, full of dead flies and she was certain a bird had fouled all over the windowsills.

Millie looked around, noting the extensive work that had to be done just to make this one room livable. 'Lord, I thought Remington Court needed redecorating! But this? It needs more than new wallpaper…'

Jeremy's sigh was deep and loud. 'They've taken everything.'

'The Germans?'

Pascal slapped his thigh. 'Germans!' He made a spitting sound though didn't actually spit which Millie was grateful for.

Jeremy spoke to Pascal. 'Is there food? Did you arrange a bed for us as I asked?'

'*Oui!*' He nodded. 'I bought bed. Come. Come.'

They followed him up the grand staircase that actually appeared to be in decent condition and along the left wing of the chateau to the turret bedroom. In here a white painted iron bed had been made up with blankets and pillows. In the turret itself stood a writing desk and a set of drawers, though one of the drawers had no handles.

'At least we have a bed to sleep in,' Millie murmured.

'Thank you, Pascal, you've done well.' Jeremy nodded, and they filed out of the room and back downstairs.

'It's such a huge house, Jeremy,' Millie said peeking into other empty stark rooms. 'There's nothing here.'

'No. We shall need to purchase a great deal and perhaps close off some rooms entirely for a year or so. We can't do them all at once. The vineyard is our main priority. We have to rebuild our orders from before the war.'

'*Cuisine!*' Pascal said suddenly and hurried along a corridor past the staircase and into the back part of the chateau. The corridor was narrow and dark, empty rooms lay abandoned filled with junk and rubbish all covered in inches thick dust.

Pascal opened a final red-painted door and stepped down into a stone-flagged floor. The kitchen was cavernous. A cooking range spanned all of one wall.

In the middle of the room was an enormous wooden table and that was all. Gaping cupboards showed their emptiness. There wasn't a stool, pot, plate or bowl that Millie could see.

However, Pascal scurried into another smaller room and came back out carrying a tray full of food and plates. He grinned as he placed it on the table. He held up a loaf of crusty bread, a bowl of olives, a wedge of cheese, thin slices of ham and a jar of what Millie assumed to be some kind of chutney. Lastly, he produced a bottle of red wine.

'Magnifique.' Jeremy shook Pascal's hand. 'Merci.'

Pascal grinned widely, pleased with himself.

The room only had windows high up on one wall and as darkness fell, a dusky gloom fell over them.

'Is there lighting, my love?' Millie asked.

Jeremy spoke in French to Pascal, who shook his head. 'Germans!' He made a gesture of someone using an axe and spoke in rapid French.

Jeremy nodded. 'The electricity hasn't been great since the Germans cut all the lines as they retreated. There is work in the town to restore it but as yet the repair teams haven't made their way out here. Apparently, it should happen in a few weeks. It was promised in the last town meeting that Pascal attended.'

'Town as in Épernay?'

'Yes. It's a few miles west from here.'

Pascal returned once more from the other room. This time he carried a wicker basket filled with candles, candleholders and matches. '*Cierge.*'

'Candles.' Jeremy took the basket from him. 'Merci.' He gave the basket to Millie and picked up the food tray. 'There are no chairs in here. Shall we take it upstairs and eat on the bed?'

'Yes, we have much to do tomorrow. An early night is what we need.'

'*Bonne nuit,* Pascal.' Jeremy headed for the corridor.

'*Bonne nuit.*' He waved them goodnight as he headed out of the back door.

Upstairs in the bedroom, Millie lit several candles and placed them around the room while Jeremy brought their luggage up from the car. There were no curtains to close or a fire lit to lift some of the staleness, but they weren't cold. The warmth of the day had seeped into the room.

Millie packed away some clothes into the set of dilapidated drawers. 'It will be some time before my family can come to visit us. I could not ask Mama or Grandmama to live in such a wreck.'

Jeremy cut the bread. 'I know it is a shock to you, how bad this place truly is.'

Millie poured out the red wine. 'True, I hadn't expected it to be a complete shell…'

'Do you want to return to England?' Uncertainty clouded his eyes.

She reached over and kissed him. 'Not in the slightest.'

'Really? I wouldn't blame you if you did.'

'What and miss out on the fun of restoring this place to its former glory? Not a chance.'

His shoulders sagged. 'What a relief. I thought you'd want to leave here in the morning.'

Millie sliced the cheese and placed it on the bread. 'Must I remind you again that I'm tougher than you know, husband.'

'Oh, I know it.' He raised his wine glass. 'To us.'

'To us and to tomorrow and every tomorrow after that,' she added.

They sipped the wine and started eating. Despite the rudimental food and the inelegant surroundings, they were content and happy. Millie had never seen Jeremy so relaxed and at ease with everything. If coming here gave him a lifetime of peace, then she was glad.

Jeremy rested back against the headboard. 'I seriously don't know where to start first.'

'First things first, we are going into Épernay in the morning and buying whatever furniture we can find.'

He sighed. 'Not Épernay, my love, for it is rebuilding. But we shall go back to Paris and get what we need. Now come over here and let us christen our first night in our new home as a proper married couple should!'

She laughed as he pulled her towards him, dislodging the food and plates and making a mess.

Chapter Fifteen

Millie stepped down from the wooden ladder and gazed at her morning's handiwork. At each of the drawing room's windows emerald green damask curtains hung straight with soft pleats and were draped back and held into place by gold rope tassels. She'd waited three weeks for them to be made and it was worth the wait. Not that she had simply sat around waiting for the curtain's arrival. No, she had barely sat still in the two months since they arrived at the chateau and her aching shoulders and back were testament to the hard work.

Still, things were happening and slowly, dreadfully slowly, the chateau was beginning to look as though it was cared for and loved.

The first room to gain attention was the drawing room or as Jeremy had started to call it the salon, as his mother's family had called it. In his mother's time it had been decorated in pale pink and white stripped wallpaper, but Millie preferred the walls to be papered in a soft white and gold floral pattern that she bought on a trip to Paris the week before. After the walls and ceiling had been touched up with new plaster, the ceiling had been painted white, except for the ceiling rose which was painted gold and a new chandelier that Millie had found in a second-hand shop in an Épernay side street had been hung.

Despite what Jeremy said, many shops amongst the numerous villages in the area were open for business and as she went in search of furniture, they welcomed her and her money very readily. For the salon she'd bought an emerald sofa with carved wooden legs, two matching winged-back chairs in cream and gold tapestry, a newly polished wooden sideboard, a small occasional table and a large rug in the colours of red, gold, and emerald. Now with the curtains finished and hung up, the room looked inviting and comfortable. Once she had some paintings on the walls, and some personal touches, the odd ornament or two it would be finished. In under a month she'd completed one room – only fourteen more to do.

Millie glanced out of the window to watch a team of men scything the long grass in the garden. Jeremy had put word out that Chateau Dumont was in need of workers and for weeks they'd been inundated with young men and women descending on the chateau begging for work. Many a man came with some form of disability as a result from fighting in the war. Jeremy tried to give them all work but it was impossible, for those with missing limbs could not dig the soil or carry a load of bricks. The guilt weighed heavily on him when he turned the very worst of the disabled away. Yet, he always gave them money and a bag of food as they left.

Widowed women came with sons and daughters, some so young Millie felt upset that families were forcing their children out to work. She decided that thirteen was the youngest age for a boy to work outside and fifteen for a girl inside. Not that she employed many girls for the house wasn't ready.

It took herself and Jeremy days to sort out the names and meet with the applicants, but soon they arranged for several teams to begin the restoration of the estate. A group of five gardeners worked around the chateau, returning the lawns and flowerbeds back from being vegetable gardens as used during the war. Greenhouses were cleared of broken glass and tables set up for the propagating of seeds, not just for the vines, but also for vegetables to feed the Chateau's growing staff.

Jeremy created another team to work in the fields and to start replanting the vines and the general work of reconstructing the damaged buildings. Pascal also selected several men to work in clearing out the cellars in readiness for the grape harvest in late August.

Millie hadn't ventured into the cellars which ran under the chateau and as far as the stable complex, mainly due to the partial flooding which had occurred during bombing, and also because the Germans had used the cellars to house soldiers, who seemed intent on scribbling German propaganda on the walls and generally smashing up the empty barrels and pulling over the bottle racks.

Jeremy had been incensed at the reckless destruction but considering how many French citizens were returning to this region to find they had no home left to live in, they could hardly feel overly victimised.

'Madam?'

Millie turned with a ready smile for Vivian, her new housekeeper. A local woman, Vivian was a relative of Pascal's and who, as a war widow, had immediately garnered Millie's sympathy. More than that within hours of her employment, Vivian had shown her hard work ethics and Millie knew she'd need such a woman to help her run the chateau.

'*Oui*?'

Vivian hesitated, her English was very good but sometimes she thought about her words before speaking. Vivian had a love of reading English novels and listening to English songs and jumped at the chance to work for an English couple not only to earn money but to practice her English on. 'Madam, will you come and see the... improvements?'

'Oui, of course.' Millie followed Vivian down the corridor and through the back entrance to the chateau. A large courtyard separated the chateau from the working buildings. With the stable off limits, Millie hadn't explored the outbuildings in any great depth, but the long stone barn closest to the chateau was being prepared to sleep the hordons of vendangeurs – the teams of pickers – which would descend on the estate in late August and early September for the grape harvest.

Although the roof had been damaged in the war, Jeremy had set builders onto repairing it straight away. The pickers needed somewhere to sleep and both he and Millie were determined to start as they meant to go along with taking care of the local people as much as they could, just as Jeremy's mother's family had done for centuries.

Millie carefully trod around the last of the debris that had been cleared from the building and entered the first half of the newly restored barn. A long table filled the space with bench seats running along either side of it. Up a flight of timber stairs showed the upper floor filled with simple wooden beds, knocked together by a few of the workmen. Glass windows that had been shattered from bombs now had new panes and the wooden floor was swept clean.

'I need new linen for all these beds.' Millie said, testing the thin mattress on the first bed. At Vivian's confused expression she tried again. 'Drab de lit?'

Vivian grinned at Millie's dreadful mangling of French. '*Oui. Vingt.*'

Millie nodded. 'Vingt. Twenty.' She sighed. She needed to make twenty beds comfortable for the pickers.

Leaving the barn, Millie glanced around. Further away towards the start of the vine rows were several more outbuildings. These were used for the storing of all the paraphernalia needed to run a vineyard. On the other side of the courtyard were the stables and carriage house.

Feeling the inclination to explore, Millie headed for the outbuildings closest to the vines. She spied Jeremy and Pascal in conversation as they walked out of the rows.

'Hello, darling. Do you need me?' Jeremy asked.

'No, I just thought that I'd take some air and have a look around. With everything to do inside and the front garden, I am rarely out here. Vivian has finished clearing out the barn ready for the vendangeurs. It looks good, but we must buy sheets and pillows, and what not. What have you been doing this morning?'

Jeremy took off his hat and wiped the sweat from his head. 'Pascal and I believe we'll get a decent harvest this year, small, naturally, as so many of the rows have been damaged by bombings but we'll definitely have a harvest.'

'Wonderful.'

Pascal grinned. *'Feté!'*

Jeremy laughed. 'Pascal said earlier that we must have many festivals.'

'Festivals?' Millie asked, surprised.

'Yes. A festival at the beginning of the harvest and another at the end, there are also festivals for the pressing and the first uncorking. You name it, and there is a festival for it.'

'Good lord, I didn't realise.' The idea sounded expensive and time-consuming to Millie. 'Are we doing all that, too?'

'Apparently.' Jeremy shrugged. 'I remember coming here one summer and my uncle had many celebrations, the locals demand it in return for their hard work. I'm a Dumont as well as a Remington, I think we should also keep up the Dumont traditions.'

'All right. I'll start making preparations.' Millie forced herself to be positive, but it was just something else she had to do on a very long list.

'Get Vivian to help you.'

'I will, but first I need to learn more about the champagne we make. I am most ignorant. Will you show me around a little more and explain how the place works as a champagne producing estate? Do you have time now?'

Jeremy smiled and kissed her. 'It would be my pleasure.'

He first showed her the pressoir – large wooden vats where the grapes are pressed to release their juice. Close to the pressoir were large oak casks which, Jeremy explained, were used for the first fermenting process. The barn held the distinct floral aromas of grapes and wine. Millie loved the smell of it.

'Would you like to go down to the cellars?'

'I would, yes.'

In the cool dark depths under the chateau, Jeremy guided her along the narrow cellars. The walls had been newly whitewashed, erasing the hateful German swastikas and wartime propaganda. In the chateau Millie could pretend quite easily that Germans hadn't occupied the rooms. All trace of them had gone, Pascal had seen to that, but down here in the gloom, Millie keenly felt their presence.

They came into a large area lit by candles. Wooden racks held hundreds of bottles and Pascal was supervising a few men in the turning of the wine bottles.

'What are they doing?' she asked.

'Riddling. After the second fermentation has completed, the bottles must be turned to collect the sediment in the neck. That's why all the bottles are at a downwards angle in the racks.'

'I see, but I thought the Germans emptied the cellars?' Millie shivered as the coldness settled on her warm skin.

'They took all they saw, yes. But Pascal was clever. He hid a great many crates in a pit behind his cottage under the muck of his pigsty. The Germans ate his pigs, but they didn't have any need to dig in the pig muck that stank to high heaven.'

'Oh, well done, Pascal!'

Pascal straightened his bent shoulders proudly. His English might not be the best, but he understood praise when he heard it.

'Despite the war raging around them, Pascal and the local women still worked the fields. Each year a harvest was brought in, obviously it wasn't of the size of the pre-war years, as the vines were destroyed, but what remained was harvested and the Germans allowed Pascal to continue the process. They just took the results.'

'Allemands!' Pascal spat to the side.

Millie looked to Jeremy. 'That's French for Germans, yes?'

Jeremy nodded and moved them further away. 'From what I can gather, the German officers were hard on Pascal, treated him and his aging mother rather terribly. When his mother died, the officers living in the chateau wouldn't allow Pascal to bury her in the village. But the soldiers, just common privates, helped him to do it in the middle of the night. To this day, Pascal won't tell anyone where she is, even me. That wound is too deep to share.

Millie's heart squeezed in sadness. 'Poor Pascal. He seems so happy all the time. Yet, he carries such a tragedy.'

Jeremy looked at her in the golden light of the candles. 'We all carry something, my love. We should know that better than anyone.'

Millie thought of their dead baby boy and placed a hand over her stomach.

Jeremy kissed the top of her head. 'Come on. Let us go up into the sunshine.'

'What about down there?' Millie pointed to a darkened end of the cellar.

'That's under the stables that were hit by a bomb. It's not safe down there until the stables above have been rebuilt.'

Once outside, Millie blinked in the bright sunshine. 'I want to be a part of the whole process, Jeremy. I need to understand everything we do here.'

'And you will, my darling. I promise.'

'Would you like some lunch?'

'In French, my dear,' he joked.

She thought for a moment. 'Le déjeuner?'

He grinned and hugged her to him. 'Perfect. But sadly, no. I have to go and check on the carpenters in the stables. I want that area as safe as possible before harvest time and we have people wandering around the place. Oh, and a man is coming to look at the well, later. We are thinking the pump has broken.'

Millie kissed him, knowing his head was full of estate concerns and in an hour or so he'd come in starving and demanding food. 'Well, I'll continue to make our home beautiful.'

She left him and went in through the kitchen door. As always, the kitchen smelled delicious as Vivian and her team of two village girls created mouth-watering meals.

Millie smiled at the two girls, Catrin and Sophie, who she knew to be sisters. They were busy peeling vegetables, but on the dresser at the side were trays of almond squares cooling. Millie grabbed one and with a wink at the giggling girls she headed for the door.

'Madam?' Vivian came in from the corridor, catching Millie in the act of stuffing a square into her mouth. *'Exquis, oui?'*

'Exquisite, yes.' Millie repeated, savouring the sweet taste on her tongue.

'I show you something?'

'Of course.' Millie followed Vivian upstairs into the right wing of the house, which was out of bounds to everyone due to the damage it received during the war. 'Vivian, we shouldn't be in this part, you know that.'

'Yes, but look, madam.' She went along the gallery and turned into a smaller antechamber that lead off from another bedroom. Vivian stopped and pointed to a large armoire.

'Oh! It's beautiful.'

'For your bedroom, oui?'

Even in the dim light of the shuttered room, its workmanship was exquisite. Millie ran her hand over the smooth wood, which was a shade of honey and had inlay patterns of even lighter wood in the shape of swirls and flowers. Gently she opened the door and stared at the bare shelves, imagining them to be freshly lined and containing her new clothes from Paris.

'Monsieur Remington will want you to have it in your room.' Vivian nodded wisely.

'It is true, we need an armoire. However, if I tell my husband about this, he'll know we've been on this side of the building and he'll not be happy.'

Vivian shrugged in the superb French way. 'It is safe.'

Millie walked back into the dark bedroom due to the window being boarded up. Bombing in the fields had blown out a lot of windows at the back of the chateau which had bore the brunt of the battles more than the front. The room was too dark to see it clearly, but Millie detected that the plaster on the walls were crumbling as in the other rooms and a mould stain was seeping down one wall from above.

She sighed and turned away. There was so much work to be done.

As Millie walked along the gallery she peeked into the other rooms on this side of the house, those which had been off limits as Jeremy deemed them dangerous until a proper inspection was carried out. Normally Millie was too busy to worry about this side of the house but since she was here she thought she would take a look. Not that there was much to inspect. Each room was empty with faded paint or peeling wallpaper and dirty windows.

She paused by the small narrow twisting staircase that led up into the attics, another area she'd not ventured into.

'Shall we, madam?' Vivian raised her eyebrows cheekily.

Millie hesitated. Jeremy was in the fields replanting the vines, he'd not know. 'Yes, lets.'

Feeling like a criminal, Millie headed up the tight staircase. At the top was a large spacious room with a dormer window on each side. Two other doors led off from either end of the room. Millie went through the one on the right, knowing she shouldn't. The right side of the chateau was off limits. Still, she would be careful.

Another dormer window lighted this room enough to see by and Millie stood and stared at the enormous amount of stuff in the room.

'There is a lot of things in here, madam,' Vivian said, edging between trunks and cupboards, crates and drawers.

'There is, and do be careful, Vivian. Look at the ceiling over there, it's fallen in.' Millie studied the far corner that was the top of the turret, and which showed a good many gaps where the shingle tiles had broken. A roofer and builder was in desperate need in this part of the chateau, but as this whole region was rebuilding, finding good suitable builders with the right skills to repair such steep rooflines was difficult. There was more demand than builders.

In wonder of possible treasures she might find, Millie walked to a pile of paintings, which were covered with dust sheets. Carefully, she moved each painting and gave it a quick glance. Some were ruined, torn, the canvas bowing in the frame but a few at the back were in good condition and she placed them to one side. One particular painting of a vase of bright beautiful flowers was worth hanging.

Further into the room she saw several more paintings stacked against a dust-covered trunk. Her curiosity piqued, she opened the trunk and peeked inside it. She took out books, lovely tomes written in French with gold embossed leather covers. There were old newspapers and notebooks, a couple of ledgers from eighteen seventy-nine, which she placed to one side to look at later. At the bottom of the trunk was a small box full of receipts.

Weirdly disappointed, Millie sat back on her heels and sneezed. What had she been expecting? Jewels? Silk and furs?

'Is there anything of interest over there, Vivian?' she asked, closing the lid of the trunk.

'Non.' Vivian sounded as disappointed as Millie.

Standing up, Millie dusted off her skirt and glanced around. 'Some of this furniture can be brought downstairs. We can use it all once it's been cleaned.'

'*Oui, madam.* This chair is very nice.' Vivian had lifted aside a dust sheet to reveal an ornately carved chair in dark blue fabric.

'I'll have the men clear it all out and we can access what will be used and what will be tossed away.'

Vivian followed her out and they crossed the bare room into the other room on the left. In here was less furniture but there were more crates and two large trunks neatly piled up in the far corner.

It didn't take long to realise the crates were full of moth-eaten rolls of fabric, old curtains and table linen.

'Rags,' Vivian muttered.

Millie sighed. 'Some might be worth saving.'

The two large trunks were behind the crates and it took a while for Vivian and Millie to move the crates aside to reach them. Incredibly, both trunks were locked.

'Why would they be locked?' Millie pulled at the heavy lock again.

'Important?' Vivian suggested.

'Do we have spare keys not accounted for?'

Vivian shrugged. 'I do not know, madam.'

Millie stared at the top trunk and then bent down to the bottom one. Initials were branded into the leather. C. D.

'Camile Dumont,' Vivian announced.

'Jeremy's mother?' An excited shiver ran through Millie. 'I must tell Jeremy. He thought his father had thrown away all of his mother's belongings after she died.'

'This was her home, madam. She has history here.'

Eagerly, Millie headed down the staircase, but heard voices as she reached the entrance hall. At the front door stood a man with a satchel. He was talking to Jeremy, who'd come in from the vines. 'Is everything all right?' she asked, noting Vivian heading back to the kitchen.

'Post and my newspapers.' Jeremy handed her a pile of letters as the man mounted his bicycle and rode away.

'What were you talking about?' She wasn't particularly interested as she sifted through the letters.

'Electricity has reached the corner of the road, about a mile along from the lane leading to here. We should have it connected here within the week. No more candles.'

Millie grinned. 'I've become used to eating and working by candlelight.'

'And making love.' Jeremy pulled her to him and kissed her.

'Definitely.' She leaned away from him. 'You are filthy, sir.'

'My thoughts or my body?'

'Both.' She kissed him again. The summer sun had lightened his brown hair and given him a tan. The physical work was defining his arms where his shirt-sleeves had been rolled up. She found him more attractive than ever. 'You need a bath, but first I have something to tell you.'

'Oh?'

'I was up in the attics with Vivian—'

'We spoke about that, darling. The whole chateau needs a proper inspection. We must stay to the left side of the house and the rooms we know to be safe.'

'Yes, yes I know but I only wanted to have a quick look,' she fibbed. She dared not tell him she'd been on the right side where the bomb damage was.

'Please don't go up there again until the builders have arrived.'

'You've located some?'

'I wrote to Monty last week asking him to find some English builders for me who are willing to travel here to France. I received a letter from him yesterday telling me some men from the village are willing to come and work for the summer here.'

'Why did you not tell me this yesterday?'

'Because my darling we were both fast asleep after dinner and I forgot this morning.'

She grinned. 'Well yes, we are working very hard at the moment and sleep comes easily at night.'

'Indeed, it does. My back is aching right now.' He kissed the tip of her nose and broke away. 'But we have achieved a lot today. The east field has four rows straightened and the gaps replanted.' He wiped a hand over his eyes. 'I'm exhausted, but happily so. What was it you wanted to show me, anyway?'

'We, Vivian and I, found two trunks in the attic and the initials on one of them is C. D. Vivian believes it belonged to your mother.'

'Really?' An interested light came into his eyes. 'Then we must get the trunk downstairs, so we can look through it.'

'I shall call in the men from the garden to do it.'

'Wait, not yet. Later, perhaps.' He tilted his head towards the salon. 'You've hung the curtains?'

'I have. Come and see. They finish the room very well.' Millie went into the salon and waited for Jeremy's opinion.

'They look as though they belong there. Are you happy with them?'

'Yes, I am. I know it is different to how it looked when you came here as a young man, but I do feel the transformation is for the better.'

'I agree. My uncle never paid much attention to the décor. It was in need of an overhaul.' He went to the window and observed the gardeners. 'In time the view out of the windows will be worth looking at.'

Millie watched Jeremy, the sudden stoop of his shoulders, which indicated to her he was thinking about something upsetting. 'Why aren't you keen to see your mother's things?'

He glanced down at his feet. 'I suppose I am a little frightened. I've forgotten what she looks like. All I've ever had was the painting at Remington Court to keep her fresh in my mind.'

'Let us have that painting shipped over here. We can hang her in the dining room when it is finished.'

'Perhaps.'

'Tell me what else is troubling you.'

'My mother is a person in my head who over the years I've created into a Madonna. What if in the trunk there are things which will shatter that image?'

'Why would there be? She left France as a young bride to marry your father and live in England. I would venture that all that's in the trunk are her childhood keepsakes.'

'You could be right.'

'I usually am.' She laughed and hooked her arm through his. 'I'll get the men to bring the trunk down into our bedroom and tonight we shall sort through it together.'

'Yes, good idea.'

'Are you hungry?'

'Starving.'

'Go and wash and I'll ask Vivian to serve us dinner. The smells coming out of the kitchen today have been mouthwatering.'

'I really don't know how we'll cope when we employ a chef. What if they aren't as good as Vivian?'

'Then I'll simply get a new housekeeper and Vivian will remain in the kitchen!' she joked.

As he left the room, she went through the letters and pulled out one addressed to her from Prue.

Dearest Millie,

I am on my way to you. I was going to send a telegram but I thought that might make you worry at the urgency of it. There is nothing to worry about, but I shall be descending on you by July 24th.

Don't worry about fetching me from Calais, I'll make my own way perfectly well enough.

With love,

Prue.

Millie groaned. Two days! Prue would be here in two days!

She wasn't ready for visitors, and especially not Prue who'd hate to live amongst the upheaval of the chateau. Nor did she have time to take Prue about the region like it was a holiday. She had so much work to do!

Then she paused. Why was Prue arriving by herself?

Chapter Sixteen

Jeremy opened the trunk with trepidation. The key hadn't been found and it'd taken many attempts with the hammer to break the ring that held the lock in place.

Millie sat on the bed, sipping a glass of wine. All evening she had been in a fix about Prue's imminent arrival. As much as he loved his sister-in-law, he could have done without her turning up so soon. He wanted more time with Millie, just the two of them. They were re-affirming their love for each other more every day. He enjoyed having just his beautiful wife to talk to at the dinner table each evening and no other, which he knew wouldn't last much longer. French families were returning to their homes and rebuilding the region, including new friendships amongst the wine growers. In the not too distant future he and Millie would have the social aspect of entertaining and being entertained by other prominent families in the area.

'I'm sure it is all innocent stuff, my love.' Millie put the wine glass on the drawers and hunkered down beside him on the floor.

'I hope it is.' A wave of staleness hit him. Carefully, he lifted out a protected sheet of tissue paper. Beneath it was an assortment of things and he withdrew each one at a time: a green silk scarf; a pair of dove-grey evening gloves; and several fans that Millie opened and fluttered at him. He smiled and continued to search through what he believed to be his mother's things.

'You know, in secret when Father wasn't around, my mother told me to call her, ma mére.'

'French for my mother,' Millie said softly, reaching into the trunk to touch a small pile of white folded handkerchiefs with C. D. embroidered on them.

'My father detested her speaking French. She had to speak English all the time, except with her maid she brought over to England with her, and me, when she could.'

'Why on earth did your father marry your mother if he was so tyrannical about everything she said and did?'

'Because he loved her. Though it wasn't a normal love, apparently. People who I have spoken to in the past all said he was obsessed with her. She was a prize much sort after in Northern France. The last Dumont female for the marriage market.' He picked up a red leather book and opened it to see childish writing. The front page read *Camile Juliette Dumont, Chateau Dumont 1871.*

'What is that?' Millie asked.

'My mother's journal as a girl. From the date she would have been about six or seven.' He fondly touched the pages hardly believing he was holding something his mother had treasured.

'How sweet. What does she write about?' Millie reached in and pulled out a ribbon-wrapped bundle of letters.

Jeremy flicked through the pages. 'She talks of her pony, her puppy which has chewed her slippers, and pressing flowers. Oh, and she doesn't like her piano tutor.'

'Girl stuff.' Millie grinned indulgently as she untied the ribbon and sorted through the letters. 'We must read these. Oh, they are written in English.'

Jeremy frowned. 'English? Who are they to?' He took some of the pile and opened one of the envelopes.

My sweet Paulina,
Today I am unwell and remaining in bed. Soames is away to London and for that I am glad. He is impossible.

'They are all addressed to someone called Paulina,' Millie announced shuffling the letters together. 'Do you know who that is?'

'I don't, no.' Jeremy folded the letter, unable to read the rest. His mother's word conjured up her voice and he had an overwhelming sense of loss. That she was speaking of his father, made him doubly sure he didn't want to read them. He needed no reminding how unhappy his mother was at Remington Court.

'Darling.' Millie's hand on his arm made him force a smile.

'I'm fine.'

'No, you aren't. Of course, you aren't. Your mother is coming back from the grave. It will unsettle you.'

He could tell from her worried tone that she thought he'd have a bad night tonight, the nightmares would come back, and maybe they would. He worked hard every day in the fields, digging and planting, tying up the vines, putting in posts, filling in bomb craters, stacking bricks, anything that would tire him out each night, so he wouldn't dream.

So far it had worked.

So far since arriving at the chateau he'd not succumbed to the night terrors or the 'episodes' during the day when he thought he was back in battles. Amazingly, he had expected to feel the torture again, especially when every day brought maimed and homeless ex-soldiers to the gate asking for work. When he had helped Monty, the nightmares had grown worse. However, that hadn't happened here. Being surrounded by the damage done by bombs and thousands of soldiers hardly affected him. It was familiar. Strangely it gave him comfort, as did the returning soldiers. They were his brothers. This land was his and he, along with them, had fought for their lives to protect it. Chateau Dumont still shone in the sun, despite the Germans. Remington Court hadn't been through a war, yet it felt dark and oppressive and haunted by his father's pining for Camile and his hatred for his son.

Abruptly, he stood and turned away from the trunk's debris. 'I don't want to do this any more. Not tonight. I'm tired.'

Millie quickly packed away the contents. 'There is plenty of time.'

'You go through it though, there might be something of interest for you to use, but I can't, not yet.' Emotion filled his throat.

'I understand.' Millie came up to him and wrapped her arms around his waist. Her touch always brought him comfort.

He kissed her. 'I thought I would enjoy learning more about my mother, but I don't think I can bear to. That letter I started to read mentioned my father and I could feel her sadness.'

'Then I shall read them, and if there is anything worthy of mentioning, then I will tell you.'

He nodded and squeezed her tight against him. Sometimes, loving her so much was like a physical pain. 'I need to make love to you.'

She smiled up at him, her blue eyes full of desire, which made him feel like a king. 'I won't complain about that, husband.'

~ ~ ~ ~

Millie stretched her back and adjusted the yellow scarf tied around her head. The summer sun blazed outside and had even infiltrated the chateau's thick stone walls. She was tired, but the library, or la bibliotheque, was coming along nicely. A group of youths from a boys' school in Epernay were under the tutelage of their craft master and were assembling carved wooden bookshelves along the walls while Millie was arranging the books to go into them. Jeremy had sent for boxes of his books from Remington Court and the Kensington townhouse and they arrived only that morning. Hopefully, the next shipment would bring her writing desk and gramophone she'd asked Monty to send over. There was nothing else she wanted from Remington Court.

'Here, madam?' Vivian came in carrying a large bowl filled with wild flowers she'd picked in the fields.

'Oui, merci.' Millie glanced out of the window, fully expecting Prue to arrive any moment, but as yet she had not turned up and it had been three days since her letter arrived. Prue was travelling alone. How Mama had allowed that Millie didn't know. What if something happened to her on route? How would she find out? She was beginning to worry.

'Madam?'

Millie brought her attention back to Vivian. 'Sorry, Vivian, what did you say?' The youths were hammering and fixing wood to the walls making a spectacular noise. Millie walked with Vivian out into the entrance hall.

'Madam tired.' Vivian held her head to one side. *'Enceinte?'*

'Enceinte?' She frowned trying to work out the meaning of the word. Then Vivian held her arms out over her stomach to indicate a pregnant woman. 'Oh. A baby? Who? Me?'

Vivian nodded. *'Enceinte, oui?'* She nodded hopefully.

Millie shivered with sudden fear. Her hands went straight to her stomach, which was rounded only slightly, but she put that down to the lovely French food Vivian brought out of the kitchen every few hours. With half of the house empty, Vivian had little to do with the housekeeping and spent her time instead cooking delicious meals and treats.

Millie hurriedly calculated her periods and couldn't remember the last one she'd had. Good God when was it? Had she even had one since she lost the baby in April? She and Jeremy had reunited in May…

A cold shiver ran down her spine. She felt the blood leave her face.

'No. No. No.' She ran from the room and outside into the furnace like heat. She whipped off her head scarf and continued running down the drive, through the open gates and along the dusty dirt road.

At the corner of the road, she stopped and bent over to catch her breath. Tears burned hot behind her eyes, but she fought the urge to cry. Instead she took a deep breath and thought rationally. Was she with child? She and Jeremy could hardly keep their hands off each other, even despite their tiredness in the evenings and then on Sundays they enjoyed long sleep-ins and gentle lovemaking when the estate was quiet and all the workers in their own homes.

The possibility of her being pregnant was rather high.

She swore soundly, and like no lady should.

In the distance a battered old truck trundled along the road, dust billowing out behind it. Millie shielded her eyes from the sweltering sun and watched the truck come closer and then slow to a stop beside her. The door opened, and a suitcase was lowered to the ground before Prue jumped down, a large smile on her face.

'Millie!'

'Prue!' They hugged each other tightly as the truck driver drove away in a cloud of dust.

'How did you know I was coming at this time?' Prue asked, collecting her suitcase.

'I didn't. I… I was taking a walk.'

'In this heat?' Prue's normally smooth tidy blonde hair was a mass of sweaty limp tendrils about her face.

'There is a lot of noise with the builders and so on. Sometimes I need the peace of a walk,' Millie lied, taking the suitcase from Prue. 'You must be thirsty.'

'I'm so excited to see it all. Imagine my very own sister owning a vineyard and a *Champagne* vineyard at that!' Prue's high spirits were contagious, and Millie grinned.

'We were expecting you yesterday,' Millie said as they walked down the road.

'Yes, well I arrived in Calais rather later than I thought I would, so I had to put up in a hotel for the night.'

'Last night?'

'No, the night before.

Millie frowned. 'Where were you last night then?'

Prue shuffled a stone with her polished black shoe. 'I stayed with a friend.'

Millie cocked her head to one side and studied her sister. Prue was seriously thin – thinner than Millie had ever seen her. Her hair was long and she wore a low-waisted dress of dun brown. In her hand she carried a black felt hat and a black beaded purse. There was an edginess to her that Millie detected. 'Is everything all right?'

'Of course!' Prue's tone was overly bright.

'Prue.' Millie stopped as they reached the gates. 'Tell me why you have come here without the others?'

'I don't have to do everything with Cece and Mama, you know.'

'I'm surprised Mama let you travel here alone.'

Prue couldn't meet Millie's eyes.

'What are you hiding from me?' Mille demanded.

'I told Mama that you were meeting me in Calais.'

'Why did you lie?'

'Because I wanted some freedom!'

'Prue!'

'What is wrong with that, for heaven's sake?' Prue marched through the gates and down the drive.

'I would say a lot,' Millie scoffed.

'I wanted to do something different, Millie. Mama was happy for me to come and see you, especially after the baby and everything. She wanted to come herself, but she isn't ready to travel yet.'

'Why didn't Cece come too?'

'I persuaded her to stay behind.' Prue shrugged one shoulder. 'It wasn't difficult. After your letters to us explaining how the chateau is nothing but a shell, and that you and Jeremy were close to something like camping in ruins, Cece thought it best that only one of us should go and not burden you more than that.'

Millie sensed she wasn't getting the whole truth from her sister but was prevented from asking more questions as Jeremy and Vivian came out of the front door. Jeremy had worry written all over his face, as did Vivian and guiltily Millie realised that they'd been concerned over her running off as she did.

'Jeremy!' Prue flung herself into his arms and hugged him tight. 'Oh, it is good to see you. I've missed you, brother.'

He smiled and kissed her cheek. 'Welcome to Chateau Dumont.'

'And this must be Vivian?' Prue shook the housekeeper's hand. 'I've heard much about your delicious cooking from my sister. I need fattening up!'

Prue and Vivian walked inside chatting about food while Jeremy took Millie's hand halting her from going in.

'Darling?'

Silly tears filled her eyes. 'Vivian told you?'

'Yes. She came running down the rows calling for me. I nearly had a heart attack.'

'I'm sorry.'

'She told me that you'd both been talking of you being pregnant and then suddenly you ran off. She didn't know what to do. We were frantic.'

'Sorry. Stupid of me to dash off. I will apologise to her.'

'There is no need. I explained to her what happened with our baby and that you are frightened.'

She nodded and wiped her eyes. 'Oh, Jeremy what if I am with child? I couldn't bear to lose it.'

'Who said you are?' He gave her a superior look that she believed he'd used many a time on an unsuspecting soldier. 'We are going to Paris to see the best doctor there is. We'll take Prue and let her shop for a few days and then we'll come home, and you'll take it easy until the baby is born. Everything will be perfectly fine. Understood?'

She nodded, too full of emotion to speak, but trusting his confidence. She squashed down any spark of happiness that she might be having a baby. It wouldn't do to get excited or even hopeful, not after last time.

Chapter Seventeen

Millie left the restaurant, barely listening to Prue as she praised Parisian fashion and juggled the number of bags she held. They'd spent the afternoon shopping, or more accurately Prue shopped, and Millie tried to be interested. However, the visit to a doctor this morning, who confirmed her pregnancy, had thrown her mind into a spin.

'We will have to sort out our dresses, Mil. We must decide on what colours we are wearing to dinner tonight. Is Monsieur Baudin's wife very grand?' Prue smiled at a man walking towards them, and he dipped his hat.

Millie grabbed Prue's arm and steered her across the road. 'Madam Baudin is a gentle, older woman with style and sophistication but she's not a snob.'

'Oh good. I'd hate for a Frenchwoman to look down her nose at me. Will there be other guests at dinner tonight?'

'One or two of Monsieur Baudin's contacts. This is a business dinner, Prue, one that we women have been invited to but which I feel will bore you senseless. The talk will be all exports and revenues.' Millie sighed and looked out over the River Seine as they strolled along side it. She didn't want to dress up and socialise tonight. Instead all she wanted to do was curl up in Jeremy's arms and discuss her fears about the baby.

Prue spun to Millie, her bags flying out wildly as she did so. 'We can go out dancing afterwards though. I saw a sign just down from our hotel that promoted a jazz band and dancing. We really should see what it's about, don't you think?'

'Perhaps.'

'Good lord, Millie. What is wrong with you today? You've been a right grump.'

'Sorry.'

'What is wrong? Is it Jeremy?'

'No, not him.'

'Yet there is something?' Prue stopped in the middle of the pavement making pedestrians divert around them.

Millie apologised to an elderly man who tutted at them. 'Prue, move aside.'

'I'll not move an inch until you tell me what the problem is.'

'My problem? What about you?' Millie stared at her sister as a passing boat blew its horn making them jump.

'I don't know what you're talking about.' Prue marched ahead.

A soft warm wind blew along the river, carrying with it the scents of the public gardens and the smell of the river below them.

Without talking, they crossed Pont Alexandre III and absent-mindedly watched the water rush below them and another boat make its way under the arch.

At the other side of the bridge, Prue paused. 'Where did you and Jeremy go this morning while I was still in bed?'

'I will tell you if you tell me why you've come to France on your own.' Millie went to the rail and leaned against it, turning her back on the frantic traffic of motor cars, and horse carriages and instead focused on the smooth flowing water which dazzled in the sun.

Prue came to stand beside her. She lifted her head, the breeze lifting her newly cut short blonde hair from beneath her felt hat. 'Very well, but you're not to be judgmental.'

Millie raised her eyebrows in question but nodded. 'You go first.'

'Jeremy and I had an appointment with a doctor. A doctor who specialises in attending pregnant women.'

Prue reared back. 'You are having a baby?'

'I am, yes.' Millie swallowed. It sounded so real when she spoke it out loud.

'That's wonderful, Mil!' Prue hugged her awkwardly with all her bags. Then she peered at Millie. 'You aren't happy about it.'

'I don't know how I feel.'

'You're worried the same thing will happen again, aren't you?'

'How could I not be?'

'It won't,' Prue said with conviction.

'You don't know that. No one does.'

'What did the doctor say?'

'He said he sees no reason why it should not be a normal pregnancy.'

'There you are then!'

Millie fought the urge to cry. 'I'm so frightened, Prue. I can't go through all that again. I had a baby boy and I never saw him.' A sob caught in her throat.

Prue dropped her bags and hugged Millie properly. 'I know how wretched you are about the first baby, but I'm confident that this time it will all be perfect. You'll grow big and fat and soon we'll have a beautiful little baby in the family and he or she will be loved and spoilt.'

'I dare not think that far ahead. I can only take each day as it comes.'

'Then do that then. I'll plan for the future for both of us. When is the little one due to be born?'

'January.'

'A winter baby.' Prue smiled and gathered her numerous bags again. 'Come on, we've got to get back to the hotel and bathe before we dress. I'm thinking of wearing the red silk with the black tassels, what do you think?'

'I think you're trying to put me off from asking questions about why you are here.' Millie matched her step to Prue's. 'I won't be put off you know. I've told you my news and now you must tell me yours.'

'It's all a bit of nonsense really.'

'What is?'

Prue looked away as they waited for a policeman to halt the traffic for them to cross the road. 'I think you'll be disappointed in me.'

'What have you done?'

The policeman blew his whistle and the crowd crossed the street to walk past the Grand Palais. The impressive domed building was lost on Millie as she watched the emotion play across Prue's face.

'I'm waiting, Prue.'

'I played false with a married man.'

Millie stopped and stared at her. 'You did what?'

Under the shade of a large tree, Prue bowed her head. 'I met a man at a party in London when I was staying with Grandmama after Papa died. I was feeling low and had drunk too much champagne. We flirted and kissed a bit.'

'Who is he?'

'No one you'd know, no one in the family knows him.'

Millie could barely believe what she was hearing. 'So, you have been having an affair with this man and he is married?'

'An affair sounds so dramatic, Millie,' Prue scoffed.

'Then explain it to me.'

'Win pursued me and—'

'Win? Is that his name?' She mentally searched her mind for any man with the name but came up with nothing.

'Yes, and you don't need to know any more than that.'

Millie cocked her head, a hundred questions on the tip of her tongue. 'Continue.'

'Win fell in love with me, but he… he is married.'

'Married. Heavens above, Prue. Why a married man?'

'I didn't mean for it to happen! It just did.'

'Do you love him?' Millie thought of her mama and knew the disgrace would likely finish her off after losing Papa.

Prue glanced at a passerby, a stylish woman dressed in a pink and white outfit that looked expensive and chic. 'I don't think I do love him at all, actually.'

'Really?' Millie couldn't hide the sarcasm. 'When did you come to this conclusion, when he was about to leave his wife?'

'Stop it!'

'What, holding a mirror up to you so you can face the consequences of your actions?'

'I've done nothing wrong! I didn't want him to leave his wife.' Fury and something else shone from Prue's eyes. 'I was stupid, I know that. It was all a mistake.'

'You've told him this?

'Yes, in Calais.'

'Calais!' Millie nearly shouted. 'You stayed with him in Calais instead of coming straight to me?'

'We had to talk it all through. He wants to leave his wife, and I don't want him to. I've told him to go back to her. It's over.'

'Did you share his bed? Answer me honestly.'

'No. It was a close-run thing, but I didn't, I promise you. He isn't the one for me.'

'Then why did you encourage him from the very first meeting?'

Staring up into the leafy canopy above their heads, Prue remained quiet for a moment. 'I wanted to be wanted.'

'Oh, Prue.' Millie couldn't chastise her for that. She'd felt something similar when Jeremy spent all his time with Monty.

'I felt very alone. You have Jeremy, Mama has her grief and Cece has her infatuation with Monty. I have no one.'

Millie walked on feeling sad for Prue and annoyed with herself. How had she missed this event in her sister's life? 'I'm sorry,' she said when Prue caught up with her.

'Whatever for?'

'For not being there for you when you needed someone to talk to.'

'How could you be? You were going through a tough time yourself. Jeremy was away, Papa had died and then the baby…'

'I am your sister. I should have been there for you.'

'Nonsense. I'll not have you berate yourself over something silly I have done. You've had more than enough to contend with. I am an adult, Millie.'

'How did you end it with Win?' Millie asked after they had walked to the next corner and turned onto the Avenue des Champs-Élysées.

'I told him not to contact me again and that we were done.'

'Will he honour your request?'

'Yes, I think he will. He has much to lose, and if I am not eager for us to continue then he could end up with nothing.'

'He sounds like a charmer,' Millie muttered about this unknown adulterer. 'Does anyone else know about this?'

'No. Just you. Cece would never understand and it would hurt Mama enormously. I beg you not to tell Mama, please?'

'I won't.'

'No one else needs to know. We were very circumspect where we met, and I've burnt all his letters. It's over, my reputation is intact, and I can forget all about it.' Prue put a hand on Millie's arm to stop her. 'I have escaped a scandal, and you and the baby will be fine. Can we please celebrate all that tonight and go dancing?'

'I don't know, Prue.' Millie's hand fluttered to her stomach.

Prue grinned. 'How about you dance the slow ones with Jeremy and I'll dance the fast ones with him?'

Millie laughed. 'Poor Jeremy! He'll be exhausted.'

'Do say yes, Mil. Let us have a fantastic night!'

'When does anyone ever say no to you?' Millie shook her head with a grin. 'Go on then, we'll go dancing.'

'Smashing!'

~ ~ ~ ~

Millie held up a roll of duck-egg blue wallpaper embossed with cream roses. She glanced from the wallpaper to the walls of the dining room and nodded to the decorator, Jean-Pierre. 'Yes, that is perfect. It is to go on all the walls, oui?'

'Oui, madam.' Jean-Pierre took the roll from her and walked over to his work station in the middle of the room. He was a quiet older man who turned up one day and said he could paint and decorate and needed work. Millie had felt assured by him and as soon as he started working, his talent shone out. Jean-Pierre was employed to decorate the dining room, but the attention to detail as he worked gave Millie the confidence to employ him for the other rooms. He had no men with him when he arrived, but Jeremy soon found some young men to help him.

Millie left the grand dining room and headed for the room opposite; the morning salon, a smaller room that captured the morning sun. In here, builders were re-plastering the walls now the new electric wiring had been finished. In the next room, Jeremy's study, the floor was being ripped out to be replaced before the plasterers could work in there.

The whole chateau rang with noise of hammers, men's voices, the scrape of tools, creaking wheelbarrows and the thump of boots coming in and out. A fine layer of dust covered everything, and Vivian and a few village girls were in a constant battle of cleaning.

Millie peeped into the salon and found it empty. Prue had said she'd be in the vines helping Jeremy and the others with the grape harvest. What kind of help she did, Millie didn't know but for the last few weeks, Prue's presence at the chateau had been welcomed. Prue's ability to find fun and laughter lifted Millie's worries over the baby, and in turn she could reassure Jeremy that she was coping just fine.

In truth, she was so busy with the creating of each room in the chateau that many hours would go by without her even thinking of the baby. It was mainly at night, when lying in bed with Jeremy's hand on her little bump did the doubts and anxiety return.

The hot summer weather continued to hold, and August was proving so hot that Millie found herself getting tired easily. She promised Jeremy she'd rest as much as she could and despite all the attention she needed to give to the builders and decorators, to Vivian and the other staff, she routinely took a couple hours off every afternoon.

Going upstairs, she found her straw hat in her bedroom. The sun beckoned, and she thought to walk to the river and sit in the shade for a while. On a chair in the turret were the pile of letters belonging to Camile. Impulsively, Millie grabbed them.

With her large straw hat on to cover her face from the burning sun, Millie strolled through the ruined orchard on the west side of the chateau towards the narrow river which was the western boundary of the estate. She'd been delighted when Jeremy had mentioned they had water rights to the river and it was used for the irrigation of the vines.

Where the orchard finished was a small grove of mature trees and here Millie sat on the grass, savouring the peace and tranquility. Several ducks swam away from her, but after she'd been there a few minutes, they ignored her and came closer. Next time she'd have to bring some bread for them. Under the trees the grass hadn't turned brown like it had out in the fields and a butterfly hovered about for a moment or two before flittering away over the water. It was a beautiful spot and Millie wished she could paint it but her ability at drawing or painting was severely lacking.

Leaning back against a tree trunk, she unwrapped the ribbon around the letters and opened the first letter to Paulina. Millie read about Camile's trip to Paris with her father not long after her mother's death. Her father had business meetings, leaving Camile to explore Paris with her maid. Millie smiled at that, for it was similar to what she and Prue had done a few weeks ago.

The next letter was about Camile's birthday party and how le père — her father — had bought her a diamond necklace, she'd also worn a diamond bracelet which had belonged to her mother. The tone of the letter revealed Camile's sadness about losing her mother. However, she had enjoyed her birthday party very much and was delighted by the many suitors who vied for her attention.

Though Père is refusing to listen to my opinion about whom I should marry. I prefer a Frenchman, but non, it must be a foreigner! Why? I do not understand it, Paulina. What is wrong with our own kind? Père is thinking a German. Mon dieu! I'll not marry a German. Le Père thinks only of business.

Do not ask about Jacques.

Millie finished the letter, which spoke of Camile riding to a nearby chateau and eating too many strawberries which stained her lips.

The next letters were in the same vein, mostly talking of the social events in the region, Camile's father hosting a grand dinner where Jacques attended, and so did an Englishman by the name of Sir Soames Remington, a business acquaintance of her father's. This made Millie sit up and take notice but not much more was said in that letter.

However, the next letter mentions another dinner with Sir Soames.

He is a bit of a bore, really. Yet, he takes a great interest in me. He is not very good-looking or as charming as Jacques...

Another letter is instantly more somber in tone and engrossed, Millie is lost to the gentle flowing river, the ducks and the birds twittering. She is in Camile's world of the early eighteen eighties and her letters are becoming desperate.

Please, Paulina, can I come to you in Egypt? Michel will allow it, I am after all his cousin and as his wife and my best friend you can persuade him! How could he say no? I must get away from France. I am in trouble and need your help.

Intrigued, Millie opened the next letter and skimmed through it to find out what trouble Camile was in, but there is no mention of it. Looking back to the envelope the date is postmarked many months later.

I am happy to receive your latest letter, my dearest Paulina. Le Père sees the English writing on the envelope and knows it is from you and always bades me to send his regards. (Us writing in English is one way to keep other eyes from knowing the contents and that is good! Also, my English is becoming excellent which I will need in the future.)

Your sudden trip to Senegal must have been of great interest to Michel and his work for the government, but I wonder if that is the same for you in your delicate health? I want to know everything.

Do not worry over me and please do not trouble yourself over my last letter. All is well or will be presently as I am engaged to Sir Soames Remington and leave for England in a month after our wedding. I am most unhappy that you cannot attend the wedding as I wish to see you most desperately. Michel wrote to Père and says his work keeps him in Egypt and sends his apologies.

Millie leaned her head back against the trunk to rest her eyes from reading the small tight scrawl. Camile's penmanship left a lot to be desired. She only had a few more letters left to read and that saddened her, especially since Camile's manner was not the lightheartedness of the first letters, where she talked of parties and social occasions and of being wooed by beaus and of the man called Jacques. Now she was marrying Jeremy's father and she sounded bleak.

Starting the third-to-last letter, Millie felt a sense of trepidation.

My dear Paulina

I am deeply concerned you are still in severe ill health. Michel wrote to me to tell me the doctors cannot make you well again. He wants to bring you back to France, but you won't allow it! Why do you prevent him from booking the tickets? You must come home. I will do my best to leave damp cold Yorkshire to see you. Soames won't like it but then he likes nothing and no one and I cannot please him. He is insanely jealous, and I cannot bear his presence in my bedchamber.

I long to escape and you are my reason to do so. Please, I beg you, change your mind and return to Paris.

Your loving friend,
Camile.
Burn this letter.

Millie quickly opened the next letter and faltered on seeing that it was written in French unlike the others. She concentrated hard and was pleased that her French was now of a passable standard to read and speak.

My sweet Paulina,

Today I am unwell and remaining in bed. I have that luxury. Soames is away to London and for that I am glad. He is impossible.

However, I have the most wonderful news. I have been delivered of the sweetest baby boy. He was born two days ago. We have named him Jeremy after Soames's father. I do not mind that for of course I cannot call him Jacques as I would wish to, and who my beautiful boy resembles…

Stunned, Millie gasped and reread the last few lines, believing she had translated it wrongly. On second and third reading the words remained the same and her meaning of them shocked her.

Jacques was Jeremy's father?

A duck quacked making her jump. Scrambling to her feet, she walked to the water's edge and continued reading.

Michel writes that you are very weak now. My heart breaks for so many reasons, for you, for my darling boy, for my cold marriage. You must make it through, for me, for Michel. Who have we got if you are not with us?

Without you I have no one.

Père is refusing my pleas to return to Chateau Dumont. He says I am married and must make the best of it. Mon Dieu! If I was another son, he would not be saying such things! A son would be encouraged to take a mistress and find happiness there. I must make do! I have nothing, only Jeremy. Jacques is lost to me, a mistake to be forgotten, but what do I tell my heart? I live here at Remington Court, which is a dreadful place of dark rooms and even darker furniture. There is no warmth. The chimneys smoke and the servants are sullen. They do not like a Frenchwoman being their mistress. Sir Soames lectures me that I should be grateful to become Lady Remington. Huh! My blood is far superior to his! Le Père is a descendant of the Great Charlemagne!

You must remember to burn this letter, not even show it to Michel, although we are close he would not like to read what I have written. I've written in French because the servants here are not to be trusted, especially Madam Jacobs. That woman is horrible!

Mrs Jacobs! Millie slapped a hand over her mouth in astonishment. That awful housekeeper at Remington Court who Millie had dismissed at the beginning of her marriage. Camile had hated Mrs Jacobs as much as Millie did!

'I got rid of her, Camile,' she said out loud, feeling the sweet satisfaction that she had at least one thing in common with her mother-in-law.

With a deep sigh, Millie opened the last letter.

I know you would not want me to weep, but I do. I sob as I write this last letter that you will never read, but write it I must, as a farewell.

Michel sent me a note telling me you had gone peacefully in your sleep, and he has returned all my letters I sent to you.

You did not burn them as I burned yours.

Michel says he has not read them, and I believe him. I am glad you did not burn them for they are my last link to you. I will put this letter in with others and then send them in a parcel to my brother at Chateau Dumont, asking him to store them away. He will do so, for he loved you also and knows how close we were.

I am grieving that you will never see Jeremy. He is the best baby in the world, Paulina, and you would have loved him as much as I do. He is my life.

I will miss you always, and forever you will be in my heart.

Your best friend,
Camile.

Millie felt Camile's pain, her grief. She knew what it was like to lose someone you loved, as she had done with her papa. Yet, she had her family and Jeremy to help her through the times when she was sad. Camile had no one, only her son, and within five years she, too, was dead. Jeremy had been left with a man who wasn't his father and who hated him.

Did she tell Jeremy the truth?

Rubbing her forehead in indecision, she watched the ducks, some which had waddled up onto the bank and sat in the sun.

What was she to do?

How would Jeremy take the news that Sir Soames wasn't his true father? Would it affect him and bring back the nightmares, the shell shock? He'd been doing so well since they arrived in France. She had expected the shell shock to return when the estate wore the wounds of battles so visibly and Jeremy was confronted every day with the scars of trenches and bomb craters which had ruined much of the vineyards, but he had shown no signs of his 'episodes'. And when they received all the ex-soldiers looking for work, she thought he would be reminded of the men he failed to save, or those who were damaged through his orders to attack. Yet, he had faced it all with such courage.

Against all her worst fears, Jeremy had not deteriorated. In fact, he seemed the opposite. He worked hard every day amongst the men replanting and getting the vineyard back into working order. He was so content here, bringing the chateau alive again. Restoring the one place he felt at home had changed him. She didn't think he was cured, for such a thing might not be possible, but for now, at least, he was the happiest she'd even seen him. How could she sabotage that? Did she even want to? What would it achieve?

She gathered up the letters, a weight of responsibility on her shoulders. She and Jeremy did promise to never keep secrets from each other again. Could she break that promise?

Walking back through the orchard, with its bent and broken limbs, she tried to rationalise her thoughts.

A part of her wished she'd never read the letters, that they had never been found in that trunk.

And who was Jacques?

Chapter Eighteen

As the afternoon sun descended over the horizon, Millie sank onto a chair, tired but happy. The courtyard was a blaze of colour from many hanging lanterns, which had crowns of coloured paper over them to send out a rainbow swirl of light. It had been Prue and Vivian's idea, and Millie was happy to let them produce a carnival atmosphere. Beneath the string of lanterns sat long wooden tables and benches filled with local people, the grape pickers, the chateau's tradesmen and staff.

She watched Jeremy drifting from one group of people to another, smiling, laughing and chatting. Totally at ease and happy. The final day of the grape harvest was a cause for celebration, or so Pascal kept reminding her.

Vivian and her girls had cooked for days and the kitchen was thick with delicious smells and tables groaned under the weight of hearty meals. Dishes of wild boar, rabbit, goose and duck were complemented with rich sauces, platters of salads, cheese and cold ham. Fresh bread baked by the dozen in the old wood stove built into the kitchen's chimney, were coated with local butter. Wine flowed, beer was drunk, and Prue had wound up Millie's gramophone, which had survived the shipment from Yorkshire.

'Everyone seems happy, Madam Remington.' Monsieur Baudin took the chair beside her. 'A successful harvest, oui?'

'Oui.' She smiled, liking the older man more each time she saw him. He had come out to the chateau to stay for the weekend and witness the end of the harvest. His wife had stayed in Paris to attend her sick sister.

'Jeremy is content, *oui?*' he asked, sipping a glass of red wine.

'Yes. He was concerned the grapes wouldn't yield as much as he wanted, especially after surviving the war, but Pascal assured him there would be enough for a good vintage.'

'And each year will only get better.' Monsieur Baudin raised his glass in a silent toast to his words. 'You will stay in France?'

'Oui. We have no wish to return to England.' Millie glanced at Jeremy and smiled. 'Our life is here.'

Monsieur Baudin gave her a long look. 'I, for one, am most happy that is so.' He turned and sought out Jeremy. 'He belongs here. France is his home.' He glanced at her round stomach. 'And the next generation.'

A roar of laughter made their gazes turn to where Prue stood surrounded by young men, all intent on winning her attention.

'Your sister is most popular.' He stroked his clipped grey beard, his eyes warm and pleasant as he looked on the scene.

'My sister always has been popular.' Millie had no jealousy. It was the simple truth. Everyone in their family knew it.

'Some women are like that. Like bees to nectar they draw people in.'

'Yes, well, Prue is certainly not guilty of hiding herself and she usually gets what she wants. Unlike me and our other sister Cece, Prue is a born people person. Everything is a game to her.'

'She is young.'

'Not that young,' Millie scoffed.

'Do not curb her happiness with rules and strictness. Let her be free to find happiness where she can.'

Millie stared at him. 'What makes you say that?'

Baudin sipped his wine. 'Youth is soon gone, washed away on regrets.'

'Regrets?'

He bowed his head self-consciously. 'Forgive me, now is not the time to be maudlin.'

He sounded wistful and Millie didn't know if she should ask another question, but she was saved by Prue putting another record on and people getting up to dance as the sun slipped down, casting long shadows over the land.

Jeremy joined Millie and Baudin and the conversation changed to the harvest and the future of the business.

A couple standing at the edge of the courtyard caught her attention. She frowned as dancers blocked her view. Millie stood and craned her neck, noticing the two suitcases on either side of the couple, then she saw the woman wave and she smiled.

'Daisy!' Millie called, waving back. 'Jeremy, Royston and Daisy have arrived!'

'About time, too!' Jeremy laughed. 'I thought I no longer had a valet!'

'You were the one who said they could stay at Remington Court longer,' she admonished just as Daisy and Royston joined them.

Millie hugged Daisy, feeling tearful. 'I'm so glad to have you with us, Daisy, and you Royston.'

'It's good to see you, Lady Remington.' Daisy shyly looked at Royston who was shaking Jeremy's hand and then Monsieur Baudin's.

'Is everything well?' Millie asked Daisy.

Daisy nodded, then glanced down at Millie's stomach and placed her hand on her own, which now Millie took notice of, showed the bump of a baby.

'Daisy you are with child, too?'

'Yes, madam.' Daisy's face fell, and tears filled her eyes. 'I'm so sorry. I told Royston that we should have written to you and let you know. I will understand if you don't want to employ me now. You must be very disappointed in me.'

'Nonsense, Daisy. Come, let us go inside and have a cup of tea. You look done in.' Millie steered Daisy away from the men and the party, which was growing louder and rowdier.

Once she was sitting at the kitchen table with a cup of tea in her hand, some colour returned to Daisy's cheeks. She glanced around the huge room and the little army of French women Vivian was in charge of for the night. 'There are a lot of people here.'

'They are all a part of getting the estate up and running again. If we are successful, then there is work for the locals and money in the region.' Millie pushed a plate of bread, ham and cheese towards Daisy. 'It is so good to see you, Daisy. Is your mother well?'

Daisy nodded and wiped away fresh tears. 'Yes, thank you, she is much recovered.'

'You must not be upset, Daisy. Sir Jeremy is delighted to have Royston back with him, as I am to have you.'

'But you were so good to us, letting us stay at Remington Court to get married and have a honeymoon. Then when my mother became sick, and you said I could stay in York and take care of her, I thought I'd lose my position for sure.'

'Why would I dismiss you for having a sick mother? You know me better than that, surely?'

'I do, madam, and you are kind and generous…' Tears ran freely down the young woman's cheeks.

Millie pulled her up out of the chair and into the corridor, stopping only when they were in the quiet morning salon. 'Tell me what is truly the matter, Daisy.'

'It is nothing, madam. I'm sorry, truly. I don't know what's wrong with me. Royston is so unhappy with me.'

'Why? What can the problem be?'

'I don't want a baby,' Daisy blurted out. 'I'm frightened, and my mother is so far away. She'll never see it or me. I have no one here and I can't speak the language. I'll no longer be working for you and be stuck in a cottage by myself while Royston serves Sir Jeremy. How will I cope on my own?'

Compassion filled Millie. 'You won't be alone. You'll have me. I know I'm not the same as your mother, or even a sister but I can be a friend.'

Daisy gave her an unbelieving look. They both knew that the two classes didn't mix.

'Listen to me,' Millie persisted. 'If after a few weeks here you still want to go home, then we will release both of you.'

'Royston won't hear of leaving Sir Jeremy again. He's been beside himself the whole time we've remained in England. He was desperate to get back to Sir Jeremy.' Daisy sighed as though the weight of the world was on her shoulders. 'But thank you, madam. I'm sorry to be a burden.'

~ ~ ~ ~

Millie woke to another sunny day and the sun streaming between fluffy clouds through the window, despite it being early October and autumn. The windows in their bedroom were still curtain-less, the old furniture still the same that Pascal had arranged when they first moved in at the beginning of summer. She really did need to start on decorating the bedroom, but since no one really saw it, this room was at the bottom of her list. She had concentrated on the downstairs rooms, and even the guest bedroom Prue slept in only had the basics, not that Prue minded. After working all day in the fields, she was too tired to care what state her bedroom was in as long as she had somewhere to sleep.

She rolled onto her side to wrap her arm around Jeremy. He moved at her touch and opened his eyes.

'Good morning, beautiful wife.' He patted her bump. 'Good morning, baby.'

'Good morning.' She kissed him softly and then stretched, loving the feel of her growing stomach against the blankets. She had a rotund mound of a belly now and she loved the sight of it for it proved their baby was growing well.

'What time is it?' Jeremy yawned and rubbed his face.

'Just past seven o'clock.'

His hands roamed over her body, slipping beneath her oversized nightgown. 'Do I have time to have some fun?'

'You do not!' She admonished in mock severity, knocking his hands away as he cupped her breast.

'You've got to be on the road to Calais by nine. Prue's ferry won't wait for her.'

'But I'll not be back until tomorrow night. Surely I can have a goodbye kiss?'

'You'll get one at the door as you leave.'

'You're a hard woman!' He shook his head and gave her puppy-dog eyes.

'Giving me that look won't work either!' As she went to get up he quickly pulled her against him and smothered her face in kisses and rubbed his stubbled jaw against her cheek.

She squealed, trying to get away.

A knock on the door interrupted their play.

Millie flung her dressing gown around her. 'Come in.'

Prue stuck her head around the door. 'I heard you two as I was going past.'

'I didn't expect you to be up yet.' Millie brushed her hair.

'I couldn't sleep. I'm so upset to be going home. It's been a brilliant summer here with you two.'

'Well, you're getting on that ferry, no arguments. I'm sick of the sight of you!' Jeremy muttered then grinned.

'I beg your pardon!' Prue pretended to look affronted.

'*You'll* miss her more than anyone,' Millie joked.

Jeremy nodded. 'That's true, you've been an amazing help around here, Prue. Since your arrival the men have worked harder to try an impress the pretty blonde English mademoiselle. I doubt half of what has been achieved wouldn't have been if you'd not made friends with every man on the estate.'

'Oh you!' Prue stuck her tongue out at him. 'Still, if it worked…' Her laughter followed her down the staircase as she left them.

'I will miss her.' Millie dressed in a woollen skirt of dark blue and a cream blouse.

'She'll be back before you know it, and your mother, grandmother and Cece will be in tow, ready to welcome the baby.' Jeremy climbed from the bed.

Millie rubbed her belly. 'You'll not forget to collect the bassinette when you're in Paris.'

'No, my love. I have a list as long as my arm. I'll drop Prue off at the ferry terminal in Calais and head straight for Paris. In the morning, I'll do all your shopping for you. I'll even put off Jacques until the evening.'

Millie whipped around, her heart thumping a rapid pace. 'Jacques?'

A tap on the door and at their call to enter Vivian came in carrying a jug of hot water and fresh towels.

'Bon matin,' Vivian said and after depositing the jug beside the basin on the side, she scooped up the dirty clothes from the day before and went out again.

'Who is Jacques?' Millie asked. She felt sick at the sound of the name. Her secret weighed heavy on her since she'd made her mind up weeks ago to not tell Jeremy the contents of his mother's letters and cause him any heartache. Sometimes she weakened, but every time she thought to tell him, something always made her stop.

'Monsieur Baudin. Why?'

'I thought his first name is John?'

'It is. John and Jacques mean the same thing really. He uses John for international business as it's easier for associates from other countries to pronounce, especially the Americans. He felt they didn't trust someone called Jacques, but plain John was no problem.'

'I see.' Millie felt a cold sweat break out on her forehead. Could this be *the* Jacques? Were there many men called by that name? It seemed common enough. 'Has Monsieur Baudin worked for the estate for a long time?'

'Oh yes, he was hired by my grandfather as a sales director for the champagne export.'

'Did he know your mother?'

'He would have, yes. Why?' Jeremy started shaving. 'I believe he was often invited to the chateau. He would have seen her before she married my father.'

She needed to dig deeper regarding Monsieur Baudin. Could he have been Camile's lover, or was it simply a young boy in the village or from Épernay that had got her pregnant? Surely, if Monsieur Baudin had an affair with Camile and made her pregnant, he would act differently in regards to Jeremy? 'We should invite the Baudins here for the weekend.'

Jeremy washed the soap from his face. 'Good idea. I will speak to him about it tonight when I see him.'

Putting Monsieur Baudin out of her mind, once dressed, Millie joined Prue in the dining room for breakfast. Her sister looked tanned, slim and stylish in a drop-waist dress of dusky rose. Her blonde hair much lighter from a summer of working outside in the French sunshine. A long thread of white beads hung about her neck and on the sideboard she'd placed her white felt hat with a pink rose stitched on the side. No wonder all the men here were in love with her.

'You look lovely.' Millie couldn't deny her sister was extremely pretty, and in her pregnant state Millie felt frumpy beside her, wearing a forest green dress over her bump.

Prue smiled. 'As do you and baby.'

'I feel fat.'

'You're only going to get bigger, and I'll not be here to see it.' Prue frowned as she sipped her coffee. 'I shall miss you and Jeremy very much.'

'You're coming back in January, aren't you, when the baby is born?'

'Of course! Try and stop me, but it'll not be the same, will it? I've had a whole summer of being free to just… well… to be free. No disapproving looks from Mama, no petty arguments with Cece, no attending social gatherings I have no interest in like Cece's sewing afternoons, or Mama's reading evenings. It's been blissful to just be outside all day and then come in to eat and sleep.'

Millie forked some eggs and ham onto her plate. 'It has been a wonderful summer. Having you here made it even better.'

'When I come back, Mama and Cece and probably Grandmama will all fuss around, and everything will have to be done properly.'

'I'm sure it'll be fine.' Millie buttered some thickly cut bread and enjoyed a mouthful of fluffy eggs.

'I'm dreading going back to Cece's lovelorn utterings of how wonderful Monty is. Did you ever find out about his past?' Prue asked eating a strawberry from the huge bowl of fresh fruit placed in the middle of the table.

'Yes. He's a fourth son of an earl.'

Prue nearly choked. 'Good God! Why didn't you tell me?'

Millie shrugged and ate some ham. 'I didn't think to, sorry. With everything going on here, I put Remington Court and Monty out of my head.'

'The son of an earl, hey?'

'The fourth son. He's not entitled to anything. The family is bankrupt.'

'Poor Cece.' Prue ate another strawberry. 'She had her heart set on him. But Mama won't allow it to go ahead if he can't provide for her.'

'He can, if she wants to be married to an estate manager. He's happy to manage Remington Court.'

'Knowing Cece it will be enough for her, too. She's not one to set her sights high, is she?'

'And what about you?' Millie asked. 'Sticking to single men, I hope? Pluck from a pool of eligible men will you, please?'

Prue grinned. 'Golly, you're never going to let me forget my mistake, are you?'

'I will. One day.' Millie laughed.

Jeremy came into the dining room and poured himself a cup of coffee. 'Are we nearly ready then?'

Prue ate another bite of croissant and finished her drink. 'Yes.'

'Coming.' Millie left the table and joined them at the front door where Prue's suitcase waited. She hugged Prue tightly. 'Write all the time and I'll see you in a few months. You've got the letters for Mama and Cece and Grandmama?'

'I have, yes. I will give them to them as soon as I get home. Rest up and relax. You need to grow a big fat baby in there.' Prue patted Millie's stomach. 'Bye-bye baby.' She gave Millie another hug and stepped back. 'I'm not going to cry, so I'll go now. Keep well.'

'And you.' Millie fought back the tears and smiled brightly as Prue walked to Tippy, the motor car.

Jeremy put his arm around Millie. 'I'll be back tomorrow afternoon. Pascal is only in the fields, or at his cottage. Do not lift anything heavy, understand? The men will be back working in the barns and gardens tomorrow if you need help with anything. Is Vivian staying in the chateau tonight?'

'No, she asked me for this Sunday off. She's worked so hard and she wanted to visit her sister in Reims this afternoon. I couldn't say no.'

Jeremy frowned. 'You'll be alone.'

'Hardly. Daisy and Royston are painting the cottage on the other side of the orchard. No doubt, I'll go over and visit them later. Daisy isn't settling well at all. I'll take her something from the kitchen as Vivian will have left the larder full of food. I'll go to bed early tonight and read. I'll be perfectly fine.' She kissed him soundly. 'Go now and drive carefully.'

'I will. Love you.' He kissed her again and walked out to the motor car.

Millie waved and watched them until they turned out of view and closed the door.

Restless, she roamed the silent chateau. Being Sunday most of the workers were in church or at home, those few that lived in the estate's cottages had today off from working.

Not knowing what to do with herself for the first time since she arrived, she wandered the unfinished rooms and mentally took notes. After a while this, too, failed to keep her occupied.

Even though the sun was shining there was an autumn coolness to the light breeze and since waking more grey clouds had gathered, hinting at a possible shower. She pulled on a thin coat from the hook by the back door and headed outside.

In a few weeks it would be Jeremy's birthday and she had to think what to buy him. Yet the main thing on her mind was Jacques. Was it Monsieur Baudin and if it was, did he know Camile had married another man while carrying his baby? She wished she knew the answers. How could she broach such a delicate subject with Baudin? He was a vital key to their business. If he took offence he could retire and leave the estate without an export manager. Jeremy would be furious, as well as hurt.

Her wanderings brought her near the stable quadrangle. Standing in the middle of the saddling yard, she gazed at the surrounding four walls of stables and barns. It was a tale of two halves. One half of the stables were intact, the other a crumbling pile of bricks and stone and gaping holes where once the chateau's thoroughbreds were housed and cared for. In the centre of the yard was a well and beside that a hand-pumped water tap.

The large stone arch in the middle of the far wall led to the drive and the front of the house, while along the wall to the right was an enormous barn. Millie thought it to be all empty, either destroyed or stolen by the Germans, but she glimpsed a carriage.

Investigating further, she noticed it was an old-style carriage, one that hadn't been used for many years. It had a broken axle and was covered in inches of dust. The black paintwork was intact, the gold Dumont crest clearly visible on the doors, but the rats and age had worn and ate the leather interiors, the seat spilling its contents of horse hair padding. In the new age of motor cars, Millie wondered whether it was worth restoring the grand old carriage, but she thought it might be worth it. After all, it would have carried Camile and therefore it was another link for Jeremy to have with his mother.

Deciding she would have it restored before it became any worse, Millie strolled to the other side of the barn. Decades of horse harnesses and tack hung from a multitude of hooks, the smell of old leather and straw was comforting.

A door led into the start of the horse stalls, but they too were empty of beasts. A sad pall of neglect hung over everything. The chateau's horses had long gone, requisitioned by the French Army at the start of the war. All that was left was the smell of horses past and a stable block.

A dove cooed from a beam in the loft as Millie went through another door and into a small office. A simple wooden desk sat under the window overlooking the yard, the walls were bare. She opened the one draw in the desk, but it too was empty.

She walked back outside feeling a little despondent. It was as though this whole area had been stripped of its personality. The vibrancy of a working noisy stable, with snorting horses, the men soothing highly-strung favourites or combing the working ponies, the clop of hooves, the steaming piles of straw, the chat of grooms going about their day was all gone.

In her mind's eye she could see how it once was, a thriving place of industry, with carriages coming and going, young Frenchmen whistling, laughing. How many from this estate had returned from the battlefields?

She'd have to ask Pascal, but the men who worked in the vines now were new to the chateau.

As she passed under the stone arch, she heard a noise. Pausing, she listened. It came from the damaged side of the stables. The noise came again. Not a bang exactly, but a soft clap. Curious, Millie walked into the first stable block on that side. Here the charred ruins of a direct bomb hit had mangled the stalls. Unlike the other side of the stables, which was whole and gloomy, this side had areas of roof missing and light flooded the block. She made her way gingerly, stepping careful over fallen beams and broken walls.

She heard nothing but her own footsteps crunching rubble.

Suddenly, she stopped. A young man, hunched half behind a crumbled pile of stones, stared back at her. He was thin and filthy and had a wildness in his eyes that frightened her.

Millie took a step back, heart pounding.

He raised his hands above his head. *'Guten tag.'*

She stilled. A German. Her throat closed on a scream. She didn't know what to do.

Around him where the debris of food, an opened tin, brown paper wrappings, an apple core. Slowly the man stood, his hands still in the air. He spoke rapid German which Millie couldn't understand, but she saw the desperation in his eyes.

He took a step, still talking.

Millie jumped back, stumbled and held on to a twisted piece of mental railing. 'Go away!'

'Englisch?' He stopped where he was, his face brightening. 'You are Englisch? I like Englisch!'

Millie inched backwards. 'English. Yes.'

'Good! Good! I know Englisch. London! I go to London. See?' His thin dirty face showed joy. 'Buckingham Palace!' he said in heavily accented German.

Millie took another step back. Every instinct told her to run.

The man pointed to his chest. 'Rolf.' He climbed over a pile of rubble towards her. Her eyes widened at his torn trousers, the stained shirt, and a knife wedged in his waistband.

Millie screamed, turned to run and slipped over a charred roof beam. She fell heavily against a stable wall and onto the blackened floor. In a whoosh of breaking timber and choking dust, she was falling again. The noise was incredible, hurting her ears as she fell into an abyss. She landed with a jarring thump that shocked her.

Timber, stones and bricks fell on top of her. She shielded her head and stomach, crying out, as something struck her then all was black.

Chapter Nineteen

Jeremy pulled Tippy to a halt in front of the chateau. He'd driven home from Paris in light rain and his shoulders ached from concentrating on the potholed roads. Tippy was packed solid with baby paraphernalia. He'd started purchasing what Millie had put on the list, but once inside the shops and seeing all the little cute things that would fill the nursery, he couldn't help but buy as much as he could fit in the motor car. Even then, he had asked the rest to be delivered next week.

Grabbing a soft yellow teddy bear from the passenger seat, Jeremy hurried inside as the rain fell heavier. He shrugged off his coat and flung it over a chair, putting his hat on top of it. Royston would collect it later and hang it up in the ante-room off the entrance hall. He liked that Royston was back. It'd become a chore to take care of his own clothes.

'Millie!' The salon was empty, not even a fire lit.

Frowning, he realised the chateau was deathly quiet. Where were the workmen? It was Monday. The place should be heaving with workers plastering or painting the rooms.

With one foot on the stairs, he heard a door open.

'Monsieur Remington!' Vivian hurried up to him, the worried look on her face made his heart plummet.

'What is it? Where is my wife?'

'We do not know!' Vivian twisted her hands together and lapsed into fast French.

Jeremy strained to hear her correctly. 'What do you mean she can't be found?' Scared, he tried to keep his voice calm as she spoke quickly again. 'In English!'

Vivian took a deep breath. 'I came to kitchen this morning. No food eaten. I went up to Madam Remington's room with hot water. No madam. Bed made.' Her face crumbled. 'No food eaten, monsieur!'

A jumble of thoughts whirled in his mind. Had Millie left him?

He raced up the stairs taking two at a time. He ran into their bedroom and flung open the armoire she'd wanted brought from the other wing. Her clothes still hung on the hangers. He yanked open each of her drawers, but all her slips and petticoats and underwear remained neatly folded. He glanced around, looking for clues, but everything remained the same as when he left yesterday morning.

He ran downstairs, nearly turning an ankle in his haste. Vivian waited for him. 'Have you searched the whole chateau?'

'*Oui,* every room.' She nodded vigorously. '*Le grenier*... er... loft? Madam not there.'

'And the grounds?'

'*Oui, monsieur.*' Tears filled her eyes. 'Pascal searching. Pascal take men.'

Jeremy ran down the corridor and outside the back door into the rain, Vivian close on his heels.

'Pascal!' he yelled as loud as he could, cupping his hands against the rain.

'Sir Jeremy!' Royston, drenched in a long dark coat and boots, came from the path that led to the orchard. 'Thank God you're back.'

'Where have you searched?'

'Everywhere I can think of. That Pascal fellow has spent the last hour walking the vines rows with some men incase Lady Remington has fallen in a trench.'

'Yes, she might have done. We've filled in a great many trenches, but there are some left in the woods and by the river we've not got to yet.' Jeremy ran for the woods. 'We need to search there. Has Daisy seen her?'

'No.' Royston ran beside him. 'We both came over yesterday evening to say hello and Daisy wanted to show Lady Remington a new baby jacket she'd finished knitting. The house was quiet, and we thought her to be taking a nap or a bath. So, we went back to the cottage.'

'You should have checked, man!'

Royston paled, the rain running down his face. 'Forgive me, sir.'

'What if she's hurt somewhere?'

'I'm sorry, sir,' Royston puffed as they ran.

'I should never have left her.' Fear clutched his heart as they burst through the woods calling her name.

They ran down the side of the river, Jeremy calling for her. His insides turned to jelly at the thought of her falling in the river and drowning.

'Millie!' He screamed her name repeatedly.

'We need to call the police, sir,' Royston said as they headed back towards the orchard.

'We need to keep looking!' Jeremy sprinted back to the courtyard and then began searching each barn. He scoured every corner, climbed every ladder leading to the storage areas above.

When every barn was searched, they headed for the stables. The rain fell heavier, a grey gloom descended over the landscape.

'Millie!' Jeremy called again and again in desperation.

'Monsieur Remington!'

Jeremy froze as he heard his name being shouted. He hurried out of the stable block, Royston by his side.

'*Monsieur Remington*! Come quick!' François, one of the gardeners, beckoned him from the small building beside the chateau that led down to the cellars.

'Have you found her?' Jeremy asked, pounding through puddles to reach him as fast as he could.'

'*Oui! Oui!*'

Lanterns were lit lighting the main passage way through the cellars. François, fast and physically fit, sprinted ahead, past the racks of bottles and deeper into the warren of cellars that spread like fingers under the estate.

Fear pulsed through Jeremy as they edged into the crumbled mass of one length of cellar which had taken a direct hit in a bombing. The lanterns didn't reach down this far, but ahead in the dark he could see the flickering glow of light.

Pascal hurried to meet him. 'She is in there.' He pointed to a destruction of stones, broken timbers and bricks.

Jeremy clambered over the rocks they'd already pulled out. Someone held up a lantern and he could make out a shoe.

Millie's shoe.

The blood left his face. Sickness rose to his throat. He groaned deep in his chest. His darling girl. The love of his life.

He started digging. Frantic wild clawing of the rocks and timbers that held her prisoner.

'Help me!' he screamed. He had flashbacks of digging men out of collapsed trenches. Of pulling at arms and legs only for them not to be attached to bodies. He began to shake, tremors convulsing his body. The darkness closed in on him. No! No! No more bodies!

'She'll be fine, sir!' Royston gripped his shoulders and yelled into his face. 'We'll get her out!'

Like a demented army they pulled away bricks, hauled at timber beams. The dust made them cough, the golden lights wobbled as the air moved about delicate flames.

Jeremy, unable to utter a word, such was his emotion, ripped his hands and nails to get to her. He would save her. She wouldn't be another body to bury. Not Millie, not his beautiful Millie.

When a beam was lifted on the straining men's shoulders, Jeremy crawled into the space it revealed and to Millie's side. His hands shook so much he couldn't touch her properly. She was hunched over, protecting her stomach. Dust covered her face. Blood had dried on her forehead.

'Millie. Darling…' He tried to feel for a pulse on her neck, but he couldn't move.

Suddenly, in front of him was a dead soldier, a young boy, blue eyes wide and staring, blood on his face.

Jeremy backed away. No, no, not blue eyes… Millie's eyes were blue.

'Sir,' Royston shoved him to one side. 'Lady Remington, can you hear me?' He moved her, manhandling her out into the open.

Dazed, Jeremy stared at her blue eyes. A gulf of grief filled his chest, his head…

'Sir! Sir!' Royston shook him. 'She's alive!'

~ ~ ~ ~

Millie woke to quietness.

The bedroom was in darkness, with just a soft glow from the lamps on either side of the bed. Outside, a half moon shone through the window. She really must get some curtains. She moved her legs and a shooting pain went up her thigh and she moaned.

'Darling!' Jeremy shot up from a chair by the bed. 'How do you feel?'

She turned and frowned at him. 'My leg hurts.'

'Yes, darling. You've quite a lot of cuts and bruises.'

'I do?'

'Do you not remember? You fell. We found you in the cellar.'

'I fell?'

'You were in the stables.' Tears slipped over Jeremy's lashes and it broke her heart to see him crying.

She reached up and touched his cheek. Then it came back to her. The sensation of falling, the hard landing that felt like she'd broken her whole body. She jerked in sudden fear. 'The baby!' Her hands went to her stomach and she felt it's hard roundness.

'The doctor says the baby is fine, but you must rest for many days, weeks even.' Jeremy voice caught. 'He says you've caused a bit of damage to your legs, but he's confident they aren't broken. He'll be back in the morning, unless I send for him. Do you want me to?'

'No. I'm just sore.' She moved a little and felt a general sense of tenderness and discomfort all over.

'I thought I had lost you.' He kissed her hands, squeezing them tightly.

'I'm sorry.' She felt so guilty for worrying him. She kissed his hands in return, noting the cuts and scrapes, the broken fingernails.

'I'm just happy you and the baby are safe.'

'Are you certain the doctor said the baby is fine?' She lay still waiting for any spasm of pain to indicate she'd go into premature labour like last time.

He nodded. 'The doctor is from Épernay, young and he seemed very knowledgeable. He served his country. I liked and trusted his opinion. He could hear the baby's heartbeat through some instrument he used. He let me hear it, too.'

'You did?' she asked surprised and awed.

More tears flowed, and Jeremy wiped them away hastily. 'I did,' he whispered. 'It's a strong heartbeat.' Jeremy placed his hands on Millie's stomach and she felt the baby move.

'Did you feel that?' she asked, crying now as her baby moved within her.

'I did. He or she is a little fighter. The doctor said the baby was a good size for six months. I told him of your past and the visit to the specialist doctor in Paris. He also thinks early January for delivery and he said he'd come out and attend to you if you wish it.'

'I won't leave this bed,' Millie promised, hot tears burning behind her eyes. 'I promise you, I won't do anything to risk our baby.'

Jeremy smiled and kissed her gently. 'Don't worry, I shan't allow it!' He pulled the chair closer to the side of the bed. 'Why were you in the stables? You know I forbade anyone to go there. What if another unexploded bomb had been in there?'

'I know, and I'm sorry.'

'Pascal found you only because he was searching in the cellars, thinking you may have gone down there and fallen, but when he saw fresh debris and fallen stone he knew something had happened. That part of the cellar is directly under the damaged stable block.'

Millie moved and felt the ache in her legs. 'I was simply taking a look, on the other side of the stables, not the damaged side. Then I heard a noise.'

'A noise?'

'Yes, from the damaged side. I went to investigate.'

'Oh, Millie, darling. You should have gone and found Pascal.'

'I didn't think. I just went in.' She stared at Jeremy, wondering if she had imagined the German man.

'And?'

'And there was someone in there.'

'Who?'

'A German man. He spoke German to me and well, he frightened me. He was like a wild man, dirty, thin, living amongst the rubble and there were food scraps round him. When he stood up, he had a knife in his belt. I went to run away, and I fell. I remember nothing else.'

'You fell and the weakened floor broke, sending you down into the cellar.' Jeremy rubbed his face.

'No one has mentioned a German being about the place.'

'He was homeless,' Millie murmured. 'I'm sorry I didn't handle the situation better.'

'Nonsense. It's not your fault. You saw a knife. Of course, you'd be frightened. I'd be worried, too. A German with a knife is no laughing matter. There are still many Germans who refuse to believe the war is over. They want to continue the fight. They don't wish to be the losers. You were right to be scared and make a run for it.' Jeremy stood and kissed her gently. 'You were actually very brave.'

'Where are you going?'

'To talk to Pascal, and to Royston. I want the whole estate searched and guarded in case this German is still about.'

'He wouldn't be though, surely? He'd have run away thinking me to be dead.'

'Perhaps, but if he'd been a decent person he'd have gone for help, not left you.'

'Come straight back.'

He kissed her again. 'I will. I'll send Vivian up to sit with you. She's been upset all day.'

When he had gone only a minute, Vivian was instantly beside her. 'Madam!' She knelt by the bed, crying and mumbling in French that Millie couldn't understand.

'Vivian, please. It is all right now. Come, sit down on the chair.'

Sniffling into a handkerchief, Vivian composed herself. 'I so sorry.'

'There's nothing to be sorry for. I was the one who got myself into this mess.'

'Monsieur Remington…' Vivian cried some more. 'I thought he would kill himself. He couldn't find you. Frantic!' She lapsed into French again and Millie found it hard to follow her.

'I'm safe now, and so is the baby.'

'Le bébé!' Vivian broke into fresh weeping.

A knock on the door preceded Daisy. 'Lady Remington?'

'Come in.' Millie smiled a welcome to Daisy.

'Le thé,' Vivian announced.

'Tea would be lovely, thank you.' Millie smiled her thanks as Vivian left the room.

'You are feeling better, madam?' Daisy asked from the end of the bed.

'Yes, a bit sore, but just relieved the baby is well.'

'Sir Jeremy and Royston have gone to speak to Pascal. So, I thought to come and see how you are.'

'Sit down.' Millie waved to the chair.

Daisy sat, her smile hesitant.

'What is it, Daisy?'

'Well, I don't want to alarm you, but I feel you should know that… well… Royston said I shouldn't bother you with it…'

'Tell me.'

'When they found you, before they managed to get you out of the rubble, Sir Jeremy… he was in a bad way. Royston said Sir Jeremy had an episode. I just wanted you to know so that you're aware. I know you mentioned that Sir Jeremy has been very good since you arrived here, and well… I just thought you should know.'

'Thank you. I'm glad you told me.'

Daisy's shoulders relaxed. 'I thought it wouldn't be my place, but I know how concerned you were about him when you were at Remington Court. My Royston said Sir Jeremy is doing so much better now he's in his mother's home.'

'He is, and it is now our home, too.' Anxiety filled Millie. Her fall had caused Jeremy to have a relapse, and that he suffered through her hurt more than she could say.

'Will you ever return to Remington Court, madam?'

Millie shook her head. 'No, Daisy. Chateau Dumont is our home.'

'Then I shall work hard to make it my home, too, for Royston won't desert Sir Jeremy and I won't desert my husband.'

Jeremy entered the room carrying a tea tray and Daisy said goodbye and hurried out.

'What did Pascal say?' Millie asked as he brought over her teacup and saucer.

Jeremy yawned, sat on the chair and took off his shoes. 'There has been no sign of a stranger around the estate this afternoon or evening. He'd have nowhere to hide after us searching the entire estate looking for you. I would say that German has moved on by now. However, Pascal will notify the police in Épernay tomorrow. His cousin is in the force, and Pascal will ask for them to keep an eye on the estate and surrounds for a while.'

'Good. I'm pleased. Come and get into bed.' She nibbled at a soft pastry Vivian had added to the tray.

He paused in pulling off his socks. 'In with you? No, I'll sleep in the other room, Prue's room. I wouldn't want to disturb you during the night or accidently touch your legs and hurt you.'

'You won't. I want you here in this bed with me. I need your arms around me. Do I need to beg my husband?' She raised an eyebrow as she sipped her tea.

He grinned and stripped off his clothes. 'If you insist.'

Once he was beside her, she cuddled up to him. 'Are you all right?'

'Me?' He frowned. 'Yes, why wouldn't I be?'

'Because I know you suffered while digging me out of the cellar.'

There was a long pause before he spoke again. 'Yes. It was difficult. So many times I've dug men out of collapsed trenches, or bombed buildings.'

'And I made you relive it all again.' She laid her head against his chest. 'I hate that I put you through that again.'

He kissed the top of her head. 'It's not as though you did it on purpose, my love.'

'You may have a bad night, tonight.'

'I'm not intending to sleep. I just want to lay here and hold you. I thought today I had lost you and I will admit that the thought of not having you in my life is intolerable. So, let me indulge in holding you.'

'I'd like nothing more.'

'My mother's letters are still on the drawers. I might read them. Have you done so?'

She swallowed, her heart twisting. 'I have, yes.'

'And?'

'There is something I would discuss with you.'

Jeremy sighed deeply. 'It'll be regarding my father, won't it?'

She jerked up. 'What do you mean?'

'He made her so unhappy. I really can't deal with thinking of him tonight. Tell me another day.'

She remained quiet and wrapped her arms around his waist. She had to tell him.

The baby kicked, and Jeremy grunted happily and rubbed her stomach. 'Sometimes the past can stay in the past, especially when we have a wonderful future to look forward to.'

She nodded and felt even more torn.

Chapter Twenty

A roaring fire filled the salon with warmth and added to the glow of golden light from the chandeliers and lamps.

Millie sat on one side of the sofa and watched Jeremy and Monsieur Baudin as they discussed France's economy. Although she had no interest in the conversation, she was happy to be out of bed. For over a week she'd remained confined to bedrest. The lovely young doctor from Épernay, Doctor Duguay, came every day to check on her and she liked him very much. After a week, her sore legs and general body tenderness grew less bothersome and Doctor Duguay announced she could sit on a chair by the bed and perhaps take gentle strolls around the room.

Jeremy, Daisy and Vivian attended to her every need and she was certain she'd put on more weight than was necessary from the inactivity and delicious food that was brought up on tray after tray.

By the second week she was bored senseless, and spent her time writing many letters to her family, knitting baby clothes with Daisy and making enquiries to hire a nanny. Jeremy had the idea to make a start on the nursery and spent days painting the room next to their bedroom in a soft yellow. Thick rugs arrived from Paris and also enough baby furniture for three babies.

Four days after he started, Jeremy held a hand over her eyes and gently led her into the completed room. She stood in awe of the bright sunny room, filled with toys and clothes. In the corner was a white rocking chair that was just for her.

Once Doctor Duguay declared she was well enough to go downstairs and resume her normal life, Millie had written to Monsieur Baudin and invited him and his wife to stay for Jeremy's birthday.

Yesterday, as the October winds and rains battered the chateau, Monsieur Baudin arrived minus his wife, who had remained in Paris to take care of her sick and frail elderly sister.

After a long dinner of many courses, Vivian brought in coffee and an array of cheeses. Monsieur Baudin gave her a dazzling smile and numerous compliments about the wonderful dinner they'd just devoured. His charm was spontaneous and genuine. Millie had noticed it on the several times she'd been in his company. Baudin was a natural flirt and delightful with it.

She also wondered if perhaps it was his charm and good looks that Camile had fallen for over thirty-seven years ago. 'Monsieur Baudin, did you grow up in this area?'

'Please, madam, I have asked you many times to call me, John, or Jacques.' He smiled and turned in his chair to give her his full attention.

'Forgive me, you have indeed told me that repeatedly.'

He sipped his coffee and relaxed in the chair. 'I grew up in a small village outside of Reims. My family were bakers. We owned the only mill for miles.'

'A mill?'

'Yes. My père grounded the wheat to make bread and my mère baked the loaves.'

'And you didn't want to follow in their footsteps?'

He shook his head. '*Non.* Years of working as a child showed me it was hard backbreaking work and I wouldn't be rich.' He chuckled. 'Besides, my old brother, he wanted to do it. As a young man I worked in various vineyards, this one was my favourite, but my calling wasn't to make the champagne but to drink it!'

Jeremy put another log on the fire. 'Jacques has a nose for it, as one might say. The best in the business!'

'*Oui!*' Jacques grinned.

'My grandfather saw the potential in Jacques one summer, didn't he?'

'*Oui.* A great man. Much respected in the industry. Chateau Dumont Champagne was on the rise and he wanted the world to know it.' Jacques gazed into the flames. 'I told him I could do that for him.' He shook his head. 'Ahh, the confidence of youth. He sent me to Paris and told me to show him I was not all talk.'

'And you did it,' Millie said, watching him carefully. 'Did you often come back here to the chateau?'

'*Oui.* It became my second home, but mainly I stayed in Paris and then of course I started to travel the world selling the champagne.'

'Did you know Camile very well?'

Jacques paused in sipping his coffee. '*Oui.* A great beauty. Everyone loved her.'

'You must have been sorry to see her move to England?' Millie didn't know how far she could take this line of questioning especially as Jeremy stood very still beside the fireplace.

'Her marriage was quickly done. I was away in Italy at the time.'

'You never got to say goodbye?'
'Non.'
'Why was her marriage so sudden?'
'I do not know.' He gave her a look that spoke volumes; sadness, interest and curiosity as to why she was asking these questions.

Jeremy picked up the fire poker and stabbed at the ashes in the grate to let more air through. 'Was that the start of our alliance with some of the Italian companies? I've read through the sales history and we sold very well there towards the latter half of the last century.'

Jacques sat up straighter. 'It was the beginning of our friendship with the Italians, *oui.* From there I was able to expand into Greece and Spain.'

Millie watched the two men as they once more discussed business and suddenly she saw the resemblance. They both smiled the same way. This evening Jacques had clipped his beard very short and it shaped his jaw much closer, it was the same shape as Jeremy's. As the truth dawned on Millie she felt utterly wretched. It wasn't some young picker called Jacques that Camile had an affair with, it was Monsieur Baudin.

~ ~ ~ ~

After breakfast the following morning, Millie was in the nursery, adding a finished little knitted jacket she'd made to the pile. From the drawer she lifted a tiny delicate little pair of socks.

'Excusez moi,' Jacques stood in the doorway and gave a small bow of his head. 'Forgive me, madam.'

'Please, do come in.

Jacques gazed around the room, touching the teddy bear Jeremy had placed in the corner of the cot. 'It is a delightful room.'

'Yes. Jeremy has done so well.'

'Becoming a new father is an exciting time.'

Millie knew Jacques and his wife had no children of their own. She waited for him to speak.

'You are curious about Camile,' he said, walking to the large window that overlooked the front gardens. 'It is to be expected as she was Jeremy's mother and the daughter of this house.'

'I have read her letters,' Millie said quietly. 'Letters she wrote to Paulina.'

'Ah, Paulina. Yes. Her dear friend and married to Camile's cousin Michel.'

'Yes.'

He stared out of the window for some time. 'You know of our affair.'

'I've worked it out that you are the Jacques she mentioned, and now you've confirmed it.'

'What else do you know?'

'I believe you are Jeremy's father.'

'What did you just say?' Jeremy's voice from the doorway made them both jump.

Millie spun around. 'Jeremy!'

A cold light had entered Jeremy's eyes. 'Perhaps we should have this discussion downstairs and not in my child's nursery.' Abruptly he left, and Millie hurried after him. At a slower pace Jacques followed.

In the salon, Jeremy poured himself a whisky, despite it being only eleven o'clock. 'This is what you wanted to talk to me about?' he snapped at Millie.

She sat down, heart racing. 'Yes.'

Jacques entered the room, but remained standing. 'It was a long time ago.'

'When was it exactly?' Jeremy demanded. 'Nine months before I was born, perhaps?'

Jacques lifted his hands in appeal. 'Before she married your father.'

'Only he isn't Jeremy's father, is he?' Millie murmured.

Jeremy stared at her as though she'd sprouted horns out of her head. 'Can you explain yourself, please?'

Millie looked from one to the other, then seeing the confusion in Jeremy's eyes, she glanced away. 'Camile wrote to Paulina that she was with child when she married Sir Soames.'

Jacques swore and spoke in French, turning away in anguish.

'She was pregnant with me?'

'Yes, you.' Millie nodded, her heart breaking for the man she loved. 'But Soames wasn't the father, darling.'

A stillness came over the room. No one wanted to move or speak.

Finally, Millie stood. 'I shall fetch the letters. You can read them for yourself.'

'No!' Jeremy shouted. 'He will tell me what he knows.' He glared at Jacques.

'Darling, sit down,' Millie placed a hand on Jeremy's arm, but he shrugged her away. 'I need to know. If Soames Remington isn't my father, then who is? Him?' He pointed to the other man.

'I must be,' Jacques whispered.

Millie's stomach clenched. Jeremy's face paled.

Jacques went to the drinks trolley and poured himself a whisky as well.

The devastation on both men's faces made tears spring to Millie's eyes. The atmosphere was thick with unspoken words and hurt and loss.

'I shall fetch the letters,' she said.

'You don't need the letters, ma chère.' Jacques went and sat on the winged back chair by the fire. He took a long sip of whisky, put the glass on the table beside the chair and then sat forward, his hands hanging limp between his knees.

'Tell me,' Jeremy whispered.

'I came to Chateau Dumont to work in the vines as a young man, but soon I was gaining the notice of your grandfather for my hard work and my talent of selecting the right wines to create a good vintage. As you say, I had a nose for it. Your grandfather liked me. I was young, handsome, full of myself, confident. He took a great interest in me, inviting me to dinners and so on. It was not the done thing, you understand. I was a poor boy, a baker's boy. Your grandmother didn't like me, and she had reason to for I had fallen in love with Camile and she with me. But I wasn't good enough, your grandmother told me that to my face.' Jacques huffed. 'Camile was forbidden. She was to marry much higher than a baker's son. Your grandmother told your grandfather to send me away to Paris, to prove myself. I thought it was a test and that if I became very good and made them rich and famous I would have Camile. Then your grandmother died, and things changed. Your grandfather wanted Camile married and off his hands. I believe your grandmother made him promise her on her deathbed to marry Camile to someone titled.'

'Why did you not come back for her?' Jeremy accused.

'Because I was away and… I was living the good life. I had money and position, women… I had to prove myself. I thought Camile would wait for me. We were so young…' Jacques shrugged. 'Her letters to me stopped arriving. I thought perhaps she had stopped loving me. I was hurt. Pride wouldn't let me return here to beg. Then I received a letter from your grandfather announcing Camile's engagement to Sir Remington. Your grandfather was so happy. Also, in that letter, were instructions to go to Italy and forge business alliances there. So, I went.'

'You left her?' Millie asked. 'You never went back to tell her you loved her?'

'Non.' Jacques threw back the rest of the whisky. 'It was the biggest mistake and regret of my life.' He waved the empty glass at Jeremy. 'Doubly so now.'

Jeremy jerked to his feet. 'I am not Soames Remington's son. All those years of him hating me and now I know why. He must have guessed I wasn't his.' He rubbed a hand over his face. 'God! I'm not even entitled to the Barony. I am not Sir Remington! My whole life is a lie…'

'My love…' Millie hated to see the hurt on his face.

'Je suis désolé.'

Jeremy's lips curled. 'I don't care if you're sorry!'

'Jeremy!' Millie went to him. 'This is not Jacques fault. He knew nothing about you being his son until today.'

'He slept with my mother!' Jeremy sneered at Jacques. 'You forgot all about her once you got to Paris, didn't you? You'd had your fun and didn't care that she was forced to marry a cold-hearted monster to save her reputation!'

'You don't know that.' Millie pulled Jeremy away for she thought he would hit the other man. 'No one knows what Camile was thinking at that time.'

Jacques stood. 'If I had known she carried my child nothing would have stopped me being with her.'

'But you could have asked her why she was marrying so quickly. Didn't you think something might be wrong? When you fuck someone the chances of a baby are rather high!'

'Jeremy!' Millie gasped at the language. Then suddenly she felt a whoosh of water between her legs that seemed never to stop. 'Oh my God!'

Jeremy frowned. 'Darling?'

Jacques stared at the puddle on the floor. *'Le bébé!'*

Millie blinked as it dawned on her. She started to shake. 'No! No! Not again. Jeremy!'

Chapter Twenty-One

Millie blew hard, puffing her cheeks to push the baby's head out. Doctor Duguay was at the end of the bed, giving instructions in French which Vivian relayed to Millie.

'I can't do it!' Millie huffed, angry and annoyed. She glanced at the clock as she rested back against the mountain of pillows Daisy had piled behind her back. It was close to midnight and she was tired.

'It won't be long now, madam,' Daisy encouraged.

'How do you know?' Millie sighed as another pain squeezed her inside like a vice. She didn't want to have the baby yet, it was too soon. It would be so small and would die as the other one had.

'Good, madam, good,' Vivian encouraged, rubbing her arm.

She wanted to yell at them all, to tell them to shut up and get out. She wanted her mama.

Bearing down, she grabbed her legs and pushed with all her might. Her head was saying no but her body was in control.

'Stop, madam!' Doctor Duguay commanded, his hands busy between her legs.

'I can see the head, madam!' Daisy near shouted.

Panting, Millie rested. It was all surreal. She felt sick and panicky.

'Poussez!' Duguay instructed.

Daisy helped Millie up for her to begin pushing again. Within several long pushes, Millie felt a sensation of sharp pain, then slithering, and finally the pressure was gone.

'You've done it, madam!' Daisy cried.

There was a flurry of activity at the end of the bed.

Millie strained to look. Where was the cry? Why wasn't the baby crying? Fear gripped her heart. She couldn't see anything. Why wouldn't they let her see?

Vivian helped the doctor who was intently working at the bottom of the bed.

Millie glanced at Daisy who was also watching the end of the bed.

'I want my baby.' Millie glared at them. Not again would she not see her baby before it was taken away.

'Soon, madam,' Vivian soothed.

'No, damn you!' Millie hitched herself up further, ignoring the blood and the mess. Her gaze was fixed on the tiny little baby lying between her feet. 'Give it to me!' she growled, hating them all. The last baby had been taken away without her seeing him. She wasn't even allowed to bury him for it he hadn't been classified as a baby. Not this time.

'I said give him to me.'

'Madam, he is small,' Doctor Duguay wrapped the baby in a blanket that had been warming in front of the fire. He rubbed the baby vigorously.

'I *said* give me my baby!' She reached for the bundle ready to scream and fight them.

Carefully, Doctor Duguay came to the side of the bed and gently handed her the tightly wrapped baby. 'He is breathing, but he is small, madam…'

'A boy.' Millie kissed his wet forehead. All she could see was his tiny face, squashed in the tight folds of the blanket. He made a slight noise, no more than a murmur and it was enough. Millie cried, the tears falling over her lashes and she couldn't stop them.

'Madam, we should get you to hospital. In Paris.' Doctor Duguay spoke, once more at the end of the bed. 'But first we deliver the afterbirth, *oui?*'

She ignored the doctor and held her son closer to her chest. 'I'm cold, Daisy. Will you fetch me a blanket, please?'

'Yes, madam.' Daisy fetched another blanket that also had been airing in front of the fire.

'Wrap it around us both.'

Once Daisy had secured the blanket around Millie and the baby, Millie relaxed against the pillows. She looked at Doctor Duguay. 'Help me keep him alive.'

Doctor Duguay nodded. 'First afterbirth, and then we take you both to Paris. You were not due for two months. He's very early. He needs to be in an incubator. Do you know what that is?'

'I know, I've been reading about them.'

'Good, then you will understand that he must be kept in one of those all the time, in hospital.'

'Then we go to the hospital.'

'Will you feed him?' Vivian asked.

Millie looked down at his darling little face and her heart melted. 'Yes. It is what's best for him. I read that, too.'

Duguay cleared his throat. 'Madam, sometimes little babies do not feed well… There are many dangers for him to overcome.'

She knew what he meant behind those words. He was preparing her for the worst. A fierce determination filled Millie until she could think of nothing else. 'But he is here, and he is alive, and we will keep him that way.'

Doctor Duguay nodded and concentrated on delivering the afterbirth, which was unpleasant, but

Millie didn't care as she held onto her son, willing him to feel her love and warmth and to keep surviving.

Vivian gathered the soiled bedding while Daisy washed Millie and helped her into a clean nightgown, a difficult job as Millie refused to put down the baby. Duguay instructed Vivian and Daisy to keep blankets on the rack in front of the fire and to alternate them around the baby every ten minutes.

'I will inform your husband, madam, and make arrangements. I'll return soon,' he said.

Millie glanced up at the doctor as the others left the room. 'Thank you so much for all you have done.'

Within minutes, Jeremy was beside her, kissing her face and marvelling at the baby. 'We have a son, my darling,' he said in awe.

'We do. Isn't he beautiful?' Millie pulled the blanket closer around her son.

'He is, as are you,' Jeremy's voice wobbled.

'We are to go to Paris, to hospital. He needs to be in an incubator. Remember that book I showed you about them? It will keep him warm.'

'Yes, and we'll go very soon. Doctor Duguay is coming with us. He's returning to Épernay where he knows there is an ambulance. So, you can lie down all the way there. I'll follow in Tippy.'

Millie kissed the baby and then Jeremy. 'We will not lose him.'

'Darling, he is so small...'

'He will make it, I know it.'

Worry creased Jeremy's forehead. 'I've been so anxious. Sitting alone down there for hours was driving me slowly insane.'

'Alone? Where is Jacques?'

'Gone.'

'Gone? Where? What do you mean?'

Jeremy shrugged. 'In all the panic and while I was carrying you up here he must have gone. When I returned downstairs when the doctor arrived, Jacques was no longer about.' Jeremy touched their baby's soft cheek. 'We do not need him.'

'Jeremy…'

'No. Do not talk of him. He left the very day his grandson was born. He didn't stay to see if either of you made it through. He means nothing to us now.' Jeremy bent over and gently took the baby from Millie.

Although her arms ached, she felt the loss of warmth immediately 'Wrap him up!' She quickly wrapped the extra blankets around Jeremy as he sat in the chair and nearly fell out of bed doing so.

'Calm down, darling. I have him and he is warm. Rest yourself. You've a journey ahead of you.'

A knock on the door preceded Vivian who came in carrying a tray of drinks and food. 'Madam, Monsieur…' She placed the tray on the dresser. 'Monsieur Baudin is downstairs.'

Surprised, Millie reached for the baby. 'You must go down and speak to him. Much was said earlier. You cannot leave it as it is.'

'The man left the house when a crisis was happening!'

'Please, Jeremy,' Millie begged tiredly. 'He has returned in the middle of the night, it must be important.'

Once he had gone, Vivian brought over another warmed blanket and carefully Millie wrapped it around the baby, admiring his tiny features.

'*Le belle bébé*' Vivian crooned. 'You have a name for him?'

'Not yet.' Millie settled back more comfortably. Tiredness overcame her in waves, but she dare not sleep, not yet. They had to get to Paris. 'You go to bed, Vivian. It is so very late.'

'*Non,* not until you have left. I can sleep tomorrow.'

In hurried movements, Jeremy entered and came beside the bed. 'You'll never guess what Jacques has brought us?'

'What?'

'An incubator!' Jeremy was jubilant.

'He's what? How?'

'As soon as you went into labour he drove back to Paris and spoke with a friend of his who is a baby doctor. Jacques hired an incubator from him and has brought it here.'

'*Hired.* Is that possible?'

'Who cares if it is hired, bought or stolen. We have one!' Jeremy shrugged. 'I think we may have to supply this doctor free champagne for the rest of his life, but it's a worthy price to pay.'

'Will it work? I mean we don't know how to use one. What if it's broken and we delay going to the hospital?'

'Duguay will know, and if it is good and he says we can use it for the baby, then we can learn what to do.' Jeremy kissed her. 'This means you and the baby don't have to go to Paris. We can stay home and be together.'

They heard a noise outside the door.

Jeremy stood and went out only to return a few moments later with Jacques, who entered shyly.

'Millie, Jacques and Royston have brought the incubator upstairs into the nursery. As soon as Doctor Duguay returns we'll get it started for the little fellow.' Jeremy smiled down at the baby.

She held out her hand to the older man. *'Merci beaucoup!'*

Jacques took her hand and kissed it. He gazed down at the baby. 'The pleasure is all mine, ma chère. I must give my grandson the best possible chance in life, since I wasn't there for my own son.' Jacques swallowed, his eyes filling with unshed tears.

Millie looked at Jeremy. 'We want you to be a part of our lives, don't we, Jeremy?'

Before he could answer, Jacques held up his hand. 'I know it won't be easy, and there is much to discuss, but I would like to be a grandfather, if not a father.' He glanced hopefully at Jeremy.

Jeremy gave the slightest of nods, his eyes wary.

Much later, as a rooster crowed in the dawn and the whole house slept late, Millie left the bed and walked into the nursery. An exhausted Doctor Duguay was sleeping in the rocking chair by the window, having said he'd stay for the rest of the night to monitor the baby. Millie wondered how they would ever repay the man for his dedication.

Jeremy sat napping beside the incubator, where their little boy lay curled up inside.

Millie stood and watched her baby sleeping.

Jeremy stirred and woke up. 'Is he all right,' he whispered urgently, kissing her cheek. 'Sorry. I didn't mean to fall asleep.'

She pointed to the slight rise and fall of the baby's chest. 'He's sleeping.' She stepped closer and peered into the box made of wood and glass with what looked like a small boiler at the side. She could feel the heat emanating from it. 'How does it work?' she whispered.

'The boiler feeds hot water underneath in the compartment down here.' Jeremy pointed to below the box. 'Tubes circulate the warm air around him. You lift this glass panel to take him in and out or to change him and so forth.'

'Will I be able to feed him?'

'Duguay says yes and he wants you to do it before he leaves today.'

Millie nodded both delighted and scared at the thought of feeding her son.

Jeremy peered in closer to the glass. 'He's like a little chicken in there. You know how they keep chicks warm in those boxes with lamps over them?'

Millie smiled. 'Yes, he's our little chick.'

'We need to name him, Millie.' Jeremy gave her a worrying look. 'Just in case…'

'He will make it, Jeremy,' she whispered harshly back at him. 'Think positively!'

'Sorry. Yes, of course.'

She thought for a minute. 'I quite like Jonathan Lionel Remington.'

'Remington…' Jeremy sighed.

She wrapped her arm through his. 'We can't change the past. We are all Remingtons.'

'I am a fraud.'

'You fought for your country, you have estates in two countries that feed and home many people. If you give all that up, then you walk away from hundreds of people relying on you for their way of life. Can you do that? Can you walk away from all your responsibilities?'

'But I'm not a Sir.'

'So? What about me and the baby? What will we be if not Remington? It is the name your mother wanted you to have. She must have thought it through before she married Soames. It was her choice. She could have contacted Jacques, but she didn't.'

'And we'll never know why she didn't.' He stared at their baby, lost in thought.

'Perhaps she felt Soames was the better option? Maybe she thought that her baby would have a better future as a Remington. At the time she wasn't to know how Soames really was, did she?'

Jeremy let out a long breath. 'You believe I should stay as a Remington then?'

'I do. It is done. In the past. We have to think of our future and our baby.'

'Jonathan Lionel…'

Millie gazed at her tiny little son. 'Lionel, after his grandfather and Jonathan is a form of Jacques, and Jacques is his other grandfather and the man who has given us this gift to keep our son alive. It's fitting.'

Jeremy hugged her to him. 'You are right, as always.'

She rested her head against his shoulder as they watched their baby sleep. 'What a journey we have travelled so far, and I believe we have much further to go.'

Jeremy kissed the top of her head. 'As long as we are together, then we can make it.'

She breathed deeply, feeling as happy as she'd ever been.

Author Note

Hello Readers,

I hope you enjoyed book one of this new Marsh Saga series.

Millie was a new era for me to write. I'd never written a story set in the 1920s before and had to research a lot about how women were stretching the boundaries of their independence and freedom. The end of WWI brought many changes, but at the bottom of it all, women were still expected to marry well and raise children. I wanted that for Millie because she is the oldest and would naturally lead the way for her sisters. Yet, I also wanted to show each sister as being unique. *Millie* was a joy to write and I hope you liked meeting the Marsh family. I've added a short excerpt of the next book, which is about Prue, Millie's sister you met in this book. However, there is an accompanying novella, *Christmas at the Chateau*, which fits between *Millie* and *Prue* that explores the family a little more. I hope you enjoy the novella as well.

After *Prue*, there will be Cece's story, and also Alice's story, Prue's friend – you will meet her soon.

Lastly, I plan to write another story which will be Grandmama's life, and how she defied the Victorian rules to be her own woman. She is such a great character I couldn't leave her out!

AnneMarie Brear
2019.

Prue

Chapter One

London, 1921.

Prue Marsh sauntered through the elegant shop belonging to Mrs Eve Yolland, dressmaker. The walls of dark mahogany shelving held bolts of material of numerous colours, arranged in shades from light to dark. Excellent light came from the large front windows, illuminating the tasteful, and discreet arrangement of accessories any woman should have the need to purchase. Assortments of beaded bags, lawn handkerchiefs, kidskin gloves, jewelled headdresses and shimmering shawls drew Prue's attention. But today, her hands merely drifted over the displayed finery, her mind wandering.

Restless.

She was always restless. Her mother said she needed a husband and house to organise, but such mundane options failed to inspire her. And that was the problem. She wasn't inspired by anything at the moment. Summer was approaching, and invitations were arriving at the house thick and fast for all sorts of entertainment, but she'd meet the same people again and it wasn't enough. She was bored.

'Prue!' Her grandmama's raised eyebrow and sharp look snapped her back to the present.

'Sorry. What did you say?'

Grandmama led the way to the shop's entrance. 'I asked if you needed more time or are you happy to move on?'

'I'm finished.' She nodded her goodbyes to Eve Yolland and her assistants, before leaving the building and stepping into the brand-new green Sunbeam motor car, her grandmama's latest acquisition.

Once Higgins, the chauffeur, closed the door and climbed behind the wheel, Prue settled back against the leather seat and sighed.

'Right, enough.' Grandmama peered at her. 'I refuse to spend another moment with you in this mood. What is the matter? For weeks you've been walking around London as though some great misfortune has befallen you. I insist on knowing the cause of it.'

'I'm fine. Tell Higgins where we need to go, Grandmama.'

'Home, Higgins, if you please.'

'Home?' Prue frowned. 'I thought we had another appointment?'

'We do or did. But this is more important. So, you can either talk on the way home, or if it is of a delicate nature,' she directed at look at the back of Higgin's head, 'we can wait until we are behind closed doors.'

'There is nothing to talk about.'

'I beg to differ.' The hard look on her grandmother's face was familiar.

Sighing heavily, Prue knew she'd not easily divert her when she had the bit between her teeth. 'Honestly, Grandmama, nothing has happened.' She shrugged one shoulder, a feeling of hopelessness descending again.

'Ah, of course.' Grandmama patted Prue's knee, nodding her head wisely. 'I understand now. Silly of me not to see it before.' She turned to look out of the window at the passing rows of houses as they entered Mayfair, where the family's townhouse was situated.

'See what?'

It took a moment for Grandmama to turn back to her, and when she did a small smile played about her lips. 'I forgot just how much like me you are. Millie has my strength, but in a quiet, efficient way, but you, you have my character, my spirit of adventure. I should have done something about it earlier.'

'Done something about it? Whatever do you mean?'

'The war interrupted things, but everything is settling down once again now. It's time.'

Higgins slowed the automobile in front of the terraced house and Kilburn, the butler, rushed out to open the door.

Alighting, Prue waited for her grandmama to accompany her up the three short steps to the front door. 'Time for what?'

'Why, to take you abroad.'

'Abroad?' Following her into the parlour, Prue slipped off her gloves, wondering if she'd heard correctly. No one went abroad now, or hadn't done for years, not since the war started in '14.

'It's high time we sampled the delectable delights of Europe, my dear. High time indeed. And you especially.' She sat down at her rosewood desk in the corner and selected several sheets of writing paper. 'You, my dear, need to explore the world as I did before I married. There's nothing better than experiencing foreign cities and people to take one out of one's self.'

A bud of excitement grew in the pit of Prue's stomach. Abroad? To go travelling. Yes! Absolutely, a hundred times yes. 'When can we go, Grandmama?'

Acknowledgements

Thank you to my wonderful friends and fellow authors, Maggi Andersen and Lynda Stacey – you both listened to me rabbbiting on about this story and giving advice where needed!

To my editor, Jane Eastgate, thank you for finding my mistakes when I think there are none!

To my talented cover designer, Evelyn Labelle, you always give me what I want, thank you!

Thank you to my family and friends. Your support means the world to me, especially my husband.

Finally, the biggest thank you goes to my readers. Over the years I have received the most wonderful messages from readers who have told me how much they've enjoyed my stories. Each and every message and review encourages me to write the next book.

Most authors go through times when they think the story they are writing is no good and I am no exception. The times when we struggle with the plot, when the characters don't behave as we wish them to, when 'normal' life interferes with the writing process and we feel we haven't got enough time in the day to do all we have to do those messages make us smile!

A few words from a stranger saying they loved my story dispels my doubts over my ability to be an author. I can't express enough how much those lovely messages mean to me. So, thank you!

If you'd like to receive my email newsletter, or find out more about me and my books, please go to my website where you can join the mailing list.
http://www.annemariebrear.com